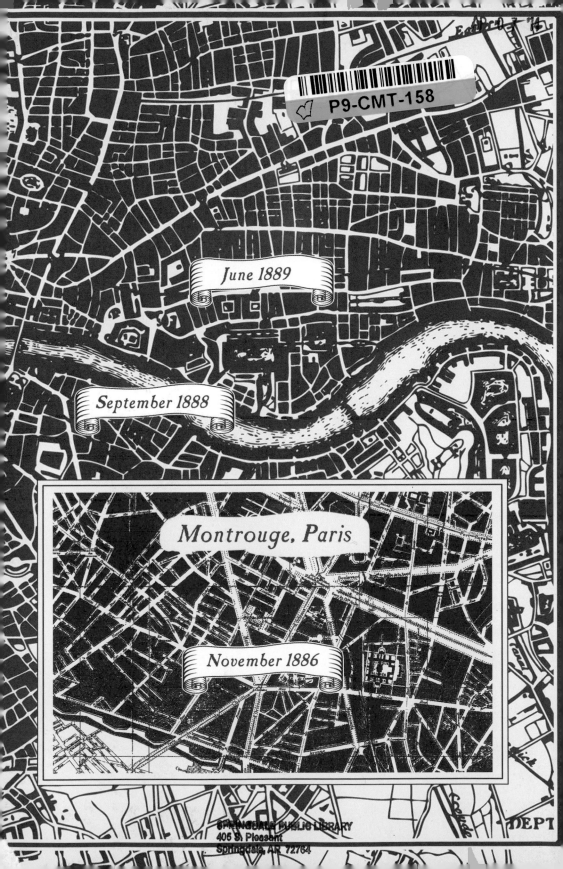

June 1889

September 1888

Montrouge, Paris

November 1886

MAYHEM

MAYHEM

Sarah Pinborough

Jo Fletcher

JF

Jo Fletcher Books
An imprint of Quercus
New York • London

© 2013 by Sarah Pinborough
First published in the United States by Quercus in 2014

Any member of educational institutions wishing to photocopy part or all of the work for classroom use or anthology should send inquiries to Permissions c/o Quercus Publishing Inc., 31 West 57th Street, 6th Floor, New York, NY 10019, or to permissions@quercus.com.

ISBN 978-1-62365-086-5

Library of Congress Control Number: 2013937917

Distributed in the United States and Canada by
Random House Publisher Services
c/o Random House, 1745 Broadway
New York, NY 10019

Manufactured in the United States

2 4 6 8 10 9 7 5 3 1

www.quercus.com

*For all the writers who have entertained me,
taught me and inspired me; some who are still among us,
and some who are long gone.*

The words live on.

PREFACE

I have stuck closely to reported factual events that took place during the period of the Thames Torso murders, and many of the players in this novel are real people from history, but for the sake of my story, and *Murder* to follow, I have taken some liberties with the characters, their personal lives, and, of course, their personalities. I send my apologies to all of them, and I trust their souls will forgive me. This is, after all, a novel, and not a history book.

Personally, if someone chooses to breathe life into *me* again, between the pages of a book a hundred years after I die, I hope that whatever is left of me in the wind and the rain will smile a little, and take whatever changes the author made to my life with good humor.

These murders, however, did take place. And they were never solved.

PART ONE

1

Paris, November 1886

He was quite handsome. A little thin, perhaps, and there was a strange mottled hue to his skin that made her think the consumption might have made a claim on him, but he had his own teeth and the air of a gent—if you could ever call an Englishman a gent—that put him a cut above her normal clientele. He was also paying her well. She smiled at him, even though he appeared less inclined to speak to her now that they were alone than when he had first seen her. That did not concern her—he was English, after all, and although his French had sounded good, it might be limited.

She didn't mind; talking could be more work than the other. There was always the chance of saying the wrong thing and then suddenly your lip was split and your eye blackened, and then there would be no work until they healed. Quiet was fine—and quiet normally meant quick, so even better.

The night was cold and she pulled her shawl a little tighter around her shoulders as she followed him down into the side streets of Montrouge to where his lodging rooms must be. A cold wind with winter on its breath twisted through the narrowing streets and they were left in midnight gloom as the glow of light from the cafés in the square faded. She sniffed, her nose running slightly, and then caught her breath as she tripped on the uneven cobbles. He grabbed her without breaking his own stride and pulled her firmly beside him.

"You're stronger than you look, Englishman," she said with a smile. There were gaps where a few of her own teeth were missing, but she

knew her smile was still pretty enough for a girl in her position. "I like that." She laughed and leaned into him, as much clumsy flirtatiousness as because she could barely see the ground beneath her feet and her head was swimming slightly. She had a head for wine—in her business you had to—but tonight she had drunk too quickly, needing that inner warmth now that the alleyways where she normally plied her trade were getting uncomfortably cold. When your skirt was hitched up around your waist and your cheek was pressed into the rough stone to try and stop them pushing their stinking tongues into your mouth, you felt even the lightest of chilly breezes.

He did not react to her laughter, but she didn't mind. He was lost in his own world somewhere, perhaps feeling premature guilt for the deed he had not yet done. He probably had a wife at home, sitting bolt upright in a dark parlor, her legs primly pressed together, everything between them religiously dry. She snorted to herself.

They rounded a corner and she was surprised when he stopped in front of a small artisan's workshop. She had not expected he would be taking her anywhere too extravagant—his coat and trousers were worn, though they were still fine clothes. She had guessed he would be staying in one of the nearby lodging houses, not the smartest of addresses, but clean and comfortable. She had been looking forward to feeling the soft sheets beneath her, and if her luck had been in, he might have fallen asleep, and then she could have slept in comfort alongside him until he woke and threw her out.

She frowned as he tugged the wooden door open; it wasn't likely to be warm in there, though at least it would be out of the wind. She had been fucked in too many strange places to feel any concern, though she was disappointed. Mainly she just felt a weariness that even the wine could not fight. Her English gent had already paid, so no doubt he would take his time. He was not doing it twice, though, no matter how many francs he had already handed over.

"I like my privacy," he muttered, as if in explanation, and he ushered her inside. He closed the door and then turned on a small gas lamp that cast long shadows across the dusty floor. Her heart sank further. The place was dirty and looked neglected. She thought she

could make out a table in the far corner, but the meager light fighting its way through the grimy glass housing did not reach that far.

He moved closer until they were standing face-to-face. He grasped her upper arms. Once again she was surprised by his strength, especially when he looked so sickly. She ignored the purplish patches on his slightly bloated face, instead staring into his blue eyes. He looked nervous, and she warmed to him for that. She was a kind-hearted girl.

"Don't worry, we'll have a nice time," she said, smiling and tilting her head coquettishly. She imagined he would like that. "Just you leave it up to me." She stretched her hand down to rub between his legs and gasped slightly—he fired up fast, this one—but he squeezed her arms tighter and pushed her farther into the workshop. She was a little shocked by his sudden roughness, and she tripped over her feet, and once again he held her up.

"You don't strike me as the rough type, cheri." She laughed a little, wanting to lighten the sudden tension. "Why don't we slow it down? Why don't you—?"

"Do you see it?" He shook her slightly. "Behind me—can you see it?"

For the first time that evening, something unpleasant unfurled in her stomach, hinting at bad choices made—the worst kind of choices. She looked into those blue eyes again. They were wide, intense, and she realized she had misread them. This wasn't nerves, or shy fear of sex. This was something else, something completely other. This was madness. Her heart thumped loudly and the last warmth of drunkenness dissipated into cool dread.

"Why don't you let me—?"

"Can you see it?" he hissed, spraying spit onto her face. She flinched, both from him and the sour stench of his breath. He was sick, she was sure about that. The chill in her gut spread into her limbs and suddenly she was trembling.

"You can have your money back. Just let me go." She tried to wriggle free, but his hands were clenched around her arms like vices. The splintered edge of the table behind her dug into her thighs. Metal clanked against metal and she saw tools spread across the tabletop. What were they for? Tears pricked suddenly at the corners of her eyes *and she sniffed them away. She was being foolish. He was mad, she could see that, but that didn't mean he was going to hurt her. The rush of blood in her ears and the panic loosening her bladder made her thoughts unconvincing.*

"You must see it," he continued, "behind me—right behind me! You must see it!"

She stared into the shadows over his shoulder. Maybe if she placated him then he'd calm down. She focused on the closed door and the lamp. They were so close, and yet so far away. She needed him to relax—if he relaxed, then she could get away. She was sure of it.

"I don't know," she stuttered, her mouth dry. Her eyes flicked from his face to the door behind him. "There's something there . . . I think . . . maybe if we get closer to the light—maybe then I could see properly?" She licked her lips. "Please, if we go near the door—where the light is—then I can look. I'm sure I can see something." She was speaking quickly and she wondered if he even understood her. She saw her own terrified face reflected in his dark orbs as he stared at her.

A frown crept across his face and settled in a ripple of wrinkles on his forehead. After a moment it twisted into a sneer.

"You cannot see it," he whispered, eventually. "You cannot." He smiled at her, and she found that she was sobbing. "But I will tell you a secret," he whispered into her ear. There was a moment's pause, and in it she held her terrified breath.

"It can see you."

Dawn was merely a gray chill when screams tore through the still-sleeping town. Montrouge rose early that day, both sleep and tranquility lost to them. Within an hour of the discovery, police were examining the remains that had been left so callously—so sacrilegiously—on the steps of the church, the town's quiet place of sanctuary from the everyday toils of life. That morning there was no quiet. Even in the silence, the horrors of the crime disallowed peace.

The torso—the head, right arm and both legs were missing—belonged to a young woman. One breast had been brutally cut off, but it was quite clear from what remained that the victim was female. The police and surgeon talked amongst themselves before declaring that she could not have been murdered where she had been found; there was not enough blood. The townsfolk had become almost one in their appalled shock, and somehow this detail disturbed them even more than if the poor woman had been cut to pieces on the church steps. If he hadn't killed her there, then in whose barn or outhouse had he committed his heinous crimes? A thorough search found no evidence, and neither did it find the missing body parts. The town did not sleep well that night, nor for many more to come. The townsfolk prayed that the wickedness that had come to their town had simply been passing through.

Later, when the torso had been taken for further investigation, it was discovered that the woman, suspected to be a missing local prostitute, was also missing her uterus.

The town prayed harder after that.

2

The Times of London
May 16, 1887

On Saturday the coroner for South Essex, Mr. C. C. Lewis, opened an inquiry at the Phoenix Hotel, Rainham, into the circumstances attending the death of a woman, a portion of whose body was discovered in the Thames off Rainham on Wednesday last, wrapped in a piece of coarse sacking.

Essex Times—South Essex, London
June 8, 1887

RAINHAM,
THE RAINHAM MYSTERY

On Sunday morning great excitement was caused on the Victoria Embankment on its being made known that a portion of the mutilated remains of a female had been picked up near the Temple Pier. The Thames Police were immediately communicated with, and on their rowing out to the pier a portion of a human leg was handed over into their possession. It appears that at ten o'clock on Sunday morning the attention of J. Morris, pierman at the Temple, was drawn to a large parcel that was floating near the lower side of the pier. On opening it Morris discovered the thigh of a human person wrapped in a piece of canvas and secured with a piece of cord . . .

The Times of London
June 13, 1887

THE RAINHAM MYSTERY

. . . careful examination of the remains (those of a woman), and was satisfied beyond doubt that they formed part of the body to which the pelvis, recently found on the Essex shore, belonged. His (Dr. Galloway) theory that the dissection was performed by a man well versed in medical science was more than strengthened. The sacking in which the trunk was enclosed was exactly similar to that found at Rainham and off the Thames Embankment.

The Times of London
July 21, 1887

THE RAINHAM MYSTERY

The various human remains, which have been found from time to time at Rainham, Essex, in the Thames off Waterloo Pier, on the foreshore of the river off Battersea pier, and in the Regent's canal, Kentish Town, the remains comprising the arms (divided), the lower part of the thorax, the pelvis, both thighs, and the legs and feet, in fact the entire body excepting the head and upper part of the chest, are now in the possession of the police authorities.

3

LONDON, OCTOBER 1888
DR. BOND

"How much farther?" The shafts of bright sunlight filling the building site above were finally petering out and leaving us in a cool, gray darkness that felt clammy against my skin.

"A little way, Dr. Bond," Hawkins said. The detective was grim. "It's in the vault." He held his lamp up higher. "We're lucky it was found at all."

Huddled over like the rest of the small group of men, I made my way under the dark arches and down the stairways from one sublevel to the next. We fell into a silence that was marked only by the clatter of heels moving urgently downward. I'm sure it wasn't just I who found the gloom to be claustrophobic—especially given what we knew to be waiting for us in the bowels of this building—and I'm sure part of our haste was simply so we could face what we must and get back to the fresh air as quickly as possible.

The workmen above had put down their tools, adding to the eerie quiet. We were a long way down, and with the walls damp and rough beside me, I couldn't shake the feeling that I was in a tomb rather than the unfinished basement of what was to be the new Police Headquarters. But perhaps I was—an unintentional tomb, of course, but a resting place of the dead all the same. I shivered. There had been enough death of late, even for someone like me, who was trained in all its ways. Recently I had begun to think that soon this city would be forever stained in cold, dead blood.

Finally, we made our way down the last few steps and arrived at the vault. It was time to work.

"They moved it over here before they opened it," Hawkins said, standing over a misshapen object nearby, "where there was better light to see it." The foreman and the poor carpenter who had found and unwrapped the parcel were keeping their distance, shuffling their feet as they stayed well clear of what lay at the detective's feet. As I looked down, I found I did not blame them.

"Dear Lord," I muttered. After the slayings of recent weeks I had thought we must all be immune to sudden shock, but this proved that was not the case. My stomach twisted greasily and I fought a slight tremble in my hands. More gruesome murder in London. Had we not seen enough? The parcel the workmen had found was approximately two and a half feet long. It had been wrapped in newspaper and tied with cheap twine, the ends now hanging loose where they had been cut open to reveal the horrific secret inside.

"We've not touched it since," the foreman, a Mr. Brown, said nervously. "Fetched the constable straight away, we did, an' he stayed with it while we fetched the detective. We 'aven't touched it."

He didn't need to repeat himself to convince me. Regardless of the sickly stench of rot that now filled the air, who would choose to touch this? The woman's torso was lacking arms, legs and a head, and across its surface and tumbling from the severed edges was a sea of maggots that writhed and squirmed over each other as they dug into the dead flesh. In the quiet of the vault we could hear the slick, wet sound made by the seething maggots. Here and there they dropped free to the black ground below.

I fought a shiver of repulsion. Whoever this woman was—and despite the physical trauma it was clear this was the torso of a woman—her death was no recent event.

I crouched lower to examine the damaged body more closely, and I held the light close as I bent down to the floor in order to peer into the largest cavity. What was left of her insides was a mess:

whoever had done this had not been content with just amputating her limbs. Much of her bowel and her female internal organs had also been removed. This killer had taken his time.

Beyond my obvious disgust, I tried to muster some other emotion, empathy of some kind for this poor creature's fate, but I could not. It was the madness of it all that haunted me, not the deeds themselves. Further to that, this woman no longer had a face with which to plague my sleepless nights—unless that was somewhere else in this dark pit, lying as yet undiscovered. But I doubted that someone would go to the lengths of removing the most personal item of the body if the intention were simply to leave it close by. From beyond the vault came the sound of vomiting. One of the younger constables, no doubt. I felt a slightly weary envy at that. Oh, to still be so easily affected by the macabre acts of others.

"You're the man who found the parcel?" I looked up at the carpenter.

"Yes, sir. Windborne's the name, sir." The gentleman in question shuffled from foot to foot, nervously picking at his cap. Even in the unnatural light, his face looked pale. He was in his thirties, perhaps more, and had the hands of a man who had worked hard and honestly for the better part of his life. "We thought it were just a bit of old bacon. I should maybe 'ave said something yesterday, but I thought nothing really of it. I didn't even notice the smell—'ard to believe that now."

"If it were wrapped tightly, the smell would have been less, and if you were focused on your work . . ." I shrugged. "Show me where you found it, if you would."

"Yes, sir." The carpenter gestured toward the dark space behind us that yawned like pitch-black night. "You'll need some light."

"What in God's name brought you down here?" Hawkins asked.

"It's where I 'ide me tools. I don't trust a lot o' the new men up there, sir," Windborne said. "I've been in me trade a long time; they 'aven't. I can't afford to 'ave me tools stolen. I know the way, but it'd be a puzzle to anyone who didn't know the place, so me tools are safe 'ere." He stopped several feet away from where the torso now lay. "I use that nook, behind a plank of wood. The parcel was stuffed in beside it."

Hawkins raised the lamp, and his arm immediately wavered slightly. "Dear Lord, look at that."

The wall at the back of the alcove was black where the rotting flesh had soaked through its wrapping, and maggots teemed across it almost as thickly as they did across the torso itself. "Well, that answers one question," I said, almost to myself.

"Which is?" the detective asked.

"Our victim has been here much longer than good Mr. Windborne knew her to be." It was cool in the vault, but I was sweating slightly. The damp air and consuming darkness beyond the small pools of light was becoming oppressive, and I suddenly feared that if I stayed down here much longer, I would not be able to breathe. I stepped back. My heart was starting to race unpleasantly, and an anxious tingle prickled at my skin. It was a sensation that had become all too familiar over recent months.

"I think I have seen all I need to see here," I said. "If you would be kind enough to arrange for the body and its wrapping to be sent to the mortuary, I will clean her up tonight." I was glad of the poor lighting as I turned back toward the stairs, sure that my face would no doubt look unhealthily pallid, were someone to study it. I quietly drew in a deep breath and silently counted each of the rough steps as we climbed until my racing heart had calmed.

These strange moments had come upon me more frequently in recent weeks, and as much as I blamed my cursed inability to sleep, I knew too that the wash of blood that was flooding London's streets this summer was equally responsible. I suffered as a child with these fleeting moments of surreal anxiety during which I was sure my heart was about to be crushed in my chest, but as I grew into adulthood, they began to fade into a memory almost forgotten. Even during my time on the battlefields with the Prussian Army they had not returned—not until this past summer. They filled me with a terrible dread, and I was left tired and drained when the spell had passed. Of course, this did nothing to help my insomnia, and

I knew that on some level the two had to be linked. I prayed that sleep would soon return, and with that, these strange fits would be dispelled.

I took the stairs with vigor, and by the time we reached the street, the combination of my brisk pace and concentrated breathing had cleared my head, and I was once again myself. I lit my pipe, and Detective Hawkins lit his. Evening was falling, and London was sinking into the gloom that existed between day and night before the streetlights flickered into life. There was a chill in the air, and as we both shivered and smoked, I felt certain that the young detective was as glad as I that we were free of the vault.

"You don't think it's *him*, do you?" The detective spoke quietly. I didn't need to ask for clarification: there was only one *him* being spoken of across London, and he even had a name now, after the letter of five days ago. *Jack the Ripper*. It had a ring to it, I had to admit. Whitechapel's fear now had an identity.

"No," I said. "I don't think so." It had been barely forty-eight hours since the deaths of the last two women, Elizabeth Stride and Catherine Eddowes. In homes across London, and in Whitechapel in particular, the bubble of hysterical chatter that was becoming a vocal demand for the killer to be caught would become hard for the men of H Division to control, should those residents decide to take matters into their own hands. "And you would do well to perhaps be loud in those assumptions yourself, Detective. There is enough fear on these streets, and Jack is getting enough publicity without our help."

"Yes," Hawkins said, "but it won't be me talking to them. I'll be passing this case on." He sounded relieved. "They've sent two inspectors over from Scotland Yard—Moore and Andrews—to help catch this Ripper. Experienced detectives, they are. CID. I'll give this to them, just in case."

Behind us two men emerged from the building site, carefully carrying the pitiful remnants of the body and the newspaper in which it had been wrapped, both now swaddled in sacking. One of them was the reserve officer, Constable Barnes, who had been called in to help mind the new building site. He had been the first among them to see the contents of the gruesome package earlier that afternoon. He had certainly got more than he had bargained for on this assignment.

We watched silently as they climbed into the waiting cab.

"How the hell did it get down there?" Hawkins asked. "And unnoticed?"

"That, my friend," I said as I dampened my pipe and stared into the darkening street, "is for your inspectors to fathom. My part of the puzzle will meet me at the mortuary."

I had fully intended to go home when my initial work with the remains was done, for I would need to be back in the morning to start the postmortem examination, and had already sent a message to Dr. Hebbert to meet me no later than half-past seven in order to get the procedure underway. I myself would be there well before that, but Charles didn't suffer with my sleep affliction, and I felt no call to drag him out too early simply because my own bed was my enemy.

Alone in the quiet mortuary, I had cleaned the torso and placed it in alcohol, both to preserve it and to kill off the teeming maggots. There was no urgency for an accurate time of death—and no way of giving one, other than that death clearly had occurred weeks before—so there had been no cause for me to work through the night, not when a fresh mind in the morning would work better.

A fresh mind had been my intention, at any rate, so I had been determined to go home to a light supper and then take myself straight to bed with a book, in the hope of getting at least six hours' sleep, though I would happily have settled for four or five. I had felt exhausted as I had prepared to leave, but yet again I found myself waking up, as I had done most evenings during these past three months. The exhaustion had sunk too far into my bones to disappear, but still my grainy eyes widened and my brain refused to quieten.

Without making any real conscious decision, instead of reaching for my overcoat, I rummaged behind the medicine cabinet for the clothes I kept hidden there: a less expensive coat and a rough hat, the kind that would disguise my normal gentlemanly appearance and allow me to blend in more anonymously at my chosen destination. I pulled them on, and once outside the mortuary, I dirtied my face a little. It would do. People tended not to pay attention to others in the dens, but I would rather not take the risk of bringing disrepute to my name.

"Thank you, good man," I said, aware that however I roughened my voice, it was still educated and at odds with my clothing. The cabbie who dropped me in the heart of Whitechapel either didn't notice or didn't care as he took my money, and that suited me perfectly well.

I took in a deep breath of night air, and then I let my feet take me through the main thoroughfares to the back alleys of the human warren that made up this rough and dangerous part of the city that now had all eyes turned on it. The hour was not overly late, but an eerie quiet hung like smog over the deserted streets, an unnatural stillness. My heels clicked against the cobbles as I sank into the sordid atmosphere of the slum.

Under the pale light of a flickering streetlamp, I caught sight of a solitary female face. Her cheeks were bloated from the drink, and although she smiled slightly, just in case I might be a gent looking for a moment of relief, her eyes, glazed as they were, were wary. I didn't blame her for it. There was no point in warning her to stay away from these wretched alleyways; her very appearance dictated that her need for liquor would make her risk the dangers. And here, as everywhere, people would always believe that the fate of poor Catherine Eddowes and the others would happen to *others*, and not themselves.

Stairwells and doorways yawned in the darkness around me, and in one or two I could make out the shapes of men, lounging and smoking as they talked quietly. They fell into a wary silence as I passed, and it was with a mild relief that I soon found myself on the main highway, with its lively gin palaces and noisy shows, where little groups of people gathered under the gaslights to listen to some enthusiastic soul expounding on the mysteries of the universe or the miraculous benefits of some such pill or another.

Watching the life around me, I couldn't help but wonder what it was about this city that its residents felt the urge to harm each other so? Ever since sleep and I had parted company so many weeks before, I had sensed a shift in the mood on the streets and behind the closed doors of homes of both the well-to-do and the slum dwellers. There was a wickedness in the air. I might laugh it off in broad sunlight, but now, in the grip of night, it was almost palpable. It wasn't the frequency of death that disturbed me— murder had always been a part of London's personality. It was the *nature* of the killings: the *intent*. Poisonings, strangulations, and now *Jack*.

My feet led me steadily toward the river. This meander around Whitechapel had been merely a distraction, perhaps a way to fool myself into believing I would not be seeking out the opium this evening, that I would simply walk myself into tiredness. It was a lie, of course, that I had only half-heartedly believed. By getting the hansom cab to drop me at Whitechapel, I had avoided the embarrassment of going directly to Bluegate Fields and the various establishments that served my needs in that vilest of areas. None of the dens were salubrious, but there were slightly less venal places than Bluegate. My choice of location would be clear for analysis, should anyone discover my new pastime and wish to pass comment upon it: if I was going to be low, then I might as well be low with the lowest. It would not take a scholar to reach that conclusion. My shame, I hoped, was my ally: it would prevent these still not entirely frequent visits from becoming a noticeable habit.

There were many in my position who would think nothing of self-medicating, of course. Laudanum would certainly be a more private way of relaxing my exhausted mind, but I feared that my will might not be as strong as I might wish it if I were to go down that path. I knew several medical men for whom that liquid was a daily necessity, and I had no wish to count myself among their number. This would do for me. As the Chinaman opened up the door and the warmth and heady scent from within embraced him, all I truly cared about was a few hours of blissful release.

Unlike the descriptions of the Chinese opium houses that filled the pages of the penny dreadfuls, this den, for want of a better word, was well swept and clean. The clientele—mainly sailors who had learned to prefer the smoke to alcohol on their travels, but also various other Orientals, the occasional shopman or steward, and here or there a beggar or thief who had come into a few pennies— did not normally arrive until half-past ten or eleven at night, as I had done. So the old Chinaman (known to me only as "Chi-Chi," the same name I used for many of the old man's counterparts in other establishments) had several hours to clean or change whatever rags and coverings required it.

I found the dens to be calm and peaceful places, with none of the restless aggression of the bawdy public houses where men and women drank too much and talked too loudly and then found any excuse to be cruel to one another or to seek a moment's feigned affection in the arms of another stinking unfortunate. The Chinese opium houses had a serene quality, a hush that hung in every full room as if noise and irritation were captured and trapped by the pall of blue smoke that curled up from the pipes and hung there indefinitely. Even those small groups who talked quietly amongst themselves did not linger on the topics of politics or war or even the terrible fates that were befalling the women of Whitechapel. Instead they let their conversation go this way and that as the smoke dictated, until, for several minutes at a time, they would stop speaking completely, and then, after a stretch of silence, one or another would eventually pick up a new thread.

Faces and bodies blurred under the glow of the oil lamps dotted here and there, and in the pipe-bowls, glowing embers twinkled like stars in the gloom. Time drifted in the thrall of the pipe, and as I lay back on the small cot, my immediate surroundings faded as my conscious floated away to pleasanter times—to fields of vivid green beneath sparkling blue skies—and the sticky heat of the den became a glorious summer sun. Somewhere Emily, so long ago lost, was laughing. I smiled as my eyes half-shut and the familiar warm rush flooded through my veins. This night, however, it was hard to hold on to such pleasant thoughts; instead, dark flashes of Whitechapel's streets plagued my mind: slashed throats, terrified eyes, brutalized bodies torn open with so much rage, the images all enhanced by the power of the smoke.

I turned slightly on my cot, no doubt muttering nonsense, as I heard the slice of the blade and the clamor of talk in public houses across the East End, almost as if I were flying across it all, my spirit free of this body and swooping down here and there to see so many strangers' faces, flushed with both excitement and too much gin, recounting the details of one grisly death after another. Those five women had been ripped apart by Jack, and now they were being torn apart some more by gossip, delivered by those with shining eyes, even more alive for their loss. This was a cruel London.

I wanted some peace, but the smoke was wrestling with me this evening, enhancing the black thoughts that plagued me, taking me deeper into my fears and forcing me to face them. Maggots crawled behind my eyes, and suddenly I was back in the vault of the new police building, this time alone in the dark with only a match burning between my fingers for light. I could feel the rough ground beneath my feet, and my breath rushed loudly in my ears. I turned this way and that, taking hesitant paces forward and back in order to seek out the stairs. *I must get out. I must get back to the light.* Something shuffled in the darkness, and I spun around, the light flickering in its death throes as the match burned close to my fingers. I let out a yelp of fear and disgust, finding myself suddenly facing the rotting torso, the corpse held high above the ground. *Held.* There was something there, behind the corpse . . . a vast shadow . . . it was leaning forward. The match went out.

I sat bolt upright, awakened from my terrors by my own scream, which thankfully manifested in the real world as a tight-chested yelp, as shrieks in dreams have a tendency to do. Chi-Chi appeared beside my cot with a damp cloth, and I took it gratefully from him and wiped my sweating face. My head was swimming with the opiate high and my heart thumped with relief that the hallucination was done. After a few deep breaths I muttered some thanks to the old man, whose dark eyes peered out like raisins from a thin, cadaverous face half-hidden by his long beard. There was no judgment in his expression, and I couldn't help but wonder how many such terrors he had witnessed during the long nights of supervising so many lost souls?

I drew deeply on the pipe and let the heady smoke eradicate the remaining stains of darkness. I felt cleaner now that the vision was done, as if I had needed to purge the day's work from my imagination. I leaned back once more, and this time, thankfully, the opium was gentle with me. I drifted for an hour or more, perhaps even came close to sleep, when the heavy tread of boots moving past me disturbed my reverie.

I had been so far lost in my own head that it took a moment to recognize my surroundings, and by the time I did, the figure had moved farther away. I frowned as I stared at the small alleyways the Chinamen used to scurry here and there, replenishing a bowl or gently evicting a customer who had run out of time and pennies.

The tall man, dressed in a long black waxy overcoat and hat, moved between the cots, his feet thumping on the wooden floor, pausing here and there to study the occupants before progressing to the next. As he turned sideways to peer down at one sleeping sailor, I could see a withered arm and crooked hand that he kept bent at his waist, the disproportionately tiny fingers curled in like talons.

Despite the heaviness of my limbs and the haze that coated my vision I dragged myself slightly upright, so that I was lying on my side, propped up on one elbow. The den had been only half full when I had arrived, but in the time I had spent in my private haze, the cots and divans had filled, and a low cloud of smoke hid the ceiling from view. The stranger moved through the dreamers, apparently in no hurry, studying those lost to the opium, just as I had seen him do in several such establishments over recent weeks. I had come to find myself slightly intrigued by him and his strange examination of the poppy smokers. Had he been standing over my cot only moments before? What was he looking for? Did he even exist, or was he merely an opium dream himself?

Chi-Chi had returned to replenish my pipe, and as he did so, I pointed at the figure almost lost in the gloom.

"Who is that man?" I asked. "I have seen him here before, I think, and in other such places."

"He come. He go." Chi-Chi shrugged his narrow shoulders. "He look."

"Who is he looking for?"

"He don't tell Chi-Chi."

"Does he smoke?" My words were thick, struggling to form against the lethargy that gripped me.

"Yes: smoke first, look after."

The strange man was almost at the far end of the room, where stairs led down to the small lower level where Chinamen came to gamble. Extra beds, for busy nights, lined the area.

"Have you noticed, Chi-Chi," I muttered, "that he looks at them strangely? I don't believe he's looking at their faces—around them, perhaps, but not at their faces. Why might that be, do you think? What is he hoping to see?"

Chi-Chi said nothing more but shuffled away as if he had not heard the questions, and as the stranger disappeared downstairs, I turned again to the pipe. I had perhaps two hours more until five o'clock, when I would have to head home to wash and change for the postmortem examination. I did not want to waste them. As I lay back down on the couch and looked up at the cloud I had created with my night's indulgence, I wondered about the man. I had seen him before—before these strange visits to the opium dens. I was sure of it. But where, and when?

4

THE PALE, MARCH 1881
AARON KOSMINSKI

"Fire!"

Sweat burst from Aaron Kosminski's forehead as he sat suddenly upright in the bed, crying out. By the time his mother and Matilda came in, Betsy was forcing her feet into her boots and wrapping a shawl around her shoulders. Baby Bertha was held tight in Matilda's arms. "Hush!" she said. "If you wake Morris again, he won't be happy."

"He's doing it again," Betsy grumbled. "It's been four nights now. He sweats like a pig and then the bed is freezing."

Fifteen-year-old Aaron was vaguely aware of his family's presence, just as he was vaguely aware of the bed and the room and that somewhere in the real world—the world that was a haze between him and the visions—his skin was freezing cold, not burning hot.

"Run, run, run, run," he cried. "They're coming!" His breath came in short bursts. "They're coming here—all of them."

Screams—people screaming. Burning wood, cold air, and so much anger. So much hate—black hate. Matilda terrified—the babies, somewhere he can't see—screaming as hands grab her. So much confusion. Morris: Morris's head is smashed red against the white of the snow. His lungs burn as he runs, he and Betsy, running and not looking back. Mother and Matilda aren't behind them—they were *behind them, for a little while, but now they're gone. He's too afraid to stop and look; he must keep running. So much hatred. So much darkness.*

"Shhh, my son." His mother hushed him softly and wiped his brow, but he was lost in the vision, unable to respond to her touch. In the vision she was no longer there—she was dead, or something worse. "You're here with us. It's just a bad dream."

"The same bad dream for four nights." Matilda snorted. "No wonder I'm so tired."

Outside, snow fell softly. Winter hadn't quite let go just yet, but its grip was loosening. For the better part of six months the shtetl had been smothered by a foot-high blanket of freezing white, but the blasts of wind that had driven the icy weather their way had fallen, anger spent, and most days there was some thaw, leaving the paths between the cramped houses and around the marketplace muddy slush. It was difficult for people to stay clean or dry as they wandered to and fro to work, or seeking work. Everything was dirty and would stay that way until the ground dried. Sometimes it felt as if they lived in grubby blackness.

The night is black. Eventually he stops running and lets go of Betsy's hand. Even in all this fear and panic he doesn't want to touch her. The softness makes his skin crawl slightly, and he remembers that awful night and the terror that had filled him—only flashes of memory now, but enough to have scarred him. Betsy doesn't notice his hand is gone from hers, or if she does, she doesn't care. She's panting from the run, and although the days have been warmer, it is now nearly midnight, and her breath pours out like smoke.

They turn and look as flames consume the makeshift town that was their home. Even from this distance they can hear the yelling, both of terror and of angry excitement. The towns have turned on them. There is so much hate. There is no sign of Matilda or Mother or the babies. Neither he nor Betsy speak—what can they say? He wants to run and keep running until they reach an ocean they can cross. That's what they have to do. They have to run.

Aaron gasped and the vision was gone. He blinked for a moment, adjusting to the sight of his home and his bed and his mother, alive and well. He shivered, and his mother pulled the damp blankets up around his chin.

"So much hate," he whispered. "They were black with it—on the inside."

His mother grabbed his hands and rubbed warmth into them, and he saw how red her skin was from all the scrubbing in the freezing air. There were cracks on her palms. It was as if he was seeing her for the first time in a long while. Loose strands of hair had fallen free of the cap she slept in, and they were run through with gray. His mother was getting old, but if they did not leave this place, she would die without getting older. He felt the truth of that in every beat of his heart.

"I told you." Matilda leaned against the wall, a frown forming lines between her eyebrows. "The same dream: four nights he's woken up shouting about fire and hate."

"Your grandmother used to have dreams." Aaron's mother pulled him in to her breast and held his head there. "When I was a little girl she dreamed of us leaving Kiev. She dreamed of old Abramanov killing his wife—no one knew what he had done apart from your grandmother, not until they found the poor woman rotting under the bed." She said sagely, "Some dreams are more than dreams."

Matilda snorted again, though her mother constantly chided her about it. Aaron could understand why: his eldest sister was a pleasant-looking woman, even in the grime and hard living that aged women fast in the Pale, but this mannerism had led to the young men calling her "horse" as they'd grown up, and that in turn had fixed her mouth in a constant expression of down-turned displeasure.

Aaron kept quiet and waited for the trembling that had gripped him to subside. He hugged his mother back, less out of a need for affection than for warmth. His bones were cold to their marrow. As he shook against the familiar stale smell of his mother's nightclothes, the vivid images that had overwhelmed him faded, but the underlying sensations remained: hatred, fear, and the desperate need to run.

He didn't need his mother to tell him that these were no ordinary dreams. He feared the visions even more when they came when he was awake, helping Mr. Anscher cut hair from lice-ridden heads or, over at the hospital, cleaning up after the doctors and patients.

There was never any warning. His head just filled with something *other*: terrible sights and sounds, like tonight's, a forewarning of the towns and villages pouring down upon them in the night and destroying or stealing everything they had. He had almost cut a man's ear off yesterday morning when the images had hit him. If he wasn't careful, Mr. Anscher would find another young man to help him, and then they would lose these rooms, poor as they were.

He had been assaulted by another vision over the past three days—one that made him realize that none of this was normal. In it he saw a vast city, bigger even than the Kiev he knew from the stories his mother and the old people of the shtetl would tell during the long summer evenings, when they gathered in the marketplace and remembered better times. Perhaps his mind had made the city up from those stories, but he knew he did not have the imagination to invent the luxury he had seen surrounding the screaming man at the center of the explosion in his vision. The cramped shtetl with its poverty-stricken residents was all he had ever known; he'd never seen a palace, let alone stepped inside one.

"Grandmother's gift?" Betsy's eyes were bleary with broken sleep. "It can't be." Her words came out through a yawn and she shuffled forward and sat on the edge of the bed, tugging an edge of blanket over her. "You always said the gift came to women."

This wasn't the first time Mother had talked of the foresight that was supposed to be in their blood. When their grandmother was alive, she herself had told them about the rotting wife, how when she had touched the baker's hand buying bread from him, she'd *seen* exactly what he would do later that night. The children had enjoyed the scary bedtime tales, but as they had grown and their grandmother had died, the "gift" became a myth, a story of its own.

"There's no such thing as the gift," Matilda said, hugging her own tiny daughter to her chest. "It's just old superstition."

"Old superstitions are not to be sneered at," Golda Kosminski snapped at her eldest daughter. "They come from truths that we are too busy to see."

"Maybe if he has the sight he can tell us where Father is. At least that would be useful."

"Matilda!" Betsy said, shocked. "Sometimes you are too *mean*." She turned and squeezed their mother's arm, still wrapped tightly around Aaron, who in turn pulled him closer until he thought he couldn't breathe. He didn't like touching Betsy. He didn't like it at all.

"It's the middle of the night and I haven't had any sleep for days," Matilda sighed. "It would appear that tonight isn't going to be any exception."

"Father's dead," Aaron whispered, so quietly that it took a few seconds before his sisters paused in their bickering and looked at him. "He wasn't lying when he said he was going to join the Army. He never got there. He died in a ditch on the way. They took his boots and his hat." His mother's arms fell away and he pulled back from her. He kept his eyes down and picked at his thin hands. They were all staring at him and he didn't like it.

"How . . . ?" Matilda's question trailed off and she stepped forward, folding her arms across her chest. "How could you possibly know that?" she finally said as she peered over him.

"The gift," Golda whispered. "The boy has the gift." This time Matilda didn't snort.

The cold in Aaron's bones was getting worse, and he wished they would start up the morning fire, even though it was hours till dawn. He didn't understand how he knew his father's fate—he hadn't been aware that he did until the words came tumbling from his mouth. But he had always been certain, in a way his sisters and mother hadn't, that his father was never coming back.

"They're all going to blame us for what's happening to the man. Tomorrow." He didn't sound like himself. Fifteen was nearly grown, but sitting there under the scrutiny of his older sisters and his mother, he felt like a little boy again—like the boy who had screamed all night when he was four. He pushed that memory from his head. Just talking was making him warmer. He had to get the coldness out.

"What man?" Betsy asked.

"The screaming man. The man with no legs." His teeth were chattering and his words came out in stuttered bursts. "They're carrying him. His stomach is ripped open and his legs are gone."

"This is all just nonsense," Matilda said, but her nervous voice suggested otherwise. "It's a bad dream—he's always been strange, ever since that night when he was small."

"Stop it, Tilda." Betsy's face burned slightly.

"Well, it's true."

"Maybe he was strange before that." Betsy was defiant. "It wasn't my fault anyway. Let's just forget it." She tucked a curl around her ear. She was the beauty of their family, just turned twenty-three and married to Woolf, the butcher's son. Her choice hadn't surprised Aaron: Betsy was steeped in blood in his mind; no wonder she liked a man who must stink of it.

"They'll blame us—all of them. They're filled with so much hate."

"Who, Aaron?" his mother asked. "*Who* will blame us?"

"The town," he said softly. "All the towns—they'll come to burn everything. They're filled with hate and anger and they blame us for the dead man with no legs, and everything else." He looked up at his mother. "We have to leave, or bad things will happen to us." He swallowed hard. "To you and Matilda especially."

This time his eldest sister paled in the shadowy light that filled the room. "It's nonsense," she said again, eventually. "The boy's talking rubbish, playing a stupid game with us." She tutted sharply like a schoolteacher. "Back to bed, everyone, or we'll die of exhaustion tomorrow."

Aaron didn't get back to sleep, and he was quite sure that Matilda, lying beside him, was awake too.

Two days later the news made its way through the shtetl, spreading as fast as dysentery. Aaron heard it at the barber's; his mother heard it at the synagogue: Tsar Alexander II had been assassinated, a bomb thrown under his carriage as he made his way to a military roll call. He hadn't died immediately, but had been carried back to the Winter Palace. According to those whispering the story, his legs had been so badly shattered that they were just a bloody pulp, and his insides had tumbled from his ruined stomach.

That night, without any further conversation, the Kosminski women and the two daughters' husbands packed up their belongings and headed out of the shtetl. They did not look back, and when they were finally on board a ship to take them to a new home in England, Aaron's dreams of hate and darkness stopped as suddenly as they had arrived. No one was more relieved than Aaron himself. He had no desire to share his grandmother's gift.

5

The New York Times
Wednesday, October 3, 1888

LONDON'S RECORD OF CRIME ANOTHER MYSTERIOUS MURDER BROUGHT TO LIGHT A PERFECT CARNIVAL OF BLOOD IN THE WORLD'S METROPOLIS—THE POLICE APPARENTLY PARALYZED

LONDON, Oct. 2.—The carnival of blood continues. It is an extremely strange state of affairs altogether, because before the Whitechapel murders began several papers called attention to the fact that there have been more sanguinary crimes than ever before known in this city in the same space of time. The Whitechapel assassin has now murdered six victims and crimes occur daily, but pass unnoticed in view of the master murderer's work in the East End.

6

LONDON, OCTOBER 1888
DR. BOND

It was just before seven when Dr. Charles Hebbert arrived at the Millbank Street mortuary, and even though I had not been there long myself, I was glad to have my friend and colleague's company. He was by nature a far more jovial man than I, and his presence immediately lifted the hovering dark cloud of my mood. Sitting alone in the mortuary I had begun to feel slightly ill at ease. I wasn't sure if it was the dregs of the opium or just my current sleepless exhaustion, but I was finding the odor and the cramped confines far more macabre than was normal, and Hebbert's brisk cheer was entirely the tonic I needed.

"So, what have we got here?" He took off his coat and rubbed his hands together as he smiled broadly and peered behind the wooden partitions that separated the other current occupants of the mortuary from our cleared postmortem examination area.

"Oh dear, oh dear," he muttered, although still with good cheer, "explosion of some kind?"

"Boiler room." I didn't need to ask which cadaver had caught his eye. "The other woman started an argument with her husband over another man while he was drunk and holding a knife. The gentleman at the end hung himself after losing very heavily in a game of cards. All within three streets."

"At least they're residents of Westminster and not ladies of Whitechapel this time," Charles said, reappearing. "Although"—and for the first time I saw his humor slip away slightly—"there has been so much murder and violence in this city of late, our Whitechapel friend aside, that I have begun to dream of it. Perhaps I should drink less coffee."

"Or more brandy," I countered, and as we both smiled, the sparkle returned to my friend's eyes. My smile, however, was a touch forced. If the city's behavior had started to affect one as well balanced as Charles, then what chance did I have of shaking my insomnia and fits of anxiety?

"Shall we get to work?" he said, and I nodded. The day—and the torso—would not wait.

By the time we'd carefully removed the remains from the alcohol, my tiredness had vanished, as had Charles's childlike joviality, and we were both focused entirely on the task of putting together the puzzle of death that had been presented to us. Even stripped of the maggots, her flesh was so badly decomposed that as we measured the length, waist and chest, we couldn't even ascertain whether her skin tone had been light or dark. The copy of *The Echo* that had wrapped her was dated the twenty-fourth of August, but we did not need that to know that she had been dead for at least six weeks.

"What do you think, Charles," I said, softly, "shall we say approximately the twentieth for her date of death?"

"I'd agree." We looked at each other across the table. "The twentieth, though?" he continued. "Is it possible it could be him?"

As always these days, when violent death was mentioned, there was no need to clarify who *he* was: the twentieth of August fell between the first two "Jack" murders, of Martha Tabram and Polly Nicholls. I could see why people would think perhaps this could be his work too, and perhaps it would be easy to claim it as such, but I shook my head. Although I had not attended the crime scenes of those cases, I had read the reports of Jack's work.

His attacks were more frenzied than this. Also, our victim had a fair amount of flesh on her, so she ate regularly, and those few organs that had been left for us, the heart, liver, and lungs, were all relatively healthy.

"She's in too fine a condition to be a street girl, and this"—I kept my eyes away from her severed neck as I gestured—"this is not his method." Ridiculously, I found the lack of the head to be more haunting than if it were there, her dead eyes glaring at me for this analysis of her person.

"And a strange method it is too," Charles said, peering closely at the large cavity at the base. "Why not just cut off her legs? It would have been an easier task than this. Less to clean up after too."

The body had been separated about an inch below her navel, as if bitten in half by some great sea monster.

"I presume he wanted to get to her internal organs—the ones we don't have—and he didn't want to open her up through the stomach for some reason of his own purpose—although who can begin to reason the purpose of a madman?"

"If anyone can, Thomas," Charles smiled, "it's you."

I shrugged, slightly embarrassed. Charles Hebbert was an excellent surgeon and had a mastery of anatomy, but he had no skill in applying what he saw on the postmortem table to the workings of a man's mind. For me, however, the two were inextricably linked.

"And what could he want with her arms and legs?" he continued, frowning. "Where are they?"

My brain tingled. I looked at the torso again, and the dark brown hairs that still clung to the skin in the brutalized remains of her armless pit.

"The arm," I said, breathlessly, looking up. "I think we already have one of her arms."

After a moment of confusion, Charles's eyes widened with dawning realization. "Of course!"

Three weeks previously an arm had been pulled from the Thames at Pimlico, and Charles and I had both examined it. Perhaps I should—we should—have thought to fetch it immediately, but as gruesome a find as an arm might be, in the days since there had been plenty more bloodshed to occupy us. I cursed my tiredness and his bad dreams.

"This isn't Jack," I said, stepping back from the table. "This is Rainham." Somehow, that thought filled me with more dread, for it meant there was, without a shadow of a doubt, another killer stalking the streets of London. A second one.

Neither of us spoke for a long while after that.

7

LONDON, OCTOBER 1888
INSPECTOR MOORE

"Did Abberline send you over?" Dr. Hebbert asked, leaning against a bench laden with recently washed surgical instruments.

"You've got an arm and a torso, and we have a madman on the loose," Inspector Frederick Moore said. "Any help you can give us, we'll take." His voice had a naturally rough edge so that no matter how politely he spoke, he always sounded as if he didn't quite belong with the middle classes. He made no effort to smooth it, for he was well aware that he also had a gravitas that belied his thirty-nine years and led to no shortfall in respect.

Despite being both older and of the same rank, Walter Andrews stood slightly behind Moore, his slim frame almost hidden by the other's thickset body.

"She's not one of Jack's," Dr. Bond said, carefully lifting the arm from the preservatives that had kept it from further decomposition for the better part of a month. It was well rounded, and the fingernails were neatly filed. Moore didn't need the doctor to tell him that whoever this woman was, she probably hadn't been employed doing heavy manual labor. Still, he was always glad to have Bond on these cases. He was a good medical man, and his forensic knowledge was respected citywide by the police. During the gruesome discoveries of the past few weeks, Moore had learned to value the surgeon's opinion as well as his craft. "Are you sure?" he asked.

"Of course I'm not sure," Bond replied, his thick mustache twitching with a slight smile, "but it *is* my definite opinion."

"I'm inclined to agree," Moore said.

"So what are we doing over here then?" Andrews asked. "We've got enough on our plate back at Division."

Moore watched as the doctor placed the arm alongside the torso and pushed them together.

"Perfect fit," Bond said.

"So there *is* a second then," Hebbert said as he and Moore stepped closer to the workbench.

"A second?" Moore asked.

"A second killer at work on the streets." Dr. Bond looked up. "I'd say whoever disposed of this poor woman is also responsible for the Rainham death."

Although Moore had not been part of the Rainham river investigation, he was aware of it, of course. If Bond and Hebbert believed the two to be linked, then he wouldn't dispute it. His insides growled with tiredness and frustration. Another murderer then.

Would he have preferred this to have been the work of Jack? Probably—each fresh body in that case was also, crudely speaking, a fresh clue, and perhaps they would have found something here to lead them to whoever was stalking Whitechapel's streets. So far, they had depressingly little to go on, and now, instead of making that hunt easier, they faced a search for another madman in their midst. He looked again at the torso.

"What can you tell us about her?" he asked.

"She was tall, perhaps five feet eight and a half inches, and somewhere between twenty-five and thirty years of age. The contents of her pelvis, including her uterus, are absent, although the positioning of her bones shows no indication that she's borne a child." Alongside Moore, Andrews had begun to scribble in the small notebook he carried with him. They worked well together; Moore led and grasped the larger picture, but Andrews was the man with the eye for detail.

"Go on."

"She's been dead between six weeks and two months, and decomposition occurred in the air, not the water. It's unlikely she died by suffocation or drowning—her heart is pale and free of the clots I would expect to find from such a manner of death."

"At least we can rule that out." Moore's answer was wry. How the hell could anyone decide how this woman had met her end? The only thing he knew for certain was that it was at someone else's hand. That was enough for him.

"Why take the head?" Andrews asked.

"I would suggest to avoid identification of the victim," Bond said.

"Makes it harder to start looking for the bastard who killed her."

"Of course," Bond lifted the arm and placed it in a vat of wine as he spoke, "given the way he's disposed of her corpse, he may have a personal reason to keep her head. Perhaps he wanted a souvenir?"

It was a grim thought. He was not a man at all predisposed to superstition, but the dark workings of men's minds could be depressing.

"And this was the same with Rainham?" he asked. "No head?"

"The Rainham woman's body was found in eleven different sections," Hebbert said. "And no, the head was never recovered. She was of a similar age to this one, and she was no working girl either, if I recall—not like Jack's Whitechapel victims, at any rate."

"And the body parts were pulled out of the river?"

"Yes." Bond nodded. "Perhaps he's getting braver with this one, leaving the torso where he did, but the arm came out of the water at Pimlico. And who knows where the rest of her will turn up?"

"What about the dismemberment?" Moore peered at the various cavities. "The cuts look relatively clean."

"I would say he knew what he was doing," Bond said. "He used a sharp knife. Perhaps a saw."

Moore glanced over at the table of tools. There were several of both such items. "So he could be a doctor?" The same had been suggested of Jack, given the mutilations he carried out on the women after murdering them so viciously. Moore didn't miss the sharp look that passed between the two surgeons.

"As we told them at the Rainham inquest," Hebbert said, "it's likely the killer had some knowledge of anatomy, but we doubt he was a medical man."

Moore didn't argue, but he took that statement with a pinch of salt. It was natural for the two men not to want to bring their own profession under suspicion or into disrepute. He didn't hold that against them—it wouldn't stop him following any leads that might point him to a surgeon, so they could be as defensive as they wished.

"It was a hot day in Camden for the inquest, wasn't it, Thomas?" Charles Hebbert shook his head slightly. "All of us crammed into that small space. I was glad to get outside, but God's teeth, the whole city stank that afternoon. Do you remember the stench coming from the canal? Worse than anything I had come across in any mortuary for a while. Juliana and her young man had come to meet me, and they'd waited so long she complained her new dress reeked."

"I remember," Dr. Bond said, smiling. "There were a fair many frock coats in that inquest that were starting to reek themselves, and probably ours amongst them. Standing on those steps while we talked was a great relief." He smiled again, and then his face fell slightly. "I remember," he muttered again.

"I say," Hebbert turned to Bond, "why don't you join us for dinner this evening? Juliana asks after you often—she's very bright you know, very interested in our work. And Mary would love to see you too. What do you say, Thomas?"

"Well, if that's all you've got for us," Inspector Moore interrupted, never that good with small talk of his own, let alone listening to that of others, "then we'll head back and leave you to finish up your work. I don't know whether to thank you or not." He smiled wryly. "Two murders by the same hand a year apart? Maybe he won't strike again for another year. By then, at least, we should have found our Jack." He spoke more confidently than he felt. He would be more than happy for Jack to take a year's absence from his work, just so they—and the rest of London—could get back to a decent night's sleep.

"Let's hope we don't see each other again too soon, shall we, gentlemen?" he added as Dr. Bond finally looked up from his workbench. "And certainly not on the streets of Whitechapel." The two surgeons said their farewells, and then he and Andrews left them to it as Hebbert again pressed Bond to accept his dinner invitation.

"The good Dr. Bond looks exhausted," Andrews said as they strode back to the main thoroughfare. "Did you see him as Hebbert was talking of Rainham? He paled and trembled—only for a moment, but I saw it."

Moore hadn't noticed himself, but then, it was often Andrews who caught the tiny details. "We're all tired," he said, "and the doctor isn't such a young man anymore." He snorted slightly. "Neither are we, for that matter. I have a feeling that we will all be tired for quite some time to come if this murderous summer continues into the winter." The October air was cold and filled with the fog from a thousand fires, all competing to heat the damp, chilly rooms in the streets around them. Inspector Moore lit his pipe and added his own small contribution. "They say this woman was five feet and eight inches tall, or thereabouts? An unusual height for a woman. Perhaps we have a chance of finding out who she was."

"Perhaps," Andrews said. He clearly wasn't convinced, but then, neither was Moore if he was honest. Even without the limited physical evidence the torso and arm provided, the odds were against them. Not only were all their resources being plowed into finding Jack, London's population was in a continual state of change. Hundreds of people came and went every day, often—and especially those who had perhaps fallen down on their luck—giving no warning and providing no destination. For many, there was no one who would care where they headed. Some ended up in the river, entirely of their own accord, providing the dredgers with a ghoulish secondary income in jewelry, pocket watches, and money. No corpse was ever brought to shore with so much as a penny piece on it. It was a grasping, desperate city they lived in, separated by such great divides of wealth and poverty. There were two Londons, he had concluded long ago: one that belonged to those who dressed for the opera, and one that was a mere survival pit for those who sold matches outside the Opera House.

Moore himself belonged to neither, but he had spent so much time trawling through the muck of one that he found the other no more than an illusion of life; he always found it strange when he was called to interact with polite society. On reflection, he decided, that was probably no bad thing. The likes of he and Dr. Bond stank too much of the gritty streets to ever be truly accepted by those gentlemen and ladies who made grand gestures of charity and talked of the "poor unfortunates" as if they in any way understood the true hell these people lived in. He smiled as he smoked. He was becoming something of a cynic in his old age.

"You know what this little trip of ours means, don't you?" Andrews pulled his overcoat tighter around his thin frame and hunched over slightly in the cold.

"Yes, yes, I'm afraid I do," Moore answered. They'd seen the torso first. This case was going to become their responsibility.

8

LONDON, NOVEMBER 1886
AARON KOSMINSKI

Even with the three rowdy children filling the small set of rooms with sound and movement from dawn until dusk, Aaron preferred to stay with Matilda and Morris in Greenfield Street than with Betsy and Woolf and their small Rebecca. *Blood*. All these years later, and he still couldn't look at Betsy without thinking of blood. When she cooked for him, his stomach roiled in revulsion at the thought of her hands on what he was eating. He couldn't understand how Woolf could touch her *intimately*, in *that* place, no matter how beautiful she was. He had made excuses so he hadn't had to see baby Rebecca until there were no remaining traces of his sister's blood anywhere, not even on his mother's apron from helping her with the birth. He loved Betsy, but he couldn't cure himself of the loathing he felt for her.

He should have been at the barber's. Matilda had given him a queer look when he had come back up the stairs so soon after leaving, but he had made some poor excuse about there being not enough work for him today. Knowing Matilda, she might check, but that was a problem for later. Not that being in the safety of their home changed things, as it turned out.

His head had been quiet since they'd fled, blissfully free of visions. Their rooms weren't luxurious, but after the Pale they were more than adequate, and the skills he had learned back then had secured him a position with various barbers on and around the Whitechapel Road. Their incomes might be small, but combined, and with Matilda's housekeeping skills, the Kosminskis had no fear of starvation. Life might be hard, but London had lived up to their hopes after their long journey fleeing from the pogroms he had visualized so violently. They were free, though the past felt like it was forever in their shadow.

Shadows. He shivered. His mouth tasted of rough metal—*fear*. More than fear, dread: endless dread. He stood by the window and looked out at the twilight. Normally he found the noise from the busy streets comforting, and he felt the safety of people—even though so many were violent and criminal or drunk and aggressive. There was always the warmth of the Jewish community, many of whom, like them, had escaped and settled in this most exciting of cities. Their past sufferings united them, and now they gathered together and told stories of the old country, even though the youngest amongst them had no real memories of it.

The old country was in his blood—his grandmother's tainted blood. And after five blissful years of freedom, it was now screaming in his veins. Something was coming—something from the old country was moving like an icy wind through Europe. For the past few weeks Aaron had awoken every morning with the taste of rot and stagnant water choking him, and there was an oppressive creeping dread that almost paralyzed him with fear. Whatever it was, it was ancient: a parasite that would bring wickedness in its wake, infecting wherever it went. And no one would see it coming.

He shivered and peered out through the brown fog that clung to the windows. Here and there dots of sickly yellow glowed dimly as they battled to break through the poisonous atmosphere. He wished for summer, where day and night did not mingle beneath the hanging shroud that coated the city most days, refusing to let more than a sliver of sunlight through. It was, he decided, like a manifestation of the awful foreboding he felt inside. When the first vague feelings of disquiet had gripped him two months previously, he had ignored them, trying to will them away by throwing himself into work and family with an unusual vigor, surprising Matilda with his willingness to do extra where he could—anything to keep busy.

But now the visions were coming thick and fast, and the constant dread was unbearable. Blood, darkness, hunger, age: they crippled him.

Paris.

His head swirled with snippets of French, cobbled streets, drunk, wine, stumbling, soft skin. And then the blood: the *feeding*.

He wanted to run, to gather up the children and flee as they had done before. Would his family listen this time? Would they leave this heaving river city that had become their home, where they had settled?

The river: black, wicked, stagnant water.

It wouldn't stray too far from a river. It would need the water.

He tried to push it from his mind, but the cold fingers gripped like a vice, digging into his brain.

His family wouldn't leave the city—and more than that, *he* couldn't leave the city. The visions wouldn't let him. That scared him the most: the visions sat like something slick, a wet dead thing in the pit of his stomach. Before, the visions had told him to flee; this time they demanded that he stay.

9

LONDON, OCTOBER 1888
DR. BOND

I had been unable to extract myself from Charles's invitation to dinner, and even once I was in the warmth of his home and seated at the table, I found it hard to shake my distraction. *Rainham.* Ever since the mention of Rainham at the morgue, my mind had taken a different turn, and I had barely been able to focus on the inspector, let alone my colleague. *Rainham.* Not the inquest itself but the reminder of how we had stood on the steps afterward and chatted, looking out over the hubbub of Camden.

"You should come here more often, Thomas." Mary smiled as Charles refilled our glasses. "You know you're welcome for dinner whenever you wish."

"That's most kind," I replied and was glad when Charles continued the conversation, asking Juliana about her recent botany studies. The study and drawing of wildlife was quite a hobby of hers. I let their chatter wash over me, making the appropriate noises when they were required, while in my mind, I was once again standing on those steps at Camden, and my eyes caught on a figure on the other side of the road. He had been standing perfectly still, and although his head had tilted downward, I had seen the glint of his eyes in the sunshine as they peered out from under the brim of his hat. He had been watching us. That in itself hadn't registered overly with me as I talked; there were always a small number of ghouls or newsmen who would gather outside an inquest. What I now remembered noticing was how heavy and waxy his dark coat was. I could not conceive why anyone would wear such a garment on a day so humid that most sane men just wanted to rip away their collars and let their skin breathe. He was a tall man, and the black coat reached almost to his ankles. One arm was tucked within its folds, even when he suddenly ducked away and moved swiftly down a side street, perhaps having realized he had been observed.

The memory had been lost to me—it had, after all, been nothing of consequence at the time—but now, *now*, it had significance. It had been him, I was sure of it. The man outside the Rainham inquest was the same man with the withered arm whom I had seen in the opium dens—but what had he been doing in Camden that day, and why had he been watching us so intently? Surely it could not be a simple coincidence? I wished I could see more of his face in my memory, and I also wished that I could trust my memory entirely. Could this be my imagination playing tricks on me through my exhaustion? The man and his obvious search for someone had become a curiosity to me of late, so perhaps my mind had simply moved him from one section of memory to another? I tried to concentrate on the dinner.

"I think it's so important that a man has a purpose, don't you agree, Dr. Bond?"

I looked at Juliana. She had grown up in the past year, and now she had a confidence in her demeanor that changed her from a child to a woman. Her eyes were lively and intelligent and her chestnut curls and skin glowed with health.

"I think it's imperative," I said, smiling.

"That's why I'm so proud of James. He's achieving so much, and he has such a brilliant mind. I have no doubt that soon his company will be the largest import business in the whole of London."

"That sounds quite something," I said. James Harrington was a little older than Juliana's twenty-one years, but he was still a young man: a fine-looking one, with a charming smile that tilted slightly downward when under scrutiny. I thought that he was not one of these overconfident sorts who filled the gentlemen's clubs these days, always competing with one another in business or gambling. He was a serious type, I decided as I saw a slight blush creep under his collar, a quiet man at heart. He would suit the exuberant Juliana well.

"Oh, Juliana," the young man under my scrutiny started, interrupting her, "I fear that although I love the faith you have in me, you are making me sound rather too impressive." Harrington squeezed her hand on the table and then turned his attention to me. "I was unfortunate enough to lose my father last year, just before I met Juliana, but the success of the business is very much all his work. I fully intend to do him credit by expanding it, but I have a lot to learn yet. I'm afraid I didn't pay as much attention as I should have to his work while he and my mother were still alive."

Sadness flickered in his eyes, but he covered it with a small smile. I remembered him now, from that same afternoon on the steps after the Rainham inquest. He had been thinner and paler, then, and no wonder.

"Unfortunately," I said, "it is perhaps in all our natures that we take the living for granted until they are no longer with us."

"Not so easy for you and Father to do, I imagine," Juliana said.

"True. Although your father's natural good cheer does rather keep us both in fine spirits, even at times like these."

"Well, I shall certainly not be taking James for granted," she declared. "I'm going to help with the company bookkeeping and whatever else he needs me to do. I'm sure I'm far better with figures than some of the men he has working for him."

"Sometimes, my dear," Charles said, his pride obvious, "I do wonder whether you should have been born a boy."

"I have to say," Harrington replied, "that I for one am very glad she was not."

We all laughed at that, and watching the couple I envied them their youth and excitement for life and each other. In the face of so much energy, it was hard not to feel old and tired, both of which I was. In fact, listening to the chatter around the table, I felt envious of the warmth with which Charles was surrounded. I doubted there were many sleepless nights in this house.

Despite my eagerness to get to the opium dens and find the stranger in the black coat, as the main course arrived, a very fine cut of beef, I realized how much I had been neglecting my appetite of late, surviving as I was on plates of cheese, bread, and cold meats. My stomach growled loudly, twice, which caused further laughter, given the informal nature of our dining, and I finished everything on my plate with an enthusiasm that made Mary ply me with more.

I had hoped to get away quite soon after coffee, but Charles insisted I join him in his study for some brandy. We left the ladies to say their goodnights to young Harrington and closed the door behind us. Charles wasted no time in pouring two large measures, and we sat on either side of the small fire gazing quietly into the flames for a few minutes. Just as the silence was reaching a palpably awkward stage, Charles shifted in his chair and leaned forward.

"London is not herself this year, wouldn't you say, Thomas?" He didn't look at me, his eyes still on the grate. His tone was quiet.

I watched as he took a long swallow of his drink before I took a sip of my own. "I think that could be considered a fair assumption," I said.

"Sometimes I look at Juliana and my heart is gripped with fear for her." The leather creaked as he leaned forward in his seat to refill his glass from the decanter. "There is so much wickedness at work in the city I feel as if I can almost touch it. We're surrounded by it."

"Perhaps *we* are, my friend, but I think your Juliana is safe." Was this the cause of his sudden melancholy? I had envied my friend his family, but perhaps I had not considered the worries that came with that. But the women in Charles's life were surely safe from the human monsters currently hunting on London's streets.

"She's not . . ." I struggled to find the appropriate words, "she's not in a position to cause alarm. She has her young man and her family to make sure she's not in any place of danger." The idea of Juliana wandering the streets of Whitechapel was one that I could not entertain. She moved in different circles; she had a different sort of life. "She's also a bright girl," I added. "She has never been childish in her thinking. Life might throw the unexpected at us at any time, this is true, but as for the London we have seen so much of this year? It won't touch her. You can be sure of that, my friend."

He smiled slightly, but it didn't reach his eyes, and as he turned to me I realized that Charles was quite drunk. I had been so distracted by thoughts of the stranger throughout dinner I hadn't paid as much attention to my host's behavior; I had presumed his joviality to be his normal good humor. But now, seeing him in this state, I realized that his laughter had been a touch too loud; his jocularity a touch forced. I looked more closely at him in the flickering glow of the firelight. His skin was flushed and his pupils were glazed.

"I dream of blood," he murmured. "Have I told you that, Thomas? Everything is coated in it. The world has turned red." His mouth turned down in a tight frown. "Quite horrible."

"I'm not surprised," I said, wanting to reassure him. "With all that has filled the news of late, and the violence that has gripped our city, it's remarkable we're still functioning at all." Despite his dreams, I envied him his sleep. Nightmares I could cope with; this endless exhaustion was something else.

"She's always in them," he said, "Juliana. Every dream."

"She is your daughter, Charles. It is entirely normal for your mind to place her at the center of your fears. The mind is a strange terrain. It has its own way of dealing with the world while you sleep."

Charles nodded, although it was clear he was unconvinced. He muttered something under his breath, the words slurring together.

"What was that?" I asked. My own tiredness was starting to feel like grit behind my eyes, and although I was under no illusion that sleep would embrace me that night, my senses were dull. As much as Charles was my friend, I had little to offer anyone in the way of good humor and support.

"I don't like to look out of the windows at night," he admitted. "It's the glass, and the darkness. It's as if everything wicked is looking into my house. Into *me*."

I had no answer for that other than a hollow dread in the pit of my stomach. This was not *my* Charles Hebbert, my cheery friend and colleague. If his thoughts could go to such dark places then what hope was there for mine?

I drank my brandy quickly, fully intending to make my excuses and leave, but Charles suddenly burst into a smile.

"Don't listen to me, Thomas. I am fine. Just a momentary bout of melancholy. Shall we have one more drink? I promise to be more cheerful." He slapped my shoulder, heading toward the decanter, regardless of my answer. "Just one more, and then I shall let you get home to bed."

I glanced at the clock to see it was already ten o'clock. I would not make the dens tonight—not, at least, in any fit state to speak to the stranger should I encounter him. I forced a smile and took another drink.

One drink became several, and it was nearly midnight when I finally rose from my chair to leave. Charles had been true to his word, and our conversation had turned to more pleasant talk, of family life, Juliana and James, and then reminiscing on the past adventures of our own youths. Yet I couldn't help but feel it was somewhat forced. Charles finally drifted off into a drunken sleep midsentence, and I left him by the dying fire and quietly headed downstairs. My own head was spinning slightly, despite having tried to avoid matching Charles's measures, and I was looking forward to lying in my own bed, even if sleep wouldn't come.

I had reached the front door when Mary emerged from the drawing room. I jumped slightly, expecting her to be already asleep.

"Thank you, Thomas," she said. "You must come again. I think your company is good for him."

"You might not thank me in the morning. I fear he is somewhat the worse for brandy. I have left him asleep by the fire."

"I shall look after him." She smiled softly as she passed me my hat. "I'm sorry he's kept you up so late. You're both working so hard; you must be tired yourself."

My exhaustion and I were such companions now that it was almost amusing to hear someone mention it so lightly. "I shall cope," I answered, "and so will Charles."

Outside, the night was cold, winter finally gripping the city now that the long, hot summer had died. The streets of Westminster were quiet. I looked back up at the house and the glass of the windows glinted black back at me. I shivered and turned away, pulling my overcoat tight around me.

10

London, August 18, 1888

She was crying. She couldn't help it, even though it was making her nose run, which was making it harder for her to breathe. *It's your own fault*: the thought came to her in her sister's voice, even though Magda had been dead two years. *If you dally in wickedness, then the devil will surely come for your soul.*

In the corner of the gloomy workshop she could just about see where the four jackets lay discarded and forgotten. He hadn't wanted them at all; they had been nothing more than a lure—a temptation—and she had succumbed. A choked whimper escaped her throat, and immediately she tried to suck the sound back in, aware of her captor busying himself with the unseen contents of an open trunk a few feet away. Her head throbbed where he had struck her suddenly only minutes before, and the rough cloth he had stuffed into her mouth was so rancid she was sure she was about to vomit up the fried fish she had treated herself to that morning, and then no matter what the man was planning she would probably die. Fresh tears ran down her face.

He coughed and spat a ball of phlegm to the floor, and she trembled. She had thought him a gentleman, but now she didn't know what he was. *Yes, you do, Ava*, the ghost of her sister reprimanded her. *He's the devil, come to tear your soul from your body. And you have no one to blame but yourself.*

She pressed herself into the damp wall as if she could somehow squeeze through the bricks to freedom on the other side. Outside, she had been sweating in the summer heat and wishing for a cool breeze. Now her entire body trembled in the chill, as if he had transported her to an entirely different world. And perhaps he had.

Not so far away, her employer—her *ex*-employer—would be working hard on her sewing machine, not giving her a single thought—and why should she? She wouldn't miss Ava or the jackets until eight that evening, when she was due to return them with the buttonholes and finishing done. Of course it had never been in her plan to return them, not once she'd met a fine gentleman who'd persuaded her to sell them to him.

More tears squeezed from her eyes as she heard the clank of metal on metal: he was removing items from the trunk and laying them out on the small workbench, muttering quietly to himself as he did so. How had someone so clearly caught by madness appeared so sane? Or had she simply been blinded to it by her own greed, by the thought of having some money in her pocket and being able to move on from her tiny, grubby room and start again somewhere else in the heaving city? He held up something that glinted in the gloom. What was that? A knife? Too big. A saw? She mewled again and fought not to release the contents of her bladder.

Food had always been her downfall. She was tall, had been even as a child, and her mother always said she had been born with a man's appetite to go with her height. She had become slimmer in these recent hard times, but even given her life of near-poverty since Magda died she still had a fair coating of flesh on her bones. Maybe that was why, unlike other employers, Katherine Jackson didn't feed her during her working hours—perhaps she thought Ava was managing perfectly well on the miserable four shillings a week she paid her. It was only a brief moment of anger, and then she cried some more, knowing this was not the truth. Katherine Jackson couldn't afford to feed her, and that was all there was to it. She too was struggling to earn some kind of living, but that hadn't stopped Ava from stealing the four jackets, which would cost Katherine dearly. She hadn't even been afraid as she'd done it, that's how wicked she was. She had smiled at Katherine and taken the garments, meeting her gaze shamelessly, and all the while her mind had been fixed on what she would treat herself to that evening—maybe a buttercake, that sweet taste she had never outgrown, or perhaps some German sausage. Her mouth had been watering all the way to where she had agreed to meet the gentleman and sell him the coats. She would be happy never to see a buttercake again. She would sew buttonholes until her fingers bled if it would get her out of this dark and miserable place and back into the stinking sunshine.

He bent over the open box and took out something she couldn't quite see, placing it with a heavy thud on the workbench before lighting a dusty lamp and turning to face her. She had thought that light would somehow appease her fear, but now she wished he would plunge them back into the gloom, where she could still pretend that perhaps he had forgotten about her. As his shadow stretched out behind him in the glow of the small light, all thoughts of food and sunshine evaporated from her mind, leaving nothing but terror. His blue eyes were wide as he stared at her, focused and curious and quite, quite mad.

"Old blood," he said, a small smile on his face. "You have old blood. From home. I didn't know what it was at first, this scent in the air every time you walked past. But then suddenly I knew: it was your blood that was driving me mad." He frowned. "And I've been so good—I've *tried* to be so good, for so many months. I thought—I thought perhaps I had control."

Ava couldn't stop herself shaking. She shook her head from side to side, as if somehow she could persuade him that she was not the girl he thought. It wasn't she who had the old blood, whatever that was; she couldn't come from his home. He was an Englishman and she was a Polish immigrant.

"It wants you," he said, softly, "and I have to give it what it wants." He picked up a knife from the table, and Ava tugged desperately at the leather ties that bound her to the lead pipes, wishing she had tried harder to free herself, wishing she had fought back harder when he'd hit her, wishing that she had never started working for Katherine Jackson three months ago.

He held something else behind his back as he came closer to her and crouched down. "Can you see it?" he whispered. "Can you see it?"

She stared at him, uncomprehending. What did he want from her? If she could just give him the right answer, then maybe he would release her. Maybe—

"It's behind me—always behind me. Can't you see it?"

Ava's eyes blurred with fresh tears. There was nothing there, nothing behind him; he was just a madman. A madman with a knife. She shook her head. No, she couldn't see it—

"*She* saw it," he said as his arm came from behind his back. He held a dead woman's head high, gripping it by the hair. The skin had turned to leather and thinned against the bones, but the mouth was forever open in terror. "They *all* see it, in the end."

As Ava screamed and screamed behind her gag, her mind snapping at the horror of her impending fate, the man leaned in closer, and she did; she *saw* it. Magda's voice had been wrong. The man wasn't the devil at all. The devil was behind him.

11

Daily Telegraph
October 4, 1888

THE WHITEHALL MURDER

Very little additional information has been allotted by the authorities regarding the identity of the victim of the atrocious crime whose dismembered remains were found on Tuesday afternoon in the new Police buildings, on the Embankment at Westminster.

Sent to the Central News Service, October 5, 1888

Dear Friend

In the name of God hear me I swear I did not kill the female whose body was found at Whitehall. If she was an honest woman I will hunt down and destroy her murderer. If she was a whore God will bless the hand that slew her, for the women of Moab and Midian shall die and their blood shall mingle with the dust. I never harm any others or the Divine power that protects and helps me in my grand work would quit for ever. Do as I do and light of glory shall shine upon you. I must get to work tomorrow treble event this time yes three must be ripped. Will send you a bit of face by post I promise this dear old Boss. The police now reckon my work a practical joke well well Jacky's a very practical joker ha ha keep this back till three are wiped out and you can show the cold meat.

Yours truly
Jack the Ripper

12

LONDON, OCTOBER 1888
INSPECTOR MOORE

"I see your lot have been busy over at Whitehall today," Waring said, paying the waiter for their two tankards of beer. "More police officers than should have been in that building for quite some time, eh?" Moore took a swallow and said nothing, but he watched the slim man carefully as he laughed at his own poor joke.

It had come as no great surprise to Henry Moore that Jasper Waring had wanted to meet him in a Whitechapel public house. The police were three days into their search of the area—a public relations act, more than with any real hope of catching their killer—and reporters were swarming the area eager for any tidbits of salacious gossip, anything they could print about any of the unfortunate women— about their pasts or those who knew them. The public was greedy for as much information as they could get; whether it was truthful or not was apparently irrelevant. Jack and his murders had proved, if such proof were needed, that there was a palpable excitement in fear. The newspapers were doing a roaring trade, and of course Jasper Waring would want to be at the heart of that.

Moore had to admit that Waring was smarter than most. He certainly had a nose for a story, and while he was no doubt relishing Jack's antics as much as the rest of his breed, Waring was a man who would always be looking for something he could claim for his own.

"Jack," whoever he might be, was the whole of London's business, and there were newspapermen better connected with the police than he who would get any information first. Not that there was much danger of that.

"Those bloodhounds turn anything up?" Waring's eyes were sharp, but still Moore said nothing as he downed half his beer. The newsman would be paying for their drinks; that was always the unspoken agreement, and he intended to make the added time on his working day worthwhile. He was tired, and it had been a cold and frustrating day of supervising the policemen and dogs as they searched the Scotland Yard building site for more—or any— of the dead woman's body parts. Their hunt had been as fruitless as the higher-profile one going on throughout the streets of Whitechapel, and eventually Moore had admitted defeat and sent the team, including Andrews, home to warm up.

"Not like Jack, this boy, is he?" Waring smiled, his expression a mix of wry and cheeky. Moore wasn't sure he liked the young reporter, but he did respect him, and they had been useful to each other in the past; if that had not been the case, he would have just gone home. God only knew he could do with the sleep. He needed eight hours straight a night, and of late he'd been lucky to get five or six before having to drag himself out of the depths of his slumber to head back to Division to trawl through yet more false leads.

As it was, now that he was here, the sheer force of life that filled the Princess Alice on the corner of Commercial Street was refreshing him. Much of the laughter was fueled by drink, and much of the drink was fueled by hardship, but at least there *was* some laughter. Londoners were strange folk, he had concluded a long time ago, never more alive than when in the presence of death. The food stands that had sprung up at the murder sites, the street theaters re-creating the tableaux of the unfortunate women's deaths: entertainment crafted by the grip of terror. Was it too much, perhaps, he wondered as he looked at the glazed eyes and flushed faces of those who filled the surrounding tables. There was something amiss in the people of the city, even he could sense that—a hysteria maybe. There had been too much violence done on London's streets this year. It needed to slow down.

"What makes you think it isn't Jack?" he said, finally addressing his companion. Waring wasn't showing deep insight: the methods of murder were so different that although both were gruesome, they were unlikely to be linked. It was Dr. Bond's opinion that there were two killers at work here, and he was very much inclined to agree.

"The letter for a start," Waring said. "'I swear I did not kill the woman found at Whitehall'?" He obviously noted Moore's look of displeasure because he laughed slightly as he raised his beer glass. "Come, come. It came into the Central News Agency. It was hardly likely to be kept a secret."

"We've had more than seven hundred such letters arrive, and it's unlikely any of them are from Jack himself. They simply add to the load of the investigation and my lack of sleep. You'd do best to ignore them," he said sternly.

"It's my job to make sure they get published, not to hide them."

"At least you're an honest bastard. There is truth in that." Moore signaled the waiter for two more drinks.

"And your lot have hardly been quick to connect them."

"There is also truth in that," Moore said. "Policemen are often politicians too. So what exactly is it you think I can do for you?"

"It's not what you can do for me," Waring winked. "It's what I can do for you." He let out a sharp whistle and turned his head to the door. Various customers glanced down at the floor as something moved between them, causing the odd smile or curse in surprise.

The small terrier came and sat obediently at Waring's feet. "Meet Smoker," Waring said. "If there's more of that woman hidden in Whitehall, he'll find her."

"We've tried dogs," Moore said. "As you are no doubt very well aware, I've spent my day surrounded by the damned things."

"You haven't tried this dog." The waiter hurried over, and Waring paid for the drinks. He waited until the man had scurried away again before leaning forward and continuing, "If there's something to be found, he's the one that will do it."

Moore stared at him. "You want me to let your dog search the Whitehall building?"

"No," Waring shook his head and tipped his glass toward Moore. "I want you to let my dog *and* me search your premises. No find, no story. I give you my word."

So there it was: the point of the meeting. But to let a reporter and a scruffy terrier into the crime scene? How would that play out back at Division? The bosses would hang him. He looked down at the eager-eyed hound; it appeared to be staring back at him, awaiting his answer. It was a confident eye, he had to give the dog that. How much harm could it do? He and Waring understood each other; the reporter would not make him look inept, no matter what the outcome. He drained his beer. He also knew he didn't have a huge amount of choice. In their strange relationship of give-and-take, it was he himself who owed the most recent debt of gratitude.

"Tomorrow then," he said, and got to his feet. "Meet me at Division at half past eleven. I'll take you over from there. And no audience." The dog, Smoker, thumped his tail against the dusty wooden floorboards.

"Tomorrow then," Waring repeated, and he also got to his feet. The dog looked up at its master, and as the two men headed out into the cold night air, Smoker stayed close at Waring's heels.

Moore headed to the main thoroughfare to try and find a hansom cab; unlike many of Whitechapel's fetid alleyways, Commercial Street was well lit and busy.

"Do you want to share?" he asked Waring, a polite gesture only. They might be many things, but friends they were not. Boundaries were respected.

"No, thank you. Smoker prefers to walk, and I enjoy the sights."

Moore nodded. That was the strange delusion to be found in all newsmen: they had a firm belief that the tragedies of the world belonged to others; their role was simply to report on those tragedies. Some found out otherwise, of course, and it had been one such event that had brought Waring and Moore together.

"Take care," he said as a hansom pulled to the side and waited for him to climb on board. "The streets aren't everyone's friend."

"Ha!" Waring laughed with good humor. "I doubt they are any man's friend, but I'm not alone in my enjoyment of them. You'd be surprised who I've seen wandering through them. The good doctor, for one. Even though he takes care to dress down and not be seen, I can always recognize a man by his gait."

Moore half-smiled. Men were always drawn to the gutter at some point or another, and he knew the doctor. He would want to understand the killer who stalked Whitechapel, and that would mean treading in his footsteps. Had he not gone the path of medicine, Thomas Bond would have made a fine inspector.

It was only just after noon when Moore led Waring and Smoker down into the vault, and it was barely fifteen minutes later that he stood dumbfounded and speechless, all words lost to him. Jasper Waring was equally silent. No matter what promises the reporter had made, he surely couldn't have expected such swift results.

"Fetch Dr. Bond," Moore muttered eventually, his teeth gritted. He didn't raise his eyes from the dog's find, but he heard feet scurry quickly away and up the steps back to daylight. The remaining group of officers were silent, each no doubt wishing that they were part of Commissioner Warren's Force who were still searching Whitechapel room by room in the increasingly vain hope of turning up something that might lead them to Jack. Moore had half a mind to send them all there immediately, as they'd been pretty damned useless here at Whitehall.

When they'd arrived in the badly lit basement of the new building, they'd placed the dog near the spot where the torso had been found. Despite the poor visibility, the terrier began digging at the ground almost immediately, barely more than a few inches from where the parcel had been placed. He was digging with such determination that Moore's heart raced in anticipation. He had not been denied, either, for there at his feet was the dog's find.

He held the lamp over it again: a human leg, severed below the knee, with the bare foot still attached.

"I told you he was good," Waring said.

Moore ignored the reporter's boast and glared up at the small gathering, those who had been unfortunate enough to accompany them. Even in the grainy light that was doing little to dispel the pitch-blackness of the claustrophobic vault, they would no doubt be able to see the rage burning in his eyes. He felt as if they were blazing the way they would if he were the devil himself.

"Why did we not find this?" No one answered. "How many pissing days have we wasted scouring this building? For *what*? For us to be saved from our own incompetence by a newsman's *ratting* dog?"

"At least we have it now," Andrews said, the only man brave enough to speak out in the face of Henry Moore's anger. "Better to find it this way than not at all."

Andrews was right, of course, even if that did nothing to appease his own rabid frustration. He also knew that every man involved in the previous search would be just as embarrassed at having failed to make the discovery. If the police couldn't find body parts that were—literally—right under their noses, then how could they expect the public to have any faith in their ability to catch the more attention-seeking Jack? It was a farce, and he wanted no part of it.

He tried to unclench his tight jaw. What was done was done. Now there was only how to proceed.

"We'll come back this evening and continue," he said, gruffly. The dog, his job done, was now more intent on getting his master's attention than digging further. "But we will conduct the search in secret, do you understand?" He glanced at Waring. "That is as much for you as them. No news reporters drawing attention to us, and I want none of the workmen to know we're here. Our killer might be among their number."

"The fog will hide us," Andrews said. "And I'll keep the number here to a minimum."

"Good," Moore said. Not that they needed a minimum; all they needed, it appeared, was the bloody dog.

13

LONDON, OCTOBER 1888
DR. BOND

I was not in the best of spirits on arrival back at the Scotland Yard worksite, but the strangeness of my own mood was only enhanced by the atmosphere I found there. It was eerie: when people spoke, it was only in hushed whispers, and through the thick night fog the few policemen Moore had with him moved like ghosts, here and there and gone as they let Charles and me into the unformed building.

Candles lit our way back down to the vault, and in that oppressive underground room those spread against the walls and in the corners seemed only to exacerbate the darkness of the shadows. I shivered, and not entirely from the cold.

"This is the dog, then?" I asked. It was a pointless question, but I felt the need to break the silence with something other than a whisper.

The small terrier was pacing a little, his tail down, and I wondered if he too felt that the air tonight was somehow unnatural. He looked up at us and whined, and then growled.

"I don't think he likes the dark," Moore said. "He's not as confident tonight." He leaned down and patted the creature's head, a gesture I found surprising, having never taken Moore for an affectionate man. There was something essentially practical about him. He was by all accounts an excellent detective, but I doubted he was ever personally affected by the cases presented to him. Or perhaps that was too sweeping a judgment. If he were emotionally affected, then I felt he dealt with such reactions far better than some—myself included, of late.

The dog whined again, and Moore released him from his lead. "Let's see what you can find this time," he said. "Bring me the head and you'll be an inspector by morning."

Moore's gruffness was soothing in this strange environment that hinted constantly at things just out of sight. I couldn't help but remember the strange vision I had had under the influence of the opium, where there had been something looming in the darkness. I shook it away, not only for the vision itself but for the opium itch it brought with it.

"Here he goes," Charles muttered as the dog wandered here and there, his nose to the ground, his short legs trembling slightly. Charles seemed unaffected by the almost supernatural atmosphere we stood in, and I wished I could be as sanguine as he and shake off my own personal exhaustion and melancholy. The past week or more had been busy—we'd had the inquest for the torso that had been rotting unnoticed so close to where I now stood, and then the wasted time of the boiled bones found on the railway tracks—at first they had looked like evidence of further gruesome murder, but once I had had time to examine them, I was left in no doubt that they were clearly those of a bear. The reporters had been disappointed at that news, and I found myself wondering at the feverish excitement for blood that had filled the streets of the city this year.

The dog reached Charles's feet and growled slightly, jumping back.

"These feet are very much not what you're looking for," Charles said, as he stepped back toward the wall to give the dog more space, and a flutter of a laugh passed around us all. At Mary's insistence I had dined twice more that week with Charles and his family, and I had been glad to find my friend in much better spirits. I found myself missing Juliana and her young man, who had gone to Bath for a few days; the young woman's company was charming, and the exuberance of youth, much as a small part of me envied it, was good for the soul.

As it was, I had spent only three nights of the past ten in the opium dens of Bluegate, where I had satisfied both my urge for the drug and my need to search for the dark-coated stranger—though on no occasion did I see the man. After my recollection of him at the Rainham inquest, this left me frustrated.

Moore coughed suddenly, just one quiet expulsion, but I jumped slightly. It was only a small movement, but enough to draw Inspector Andrews's attention to me.

"Are you all right, Doctor?" he asked. "You look pale."

Even in the gloom I could see him studying me with a mixture of concern and curiosity, and I forced a smile. "If I'm truly honest, I, like the dog, am no great fan of small spaces with no natural light."

He returned my smile and the answer appeared to satisfy him, but his eyes still rested on me, and I wondered what he was thinking. Had my behavior become unusual? Did my increasing itch for the poppy show?

"He's digging," Charles said, breaking the moment, and we all turned to look. It was true: the dog might have been unsettled, but he couldn't fight his nature.

"That's where the leg was found," Andrews looked at Moore. "Perhaps there's still a scent there."

Moore said nothing. His gaze was intent on the terrier, who had lost all interest in everything except what secrets the ground might hold. The earth looked hard, only small pockets of dirt flying up with each scrabble of his claws, but he continued to dig, determined.

We stood in silence and watched, anticipation growing. This was not an animal who was simply confused by a scent; the dog was digging with purpose. My own heart thumped in my chest. There was more of our mystery woman to be discovered here, I was sure of it. After several minutes of mounting tension, a flash of something other than darkness appeared in the light of the candle Moore was holding over the animal: fingers, bent as if clawing their way out of the ground.

"He's got something!"

Suddenly, where there had been stillness and silence, there was a flurry of activity. The dog was eager to retrieve his prize, but he was dragged away and back upstairs to where the newsman was waiting for him. Moore and Andrews crouched by the broken earth and excavated the rest of the limb: an arm, removed at the shoulder, just like the one pulled from the riverbank.

"How much further down?" Andrews asked after we had stared silently for a few moments.

"Ten inches or so," Moore said.

I looked at the earth around me. It was hard and trodden down. "Then it's been there for quite some time."

"We need to confirm that it matches the rest," Moore said. Charles stepped up.

"I'll take it back now. Get it done."

"Thank you," Moore said.

"No need for you to come, Thomas," Charles said. "We all know what the outcome is likely to be. This won't take both of us."

He was right of course. We did all know that the matching of the limb to the body was likely to be a mere formality.

"Get more men here," Moore growled. "I want to find the damned head."

As it turned out, Smoker refused to hunt anymore once the other men arrived at the scene. Instead, he sat stubbornly beside his master. I wondered if perhaps he had found all the treasures the ground had to give up; I certainly didn't think that the killer would have left the head here: a head was a clue, and while this man might be taunting the police with his choice of location for the body parts, I doubted very much whether he wanted to get caught just yet. After I had examined the ground from which the limb had been pulled, we headed back up to the dank night air, leaving the new body of men to continue scouring the ground once again. Andrews and I stood with Inspector Moore as he smoked.

"Both limbs rotted in the ground," I said quietly. The fog had a grip on the city now and it felt like a shroud, separating those of us who dealt in death from the life that filled the streets. "They've been there for weeks—as was the torso, I suspect, despite Mr. Windborne's insistence that it wasn't there before."

"To bring the body here unnoticed," Andrews said, "how could that be possible?"

"The billboards at the Cannon Street entrance appear scalable," I said, adding, "perhaps not for me, but for a younger man."

"Maybe our killer is one of the workmen," Moore said, exhaling smoke. "They come and go, and they have easy access to the vault. The torso itself would have been bulky, but the arm and leg could have easily been wrapped and concealed as tools. Or if not the killer, then perhaps an accomplice. I'll start re-questioning them tomorrow."

"What do you think, Doctor? You have a mind for these things." He looked at me, his eyes sharp flints in the gloom. I examined my thoughts. He was right: I did have an instinct for seeing into the minds of violent men through their actions. I often wondered, while lying sleepless in my bed, whether that "gift" could be the root of my problems. I could see evil too clearly at times.

"I doubt that the man we're looking for would leave the evidence of his crimes at his own workplace. That would be arrogance to the point of stupidity—a quite different kind of madness, or perhaps the action of someone who wants you to catch him. I don't think either of those is the case here, unfortunately. Neither do I think he has an accomplice. I doubt he would risk a second person's knowing about his deeds, no matter how close they might be."

"That doesn't help me," Moore said. "I was very much hoping you were not going to suggest that a stranger managed to get into our new Police Headquarters and deposited three parts of a body with no one noticing."

I smiled. "Of course, I could be wrong. These are just my thoughts, not proven facts."

A police constable emerged from the gloom ahead and reported, "It's still quiet out there."

"Good," Moore said. "I am in no mood to face blood-hungry newsmen tonight."

"A few passersby stopped to look," the constable continued, "but I think it was more curiosity about the original find than any news of recent ones. There was only one man I had to move on. He was just staring at the site. Very strange."

"A man staring at the site and you didn't think to perhaps bring him inside for us to talk to?" Moore's voice had shifted into something close to a snarl, and I understood why: anyone behaving even slightly suspiciously was enough to consider as a suspect, especially when there were no other leads to follow in such a case. Hunting ghosts was no easy task.

"He had a withered arm," the constable stuttered quickly. "He'd never have managed to carry a torso in here."

The words were like ice hurled at my face. *The stranger from Camden?* "What was he wearing?" I asked, before I could control myself. Both Moore and Andrews turned to look at me and I cursed myself, but still I stared at the young man in front of us.

"I couldn't see," he said, even more nervous now that I was so intent on his information. "A long black coat, I think. Waxy."

So it *was* him! My heart thumped once again. He had been here, and not so long ago. If I could make my excuses now, then I had half a chance of finding him tonight.

"Did I do something wrong?" the constable asked, his eyes flicking between his two superiors. "If I had thought . . ." His words trailed away.

"Do you know that man?" Moore asked.

"No, not as such," I answered. "I imagine he is just a ghoul, drawn to such events. He's probably been at Whitechapel too, I wouldn't wonder." I kept my tone light. I didn't want to examine my own reasons for keeping this secret from the two inspectors. I told myself I really had nothing to tell—and I certainly didn't want to share my visits to the opium dens with them.

"Where have you seen him?" Andrews asked.

"If it is indeed the same man, then he was outside the Rainham inquest. I recall the withered arm."

"As you say, probably just a ghoul," Moore said. He did not sound entirely convinced, but I knew his irritation was directed not at me but at the young officer. Andrews was watching me.

"To remember a stranger from over a year ago," he said, eventually. "I wish I had your memory for detail."

"Ah, that's age," I said, forcing myself to smile. "I can remember things from a year ago, but don't ask me what I ate for supper last night. How is the Whitechapel search going?" Presently, all the men in the area were being questioned as part of the search for Jack. I needed to change the subject of our conversation for the sake of my own nerves and Henry Moore took the bait, snorting derisively.

"It would perhaps have been more effective if we had not adhered to the law so thoroughly. We should have just searched by force and not with permission. There's been plenty of time for our Jack to move anything suspicious."

"But still," Andrews said, "it's better than doing nothing, in the eyes of the populace, at any rate."

"Oh yes," Moore said, "for now, we have the residents with us." He dampened his pipe. "Until he kills again, of course. And then we're fucked."

There was nothing to say after that, and for a while the three of us simply stared out into the fog and listened to the sounds of the search going on in the building behind us. They would find nothing more, I was sure of it. Waring's dog had done their job for them. And what was the stranger's interest in these cases? I wondered. And what was he looking for in the opium dens?

I had to find him.

14

THE EAST-END MURDERS

We are requested to publish the following:—

Sir Charles Warren wishes to say that the marked desire evinced by the inhabitants of the Whitechapel district to aid the police in the pursuit of the author of the recent crimes has enabled him to direct that, subject to the consent of occupiers, a thorough house-to-house search should be made within a defined area. With few exceptions the inhabitants of all classes and creeds have freely fallen in with the proposal, and have materially assisted the officers engaged in carrying it out.

Sir Charles Warren feels that some acknowledgement is due on all sides for the cordial cooperation of the inhabitants, and he is much gratified that the police officers have carried out so delicate a duty with the marked goodwill of all those with whom they have come in contact.

Sir Charles Warren takes this opportunity to acknowledge the receipt of an immense volume of correspondence of a semi-private character on the subject of the Whitechapel murders, which he has been quite unable to respond to in a great number of instances; and he trusts that the writers will accept this acknowledgement in lieu of individual replies. They may be assured that their letters have received every consideration.

15

London, October 1888
Aaron Kosminski

The dank streets outside were finally emptying of the dark-uniformed policemen who had overrun Whitechapel for the past few days, but the sense of tense excitement still hung in the encroaching fog. Handbills and flyers seeking information, thousands of which must have been handed out, now littered the streets. They were trampled into the dirt and mud underfoot until they were no longer visible, but people still talked about their contents, the search for Jack and his grisly souvenirs, even if no gory innards had been discovered in the room-by-room search of their homes.

Not that Aaron had been outside much during the search. Matilda had thought it best he stay inside. It was no secret that hundreds of anonymous accusatory letters and cards were being sent to the police. Aaron had barely worked in two years, and he was known in the overcrowded houses and roads around them as being "something of a strange one"—no doubt the most polite of several descriptions—so she and Morris, after much whispering between them, had encouraged him to stay inside and help with the children.

He hadn't minded that at all. Going out was something he— or the awfulness inside his head—forced him to do, to seek *it* out, however much he didn't want to. Not that he felt much safer confined to their rooms, even with the police methodically searching every room for streets around. Even if they found their "Jack," they wouldn't find what terrified him. Jack was merely a side effect of the mayhem that followed in the creature's wake, the wickedness it hid itself within. Everywhere one turned in London these days there were fights and foul words. Tempers were like dry tinder, just waiting for a spark to set them off. It might be more apparent in the hard-scrabble lives in the rough, dimly lit areas like Whitechapel, but he could feel the tendrils stretching out into the large houses of the rich too, where it simmered more quietly. Hatred, violence, evil, all carried on the water.

He wished he could *see* more and *feel* less. What use were these awful half snippets of thought, the hours of dread? They served no purpose, other than to feed his sisters' growing conviction that he was mad—and perhaps he was. His hands trembled constantly, and he barely slept. Even if someone would employ him, who would trust him with a cut-throat razor?

"What did you say to them?"

He'd known Matilda was standing in the doorway behind him before she'd spoken. He could feel her eyes, staring at his back with a mixture of worry and disapproval. She'd be rubbing her hands on her apron. He could almost hear the skin rasping against the worn fabric. She didn't care what they'd asked him—she already knew that. She cared only for his answers. They all knew the questions: the police had spoken to hundreds of men throughout their laborious search of Whitechapel, and they'd asked the same things—times, places, habits—all the while other officers were looking under beds, rummaging through drawers, examining knives.

Aaron shrugged. He couldn't quite remember what he'd said. He was sure he'd answered their questions perfectly adequately, but he was also aware that it wasn't his softly spoken words they'd been paying attention to. It was his nervous twitches, shaking hands and tired, straying eyes. He knew they were suspicious, but what could he say, that they were on the same side of the fight? He could feel the terrible evil at the core of the city, and he wanted to find it as much as they wanted to find the side effect—this Jack? They'd have him in Colney Hatch as soon as he'd opened his mouth. Perhaps Colney Hatch was where he belonged—he might even find something like peace there.

"I just answered the questions," he said.

"Good," Matilda said, although she sounded less than convinced. She knew as well as he did that although no trace of anything even remotely suspicious had been found in their rooms, that wouldn't stop the police looking at him.

"They made me write something," he added.

"They did that to lots of men, so Molly downstairs says. Her Harry too." Matilda's accent was still strong, but she'd picked up the patterns of the language well in their years here. It was a strange mixture of the old country and the new one, and that made him shiver too: the thought of the old country. "But if you ask me, he's long gone from here. They won't find him."

He didn't turn around, and after a few moments, she sighed and went back to her cooking. He stared out of the window and picked at the edges of his dirty fingernails, trying to stop his hands shaking. He would have to wash later; Matilda would insist on it. But the water bothered him. It made him think of the river. And that in turn made him think of Betsy's blood, all those years ago in their childhood bed.

A dank, dark stagnant river of blood: that was what filled his head most days. It tore at his skull.

Perhaps this was just madness, after all.

16

LONDON, OCTOBER 1888
DR. BOND

Several of the attendees were still milling around Westminster Sessions House as Inspector Moore, Inspector Andrews, and I emerged. They were mainly the workmen and ordinary people who had been called as witnesses. For them, although they had naturally been quite nervous, there was a sense of excitement. Today had been something of an adventure—a change from the monotony of their daily existence; doubtless they would shortly celebrate that fact with several flagons of beer. Once again I pondered the strangeness of life: I attended so many inquests that they were sometimes barely more than an irritating interruption to my day.

I would rather have made my escape from the building more quickly, my overwhelming objective being to see whether the stranger in the black coat had observed this inquest from afar, as he had before, but given the verdict and Jasper Waring's propensity for chatter and questions, we three had been held up longer than expected, and I could hardly have fled without looking rude, at best.

Now I scoured the green opposite us, but I could not see the object of my curiosity. Had he been there and left already? It was possible—but why just loiter and observe? What was to be gained from it? If he had some interest in these deaths, which it was clear to me he must, then why not simply approach one of the inspectors? I thought again of the strangely intent way he had moved amongst those in the grip of opium stupor. How did that activity—one I could not deny I was craving for myself—have any bearing on these awful murders? There was, of course, another option: perhaps the man was simply quite mad, and there was no connection.

"No other evidence to offer at this time," Moore muttered, as Detective Inspector Marshall, who had represented Scotland Yard at the inquest, tipped his hat in our direction and then hurried down the steps to his waiting hansom cab.

"To be fair," Andrews said, "we have no other evidence. All we have are body parts and some old scraps of newspaper the torso was wrapped in."

"That may be true," Moore grunted, "but hearing it spoken aloud still makes me feel like a fool. I wonder if our Inspector Marshall is one of those who think these killings are Jack's work?"

With no distraction in the form of the stranger to be found, I returned my attention to the conversation. "Ah," I said, "but as yet this, unlike Jack's work, is not a case of murder."

The irony in my voice was clear, and Moore snorted slightly; an animalistic burst of humor. "Found Dead. A verdict as useful as a fucking Bible in a Bluegate brothel."

I was used to Henry Moore's colorful language, but a fine-looking woman in a crisp blue dress coming down the stairs alongside where we stood turned suddenly and stared. I nodded at her by way of an apology, but she did not acknowledge me; instead she muttered something under her breath and stalked off. I noticed that her mouth tugged down at each side, the lines too deep for a woman of her relatively young years. I imagined she was predisposed to surliness, and I fought the sudden urge to curse at her myself, and using language much fouler than that which Moore had spoken. I was having these strange moments more frequently of late, and I could attribute this sudden compulsion to act entirely out of character only to my constant tiredness. I turned back to Moore and focused.

"Yes," I said, glad to hear my voice sounding entirely normal, "I fear that is my responsibility. However, without a way to determine an accurate cause of death . . ." My sentence trailed away. It didn't need finishing. The jury had been allowed two options: "willful murder" or "found dead," and the only one that could, in this case, be seen as provable fact was the latter, however farcical it was to all those of us who had stood in that vault and looked at the moldering remains of our poor anonymous woman.

"Of course she was bloody found dead," Moore grumbled. "Some bastard cut off her head and her limbs. If she'd been found alive, I would have been more than bloody surprised."

Inspector Andrews smiled but said nothing. I couldn't help but notice once again what an unusual pairing these two men were: one so gruffly obvious and the other quiet and observant. Their mutual respect, however, was clear.

"Is it true," I asked, "that some of your colleagues at the Yard don't believe that the Whitehall case and the Rainham one were even committed by the same person?" I had heard that rumor, but I found it hard to comprehend. The patterns between the two were so obvious only a simpleton would not see it. Moore shrugged in response; of course it was true. And of course there were plenty of fools—mainly those with political sensibilities—within the ranks of the Metropolitan Police Force. I myself had met several during my years of working alongside them. But the police had bigger distractions at the moment, and I could see they did not want their concentration divided.

"It's Jack, isn't it?" I said, wearily. "They're only concerned with Jack."

"And perhaps with good cause," Andrews said, his soft voice reasonable.

"Perhaps," I countered, and then, without any further discussion, we started to make our way down the steps. The inquest was over, and we were all busy men; the world would not allow us to linger for long. I stared over at the green, where nursemaids dressed in starched uniforms wheeled babies around in the fresh air, and men sat on benches, pausing for a moment to enjoy a breath of peace on this crisp autumn day. There was no black-coated stranger among them.

As I stared at this vision of normalcy, I felt the strange sense of the unnatural wash over me again. My words came almost of their own accord—I certainly had had no intent of speaking them, even if they did fill my mind.

"But this," I muttered, my feet pausing as we reached the pavement, "this chills me more than Jack's work. This is . . . colder. This is something . . . *other*." The brightness of the green against the darkness of my mind threatened to overwhelm me, and as my heart thumped loudly in my chest, the world around me was lost for a moment.

"Dr. Bond?"

I wasn't sure how many times Andrews had spoken my name by the time I came out of whatever trance it was that had gripped me. I found him looking at me with obvious concern.

"Are you sick?" he asked. "Forgive me, but you do not seem quite yourself."

"I'm fine." I smiled weakly and fought to compose myself, despite the sudden sweat under my clothes. Was this simply a need for opium? Had I become so dependent on the poppy that a lack of it would bring out such a reaction? "Sleep and I are not the best of bedfellows, I'm afraid."

Andrews nodded as if my explanation were enough, but still his eyes bore into me.

"Now, if you'll excuse me, gentlemen," I finished, stepping toward a hansom before either could question me further, "time waits for no man."

It was a relief to feel the sudden jerk as the wheels began to roll. Peace, that was what I needed: a few hours' peace, and then I would start my search.

The hours passed interminably, but finally I found myself back in the grim streets of Bluegate Fields, looking the worse for a change of

clothes and with my face dirtied, making my way to the den where
I had last seen the stranger. I had always varied my choice of den as
well as the hour, for fear of standing out because of any regularity
of habit, but if I were to find this gentleman who had so fired my
imagination, I was going to have to follow some sort of schedule
of my own in order to fathom his. From the nature of his actions,
the *searching*, I concluded that he must be following a pattern of
some kind; that, after all, was the nature of searching. It had to be
methodical, even in the hellholes of Bluegate Fields.

I had also to admit, even if only to myself, that such was the
nature of the smoke of the poppy that I was not always clear about
which of the various dens I had visited most often. My memories
of the stranger were clear and sharp, but my surroundings were
merely a blurred haze.

I walked quickly through the narrow alleyways, trying to keep
my pace purposeful and confident. The dirt I had rubbed into my
cheeks might fool a casual glance, but it lacked the ingrained quality
that would mark me as one of the hoodlums who belonged, and
neither did my eyes have the sharp, feral sheen common to those
who had survived here. This was no place for the fainthearted to
wander at night, for these were streets filled with villainy. The worst
kind of brothels proliferated, where whatever fleeting pleasures the
sailors stumbling in from the nearby wharves might enjoy were as
likely to be accompanied by the pox or some other fatal infection.
And any seaman innocent—or foolish—enough to carry with
him more than just the fee for his evening's pleasure was unlikely
to find himself still in possession of money or goods at the end of
his encounter.

It was with no small amount of relief that I knocked on the
familiar door and was ushered silently inside by the Chinaman's
ancient, bowed wife. This was one of the largest of the dens that I
frequented. Some were no more than a single room in an Oriental's
cramped house, but this one could hold forty or more clients,
though this evening it was quieter than normal. On seeing me,
Chi-Chi spread one of his cloths over a vacant cot in one corner.

His brown cigarette was clamped between his teeth, and he said not a word as I sat down gratefully and waited for him to gather the tools of his trade and bring them to the low table beside me. I found my mouth watering as he picked up the long pipe, dipped a pin into the treacley liquid, and held it over the flame until it had bubbled and grown into a ball the size of a pea, and I realized I was like a child waiting impatiently for a promised treat. Although the surgeon in me enjoyed watching the precision with which he prepared the opium, the rest of me wanted to grab him and shake him to make him work faster. I should have been ashamed of myself, I knew that, but instead all I could feel was the need to have the drug coursing through my system. That need eclipsed all else, momentarily at least.

Eventually, Chi-Chi dropped the small brown ball into the ceramic bowl and lit it. I puffed greedily, relishing the sweet taste and the immediate rush of tingling sensation that flooded my brain. I could feel the veins in my head throbbing as my body absorbed the smoke.

I lay back on the bed. Around me the grimy gas lamps glowed like stars in the firmament. They detached from the walls and danced before my eyes, leaving trails of light and color behind them, and my mouth opened in wonder. I tried to focus on the purpose of my visit this evening. I needed to ask the Chinaman about the stranger—it had been my firm intention to do so before I took the pipe, but my need had been too great; it had overwhelmed me. I should have felt shame at that, but all natural sense was rapidly being lost to me. I made up my mind that I would close my eyes for just a moment and then I would call him back. That was what I would do.

My mind drifted, and for a while I was floating amid the kind of visions of the fantastic that might be considered madness by a rational mind. I was aware of my body, but as if it were something distant from my mind.

When a partial lucidity returned to me, and once again I became hazily aware of my dimly lit surroundings, Chi-Chi, with that innate sense peculiar to the Orientals who ran these establishments, silently appeared by my side and began the job of replenishing my pipe, knowing my habits of quantity perhaps better than I did.

The room before me had filled with more clients, and I wondered how many hours had passed since I had arrived. Time means nothing in the dens; indeed, I believe it moves at a different pace for each smoker. For those whose visions brought sudden, unwanted terrors, the minutes could feel like eternities, while for others who smiled and drifted more pleasantly, surely the reverse was true, and an hour could be over in a heartbeat—just as it had been so for me.

My arm felt incredibly heavy, but still I raised my hand as best I could, in a bid to stop the old Chinaman in his work for a moment. Although my subconscious might have very recently taken flight, my body was very much anchored to the bed.

"No want?" he asked. His dark eyes stared at me, endless pools of alien thought.

"There is a man who comes here," I said. "He wears a black coat. It's long, and coated in wax. He has a withered arm." My words slurred as I tried to keep my sentences short and focused, as much for my own confused mind as to ensure that the Chinaman understood me.

"You talk of him last time," he said, and I wondered how much this man remembered of all his clients. We came here and dreamed in front of him—perhaps he was the guardian of all our souls.

"He is looking for someone," I said. "I might be able to help him." This was only a partial lie—until I knew for whom he was looking, I did not know whether I could help him or not.

The Chinaman remained still, his expression unreadable.

I continued, "He takes the pipe and then wanders amongst those who lie here. He studies them." I felt as if I were talking to myself. Perhaps I was. Maybe this was all part of the opium dream. "Although how he has the wherewithal to move at all astounds me," I muttered, thinking of my own weakened state. "He must have the constitution of the devil."

"He does not smoke this. *This*, but not *this*."

The Chinaman spoke quietly, and the words took a moment to filter through my dulled senses.

"What?"

"More expensive."

For the first time, the Chinaman looked slightly awkward, a moment of universal humanity on the wrinkled foreign face.

"Is rare. He ask I no tell."

"But you've told me," I said, "and I must try it."

"Very expensive."

"I have money." I reached into my pocket and pulled out a handful of shillings. I had more tucked inside my shirt, but I had no intention of revealing that, not in a place like this. Although the Chinaman seemed like a decent enough sort of chap given his situation, I had no desire to find myself robbed, murdered and thrown into the stinking Thames on my departure.

He looked down at the palmful of coins and selected three before disappearing behind the curtained doorway that separated his place of business from what I imagined must be his home.

I wasn't sure quite what I was expecting, but Chi-Chi returned with a small silver container, about the size of a thimble, containing a liquid of much the same consistency and color of that which I had smoked earlier. Was this some kind of ploy? As there was only one way I was going to find out, I lay on my side on the cot. Once the preparations were complete, I drew in a deep lungful of the smoke.

At first the sensation was familiar to me, but then it changed and settled into an excited tingle in my veins. The world did not blur about me, and my body was no longer heavy—if anything, I felt as if I could walk on air, should I so wish. I smiled and drew in more, until Chi-Chi, watching me carefully, took the pipe from me. For the first time in our acquaintance, I saw how sharp those dark eyes really were. Previously, the world had become a swirl of colors and fantasies of the mind. This time, although my body was experiencing the expected pleasant sensations, my mind was quite clear—in fact, the world around me was almost *too* real as I looked at it. The negative empty shapes between each item competed for my attention as much as those articles themselves. The room around me had changed its dimensions, almost flattening, and yet becoming perfectly clear. It felt as if I were seeing the world as it saw itself.

I sat up, a restless energy filling me, and looked at Chi-Chi once again, and I gasped out loud. Around his head was a strange glow, an aura of reds and rich purples that clung to his dark hair. I was quite certain that somewhere within the colors, an Oriental dragon danced.

"What is this?" I asked.

"Those who can see, see," he answered. His accent had evaporated.

"Those who can see?"

Chi-Chi shrugged and got to his feet. "Some can see. Others, no. The man can see. Perhaps you also, can see." He picked up his tools and disappeared back behind the curtain, then emerged again and scurried over to a client who was feebly waving a hand from his cot.

I sat for a moment, unsure what I ought to do next, and then I thought of the man I sought. What did he do after smoking this strange opium? He looked at the dreamers—so that was what I would do. I got to my feet, expecting the world to shift beneath me, making me nauseous, as often happened, but I was steady. Neither could I feel the aches and pains that had settled into my bones as the years passed. I felt younger—more than that, I felt *awake*, and I found myself holding back a giggle at the sheer relief of having shrugged off the exhaustion that had enveloped me for months on end. The opium dens had always brought me some measure of oblivion, but I knew it was a false rest. Now I felt the kind of energy that came only with having eight hours' good sleep each night, and I wondered how long this would last. If anything were to turn me into an addict, then surely it would be this.

I brought my attention back and considered the stranger's practices. I began to move between the cots spread around the large room. Some were arranged like shipboard bunks, stacked one atop another. No one noticed my activity other than Chi-Chi, who ignored me. I did as I had seen the man with the withered arm do, and I leaned over those lost in their own wild imaginings. As with Chi-Chi, they all had some hue of color around their heads, varying through the whole spectrum of the rainbow, although it was the rich blues and greens, those colors of the sea, that proved to be most common.

If I looked carefully I could see seagulls and fish, darting this way and that in some of the worlds swirling around the dreamers' heads. In others, those the shades of murkier waters, I saw here and there a man drowning, a vast whale, and other monsters of the deep. These latter images appeared most commonly around those who twitched and moaned in their half slumbers, and I wondered what was it that I was seeing: the nature of their torments? Their fears, even their very souls? I wished for a mirror so I could see myself—but what would I see there? What colors danced around my own tired mind?

I continued my studies, but fascinating as the sights I saw were, I had as yet no idea what exactly the stranger was seeking. I could not tell if he even saw the same visions as I did, for surely the visions were simply a product of one's own mind. I was under no illusion that what was appearing before me was in any way "real" despite appearances.

After half an hour or so, I had finished examining each of Chi-Chi's clients, and I decided that I should wander to another den and study whoever was there. My meager plan had been to wait here for the stranger, but that was before the opium haze had hit me; now my feet and my mind were restless. This evening's drug was showing no signs of releasing me as yet and so, feeling far more brave—or perhaps foolish—than usual, I went back out into the dark streets of Bluegate Fields.

The cold air stung my face, and the fog dampened my skin, sending pleasant tingles through my body as I turned up my collar and strode forward. I could hear raucous noise coming from some of the wretched, overcrowded buildings around me, but I passed no other living souls. This would normally have been a relief to me, but my curiosity to see more of these strange auras was overwhelming my usual instinct for survival.

I rounded a corner into a narrow alleyway and stopped suddenly. The den toward which I was heading was closer to the other end, and a glow of light cut through the heavy mist. The door was open, and someone was leaving. I stared as the tall figure exited, and then the light pinched out as the door was closed behind him. I stumbled forward a few paces to get a clearer view—could it be the stranger I sought? Knowing full well that the opium could be playing with my sight, I scurried forward, sucking in the dank air as I broke into a jog.

The man had turned away from me so I couldn't see his arm, but his gait was familiar, and he was of the right height to be "my" stranger, as I thought of him. I was perhaps ten feet away when he spun round, his tall body crouching slightly as if in preparation for a fight.

"I'm sorry," I said, sounding slightly breathless. "I had no intention of startling you." I stopped where I was and pulled off my hat, then rubbed at my face in an attempt to try and remove my poor disguise. "I've seen you—at the inquests."

He stared at me, and for a long moment he said nothing. I could not place his age other than between thirty-five and fifty. He was taller than he had at first appeared, perhaps four inches over my own five feet eleven, and his face was like leather, worn and rough in a way that could only come from being battered by both life and the elements. His eyes were little more than black pits in the gloom, yet still they managed to bore into me. The straggling ends of his long dark hair reached to his shoulders, but he was clean-shaven, no mustache nor hint of whiskers gracing that scarred visage. I saw no aura around him, but it was perhaps muted by his hat, or maybe the effect of the drug was wearing off. His arm, as I had seen before, was bent at his waist and as thin as a twig in comparison with the rest of his impressive form, and the fingernails at the end of the crooked hands were long and dirty.

None of this shocked me. What drew my eyes and held me in place where I stood was the glint of the heavy gold cross that hung beneath his priest's collar. Was this why he always wore a heavy overcoat, to disguise his true calling? But why? Although the robes he wore were unfamiliar to me, they definitely belonged to some religious order, and if so, why would any man hide his love of God, if he had taken such vows?

"You are mistaken," he said, eventually.

He had an accent, but from where, I could not determine. I could hear the lilt of Italy in his words but he spoke like a man who had not been in his native country for a long time.

"The Rainham inquest," I said, more firmly now. "I saw you there. And then you were at the Whitehall site." Now that I had found him, I was determined to get at his purpose, though I found myself at the same time almost at a loss as to what to say, without sounding like a madman myself.

"And I have seen you in the dens. You are looking for something, I believe."

His back stiffened. I have a natural ability to analyze the actions of men, and with the opium and excitement both rushing through my veins, my senses were more acute than ever. He had risen slightly from the fighting stance he had adopted as he had turned to me, and I knew I had surprised him. He *was* looking for something.

"Do you know something that would help the police? Do you have suspicions about who might be committing these awful crimes?" I asked. I took a step forward, and he took one backward, as if we were engaging in an awkward waltz. I was careful in my choice of words, not wanting to sound as if I were in any way accusing him of wrongdoing, for I did not believe him guilty—not with that disfigurement, and certainly not now that I could see he was a man of the Church—albeit one who had clearly seen some hard times. "What is it you are looking for? Perhaps I can help?"

He smiled then—a wide, cynical grin that revealed surprisingly white and healthy teeth—and a quiet laugh rumbled from somewhere in his chest. There was no humor in either gesture. He was laughing at me as if I were a particularly stupid child.

"You can't help," he said, and he turned away, his long stride taking him farther from me.

"Is it something in the visions?" I asked, the pitch of my voice rising in desperation.

He froze where he stood, and in the silence I could hear my own heart beating loudly in my ears. Slowly, he turned once more, and even shrouded as we were in the grip of the dark night, I could see that his face was filled with such anger and venom that it was my turn to remain welded to one spot.

"You know *nothing*," he growled at me. "You are interfering in things you do not understand."

"I took the drug," I said, determined not to show my sudden fear. "I saw strange fantasies around the heads of the smokers. Is that what you look at?"

"Stay away from the visions, Dr. Bond." His mouth twisted into a sneer. "They will drive you to madness."

I opened my mouth to speak again, but the priest spun and broke into a sudden run, disappearing into the fog. I had never seen a man go from a standing position to sprinting so fast, and by the time I had forced my own legs into movement, he had vanished, though I searched the surrounding streets. Did he have rooms in this Godforsaken place, or had he simply hidden in one of the various alleyways, hoping that I would be unlikely to find him?

After fifteen minutes of running this way and that, I gave up, panting and sweating, and rested against a brick wall. The priest was gone, and as exhaustion hit my body again, I knew the drug was finally releasing me.

It was only in the hansom cab on the way home that I realized something else, and a far more natural shiver of excitement and fear ran through me.

The priest had called me by my name.

I had thought that I would not sleep when I got home after my encounter with the stranger. As I climbed the stairs and passed the clock on the first-floor landing, I was surprised to note that it was after three in the morning. I paused and stared at the heavy hands as if expecting them to roll back and correct what must have been an error. Instead, they slowly clicked forward one minute. I turned my back and headed up into the gloomy darkness, finding my way to my bedroom without need of light. My mind was elsewhere: how long had I been studying the dreamers before leaving that first establishment? I had thought it perhaps only thirty minutes, but it had become apparent that my mind and understanding of time had not been as clear as I had thought it. That disturbed me more than any opium vision ever could. Where were the lines between fantasy and reality in this new version of the drug Chi-Chi had given me—could I even recognize them? Had I even seen the stranger at all, I wondered, or was that just part of the drug's magic?

My bedroom was cold, and although the fire was set behind the ornate guard, enough to warm me through the last hours until morning, I didn't light it. I rarely did, these nights when I sought refuge in the poppy, for I did not trust myself not to set either the room or myself on fire, regardless of how convinced I might be that the effects had worn off. Perhaps I might change my mind once the city was held in the grip of winter and ice once again formed on the inside of my windows, but for now I simply crawled between the freezing sheets and pulled the heavy covers over my head, letting my breath—loud and steady in that tiny space—go some way to warming me.

I expected to lie there, awake, until the clock downstairs had ticked around to morning, but within moments I had sunk into a slumber close to oblivion. If Mrs. Parks, my housekeeper, hadn't shaken me awake then I think I could have slept all day.

"It's half-past ten," she said, before I had even opened my eyes. "You have a visitor. A young lady." Her disapproval was clear in the sharpness of her tone and the stiffness of her spine—not that a young lady was calling on me but that I was still in bed so late into the morning. The fire was dying down in the grate, and she stoked it up. She gestured toward the small table in the corner. A tray sat on it. "I brought your breakfast up and lit the fire at seven," she continued, "but I couldn't wake you. For a moment I thought you might be dead." The words were matter-of-fact, as if my demise would be nothing more than an irritation to her, but I knew that was not the case: Mrs. Parks was fond enough of me, in her own way. Perhaps not on this particular morning, mind you, but fond all the same.

"Of course, it'll be inedible now. And it was the last of the eggs."

Having hauled myself half-upright, I tried to make some noises of apology, but I had discovered that even the slightest movement made my head throb. Still struggling to order my thoughts, I managed a strangled groan.

"A man in your position!" Mrs. Parks almost tutted midsentence. "Well, you should know better than to be up drinking all night. However hard you might be working, it's not good for you—it isn't for any man."

"But," I started, forcing the words out despite the agony it caused to flare up behind my eyes, "you're mistaken." Quite why I felt the need to excuse myself to my housekeeper, I knew not, but I did, even as she continued with her disapproving glare. "I was feeling quite unwell—I still am." The last sentence was not a lie, even if the first was. I felt terrible.

She pulled open the curtains to reveal a thankfully gloomy day. My eyes were not ready for brightness, and I am quite sure that if sunshine had burned through the glass, I might have clawed them out from the pain. As it was, I was barely more than squinting. She turned back to face me, and pursed her lips before saying, "Then no doubt it was some malicious spirit who tossed your coat and shoes carelessly in the hallway." She paused and arched an eyebrow. "And left the good crystal brandy decanter—empty, I might add—lying forgotten on the stairs."

My mouth dropped open in confusion. *Brandy?* Suddenly the cause of my awful headache was clear, but truly, I had no memory of drinking. As far as I was aware, I had come in, seen the time, and gone straight to bed—or had I, in fact, come home earlier, got drunk, and then climbed the stairs to bed? The uncertainty of it all made my stomach roil, sending a wave of nausea through me. The priest might prefer this special opium of Chi-Chi's, but I did not care for its effects. I enjoyed the liberation that came with the drifting visions as I lay on a cot, when my exhausted limbs were too heavy to do anything other than lie there, but this strangeness in behavior and loss of time did not suit my practical mind and nature. There were holes in my memory that I could not fill—either that, or I was going mad.

"I have taken Miss Hebbert into the drawing room. I didn't tell her you were still asleep. I presume you'd like me to put a pot of coffee in there?" She looked me over again. "A large one?"

"Miss Hebbert?" I said weakly.

"Your visitor." Her voice had taken on the slow pace normally used when speaking to a small child or the elderly. "The young lady, Miss Juliana Hebbert."

Despite my dreadful headache, I found that I was able to get up much more quickly than I had expected.

When I came into the room she was standing with her back to me, staring into the fire. Mrs. Parks had lit all the lamps throughout the house in a bid to dispel the miserable October day, but rather than creating the warm and comforting atmosphere I had been expecting, strange shadows gripped the room in shapes both hideously deformed and claustrophobic as the lights flickered through the colored glass or crept up the walls.

As Juliana turned, half her face appeared to be eaten up by darkness, and for a moment I was filled with a dread I could not understand. I trembled as colors flashed around her head—too fast to capture any image within them—and then my headache disappeared instantly. I gripped the door handle to steady myself.

"Dr. Bond?" Juliana's smooth brow furrowed slightly. "Are you unwell?"

I blinked rapidly, and to my great relief found that the strange moment had passed. The shadows were as they had always been, tired dark spaces clinging to the corners of the room, and the left side of the young woman's face was perfectly visible, despite being more shaded than the other. No colors danced around her head, and my own was throbbing again. It was surely the remnant of that strange drug taking its toll.

"I'm sorry." I smiled and headed over to where the tray was laid out in order to pour us both coffee. "I think perhaps I might be slightly unwell—or perhaps I am just tired. Please, do sit down."

There was a chair on either side of the fire, and she took the farther one, smoothing down the blue fabric of her dress as she sat. The seal fur trim around the border of her matching jacket and cuffs enhanced the soft hazel brown of her eyes, and the bright blue felt hat accentuated her soft brown curls. Juliana Hebbert was a beauty, there was no doubt about that; though she was nearly twenty years my junior, I was by no means immune to her natural charms.

"I'm very sorry to have disturbed you," she started. "I didn't think—you have been so very busy, and I'm sure you need all the rest you can get."

"Not at all. Visitors are always refreshing." I willed the pulsating headache to fade. "And you are welcome to call at any time." It was only when I handed her the cup and saucer that I noticed she was clutching a slim volume in her gloved hand. As she placed the drink beside her, I noted there was the slightest shake in her hand. I looked at her more closely. There were shadows under her eyes, and not the sort that would fade in the presence of direct sunlight. I wondered what concerns this bright, vivacious young woman might have?

"I presume, however, that there is a purpose to this unexpected pleasure? All is well with your family, I hope?"

"Yes, yes," she said, a smile fluttering across her face like a nervous butterfly. "It's nothing like that. I just—well, I—" She half-raised the book. "While we were in Bath—James likes to take the waters there; he has a weak chest, you know, from a terrible infection he had a while ago, and sometimes it can still make him quite ill . . ." Her words were coming out in a flurry, and as my curiosity became more engaged, my nausea and headache finally subsided. I had seen Juliana animated before, but never with this slightly anxious edge. I took the seat opposite her and sipped my own coffee as I waited for her to finish speaking.

"Anyway, while we were there—and it is very relaxing, and you should probably take a visit there yourself, if you haven't already—I thought of you and your sleeping problems, and I remembered seeing a book on my father's shelves on that very subject. It contains sixty remedies that are 'tried and tested,' according to the author, so I thought I would bring it to you."

She held the volume out, and I leaned forward and took it. "How very kind of you." I was, indeed, truly surprised—first, that she had been thinking of me at all, for I was, after all, quite middle-aged and dull from the perspective of one so young and vibrant—and second, that she had gone to the effort of visiting me with such a helpful gift on so gloomy a day.

I flicked through the pages before looking up. "I shall try a different one every night until I find the winner."

She smiled at me, evidently relieved. I had no desire to tell her that all these "tried and trusted" remedies were old wives' tales, or that I had tried each already—she was trying to help, in her innocent way. I doubt she had missed more than one or two nights' sleep in her entire life.

If there were a remedy for my sleeplessness, it would not be found in this book—and it dawned on me that maybe I did not want it found just yet after all, for my insomnia had become a tool in my investigation into the stranger in the black coat. If my body suddenly reverted back and I regained my normal sleep patterns, then my nighttime adventures in the dens would have to stop— and I had begun to realize that no matter how awful I had felt on awaking this morning, I had every intention of returning tonight and tracking the fellow down—I would even take that pernicious drug again, if I had to.

"Good." She smiled, looking genuinely pleased, but I was still convinced I could see the hint of something troubling her in the slight twitch at the corner of her mouth. She leaned forward a little and looked as if she were about to say something more, but then she stopped herself, instead rising to her feet.

"I fear I have kept you from your day for long enough, but you must come for dinner more often now I am back—in fact, I shall insist upon it. We all enjoy your company, and dining alone can be such a sorrowful affair."

"That is most charming of you," I said, meaning every word, "but I would hate to become an imposition. I know your father works as hard as I, and I'm sure your fiancé does too. They would surely prefer to dine alone with their loved ones, without the effort of constant visitors."

"Yes, they do work hard." Her smile wavered again. "But they are also out a lot in the evenings, at Father's club." She was trying very hard to cover it, but her face was suddenly awash with sadness, and like all old fools in the presence of beauty, my heart melted.

"Then I shall be delighted to join you," I said, a small flush creeping up under my collar. I was under no illusion that she would ever love me—and even I could see how ridiculous such a situation would be, should that ever occur—but surrounded by death and darkness as I was, it made me happy enough to know she considered me a friend.

"Good," she said, and she turned to leave.

"Juliana." I could not ignore the sorrow she had been trying to disguise. "Is there something worrying you? You know that you can talk to me, if there is . . ."

"It's nothing." She smiled, more brightly this time. "Nothing that good company at dinner won't cure."

"Then I shall do my best to provide it," I said.

The rest of the day passed without incident, and after Juliana's visit, even my walk through the damp fog to spend a few hours at Westminster Hospital did not manage to dispel my sudden good mood. I had been certain, after waking up so out of sorts, that I was about to suffer one of the anxiety attacks I had come to fear, but as yet there had been no sign, and I put that down to the distraction brought about by her company. Although she had not wanted to talk, it was clear to me that something was troubling her—but if it was simply loneliness, then I could happily help ease that. I wondered whether I should talk to Charles, but I decided that for now at least I would leave it be. I had my own unorthodox ways of dealing with the stresses of our work, and I could hardly begrudge Charles his—at least he did not spend his nights wandering unsavory places such as Bluegate Fields in search of oblivion.

Once the headache and nausea from my brandy consumption finally eased, I discharged my various duties at the hospital with no real effort. I had been a Surgeon at the Westminster for so many years that my routine—unless something completely unusual presented itself—was no longer taxing, and I was permitted the free rein that came with the position. I lectured the students and presented papers, and I had gained enough respect that none would query my behavior if they found it somewhat erratic—and if it were noticed, it would no doubt be put down to the forensic work I did on behalf of the Metropolitan Police.

By the time I returned home, just after five, Mrs. Parks had almost forgiven me for the previous night, and when I told her that I was indeed hungry—not the answer she normally had from me—she hurried about cooking me a fine early dinner of roast pork, the sort of meal I used to eat before this most recent and most affecting bout of insomnia and anxiety had gripped me.

Once the plates were cleared away, she left for the night and I sat by the fire in the drawing room and waited for the clock to finish its crawl round to night. As I gazed into the crackling flames, I thought of Jack and the second killer who intrigued both the mysterious priest and me—the man I was coming to think of as "the Thames Killer." It was a less dramatic moniker than the one "the Ripper" had coined for himself, but I found it more chilling—colder. What were those two doing tonight, I wondered, planning more mayhem on the London streets? Or perhaps staring into a fire somewhere else in the city and wondering what men such as Inspector Moore and I were thinking?

Moore and Andrews were no doubt assisting Abberline; I could picture the three inspectors trawling through all the interviews conducted during the search of Whitechapel, looking for something, *anything*, that could lead them to find Jack and restore some calm to the streets. I didn't envy them their jobs, damned as they were by both sides if they failed.

Jack the Ripper and the Thames Killer: they were shadows in the dark corners of my mind, unformed but threatening, both monsters, and yet so different in their approaches. How anyone could think they were one and the same man beggared belief, but that was the easy way of thinking, and for many, that would always be preferable to hard truth.

The fire crackled, and the remnants of my earlier good mood disappeared into the smoke as my thoughts drifted. I had left the curtains open and now the night crawled in around me. I thought once again of the wickedness that appeared to come alive in the city at dusk, and how most decent people were happy to shut it out with the pull of a cord, as if something as simple as brocaded fabric could hold it out. What had Charles said to me in his study that night? He didn't look out of the windows because of the darkness. *I feel like everything wicked is looking into my house. Into me.* His words rang crystal clear in my memory, and I understood them.

I had never been a superstitious man, but yet again I found myself wondering about the evil that had gripped so many men's souls of late. London was never a city without crime, but this year there had been so much mindless violence that even without the two leading performers, I would have been disturbed. Something was reaching into men's souls and dragging out their hidden darkness, leaving them dumbfounded by their actions as they were led away to the gallows.

I was glad I had already emptied the brandy decanter so thoroughly, for I would have doubtless poured myself a very large measure to aid my courage for my outing into that shrouded night. I was determined to find the priest, but I would be a liar if I said my heart did not tremble slightly as I stepped out into the cold.

The chimes of ten o'clock were ringing out as I stepped through the increasingly familiar streets of Bluegate Fields, my coat wrapped closely around me. I carefully selected an alleyway that sat between two of the dens in which I had seen the priest during the past weeks, and I waited in the shadows, invisible in the darkness. My skin itched in the cold, and I knew the cause was the proximity of the opium. My willpower was strong, and I knew I would not give in to the cravings tonight, but I could no longer deny that my body had developed an overfondness for the poppy.

It wasn't an icy night, but the air was invasively chilly, and as the hours ticked by, my feet became numb in my boots, and despite my hat, gloves, scarf, and coat, I was frozen to the core. Standing there in the darkness, I began to feel as if I had become truly invisible to the world beyond the small, forgotten doorway that hid me. Every now and then I would hear uneven footsteps and laughter as drunken men and women wandered back to whatever dreadful slum they called home, if only for that night, but not even those who passed directly before me turned their heads to glance my way.

Was this how it was for Jack and the Thames Killer? Did no one's hair prickle at the back of the neck when passing by the hiding places of those dangerous men? Did no one feel their murderous eyes upon them, evaluating their potential as a victim before making their decision whether to let them continue to breathe or not? So much for instinct, I thought as another pair of cheaply shod feet stumbled by, their owner mumbling incoherently to himself.

For the first time in my association with this vilest of London's villages, I felt like the hunter rather than the prey. There was a power in being hidden, *unseen*. The streets once again fell into silence, and I pressed myself against the rough wall and fought the chattering of my teeth, which I was sure must be loud enough to draw all manner of ruffians to where I stood. I might have had illusions of power from my place in the darkness, but illusion was all it was. I had no weapon—I was no Jack with a blade ready to tear apart some unfortunate woman. I was simply a tired, middle-aged, middle-class man whose curiosity had got the better of him, and who hoped that some answers would help him to sleep.

I sniffed and waited, unsure exactly how long I had been there, but not wanting to strike a match to check the time on my pocket watch. Those who frequented the opium dens must already be in a stupor in their cots, or perhaps they preferred to use the busier roads to pass from one establishment to another. I doubted this would be the case for the priest though: he might have a crippled arm, but he did not appear to me to be the kind of man to fear anyone—or anything—that might be lurking in an alley, most certainly not me. That had been quite clear the previous evening. I remembered how fast he had moved to lose me, and I hoped I would not have to burst into a run tonight. It had been a long while since I had been forced to physically exert myself, and with the icy chill already gripping my limbs, I wasn't entirely sure I was capable of walking, let alone running anywhere.

As it happened, I did not have to wait long to find out. I recognized his step before he passed by in front of me—there was a confidence in the fall of his feet lacking in those drunks and edgy villains who had thus far passed my way. My heart thumped so loudly in my chest that I was sure he would sense me here—that he would turn into the shadows and with a roar, drag me from my hiding place and throw me into the river, or maybe beat me unconscious in this God-forsaken place. Why I felt that so much violence could lurk inside a man of the cloth, I did not know, but somehow, over the weeks of my growing obsession with the priest, he had become something more than human, and the previous night's strange encounter had solidified that fantasy in my overheated imagination.

But he did not turn. I saw his tall hat and long waxed coat for barely a moment as he strode by me. I held my breath, and my muscles screamed silently as I cautiously pushed my body forward so I could peer out into the gloom. The priest was several feet ahead, but despite my terror that I would lose him once again, still I waited a few seconds longer before falling into step behind him. If I grew too close, he would sense me or hear me, I was sure of that, so I willed my shoes to be silent against the uneven cobbles and my breath came in shallow bursts, the steam disappearing into the heavier mist. Winter was not my favorite season; I found it heavy on the soul, but tonight I was glad of the smoky fog as I moved through it like a ghost, never losing sight of my target.

He stopped and went into one more den, a brief ten-minute visit, before reemerging, head down, and continuing on his way.

The dens must have been quiet tonight, and my guts twisted with longing as I passed a doorway I would normally be eager to step through. Tomorrow there could be opium, I promised myself, but for now, I needed my wits about me.

He walked through the streets, ducking through side roads so narrow that two men could barely walk abreast, where the darkness was so complete that he all but disappeared ahead of me, leaving me solely dependent on my hearing. His footsteps were deadened taps cosseted by the lapping of water and creaking wood, and now I realized we were near the river, down by the wharves.

Finally he came to a halt outside a decrepit tenement building, which leaned uncomfortably against the one beside it as if needing the support to keep it standing. Catcalls and laughter came from somewhere above—disjointed, rough voices that could quickly turn from humor to aggression. I had heard voices like those before, edged with gin and sharp with hardship: people who turned on a coin from one mood to another.

The priest stepped through the doorway, and before the door closed, sealing him off from view, I saw him begin climbing a narrow staircase. I had no fear that I would be locked out—the door was barely held on its hinges, and in buildings such as these, where individual rooms were rented by the night or the week, there was no call to secure the main entrance. This was a transient city in which we lived in. Only the hardy survived, and even then, they often wandered. Those who ended up in Bluegate Fields did not rent by the year—their lives could not be guaranteed that long.

I stared up at the building and hoped that the priest's rooms were on this side of it. I could not have risked following him up the stairs—he would have spotted me straight away, and I did not want to bring a fight on myself in a place like that. After all, I wanted only to *speak* to the man; I was not *accusing* him of anything.

I scanned the windows, studying those in darkness until one, on the second floor, started to glow from lamps or candles lit within. I took a moment to lock its position in my head and then, with my heart somewhat in my mouth, I entered the building.

Although not warm, there was a humidity in the small hallway that could only come from too many bodies being crammed into one space for too long a time. The night breeze came in behind me, but it did nothing to dispel the lingering smell of stale sweat and smoke from poorly lit fires, the scents that were ingrained into the fiber of places like this. The staircase was narrow and the banister rickety, but I climbed steadily, keeping my head down, and the noises of the life around me filled the cold air. Babies cried and women soothed them as best they could, and I wondered how many families lived here, crammed into one or two rooms and praying that the next week they would have the money to pay those who preyed on them, anonymous landlords operating through lawyers who sat in much warmer, much larger houses counting their ill-gotten pennies.

I was glad that the priest was only on the second floor. As much as I pitied those who found themselves living in such dire premises, I was aware that I had plenty to fear from some of them. My poor disguise did little to hide my class, and my clothes, however dirty, were still of a finer quality than any here could ever expect to own. Terrible situations created terrible deeds: there would doubtless be plenty in this building alone who would rob me and think no more of it ten seconds after it was done.

Thankfully, I reached the doorway unseen. I raised my hand hesitantly to knock on the scuffed wood, but before my glove had even made contact, the door was pulled open and once again I found myself face-to-face with my mysterious stranger. His eyes were dark pits of glowing coal as he stared down at me.

"For a moment, Dr. Bond, I thought you might be going to the wrong rooms. That could be a dire mistake in Bluegate Fields."

"You knew I was following you?"

He shrugged before silently stepping aside to let me in. Suddenly, I felt a fool. I had been so confident, imagining myself the hunter in these mean streets, and all along my strings were being pulled like a puppet. I had done exactly as he had expected of me.

"Most men are predictable," the priest said, as if in answer to my silent thought. He closed the door behind me and I looked around the small room. The bed in the corner had a meager coating of blankets; there was one chair and a small table. Unlike the broken windows in the hallway, his were at least whole. A small fire burned in the grate, sending small spirals of smoke dancing in an eerie fog throughout the room.

"Sit." He nodded toward the chair and sat on the edge of the bed. He kept his coat on, but the heavy crucifix shone in the light from both the fire and the candles he had lit before my arrival. I stared at it as he stared at me, until finally I took off my hat and placed it on the table. He looked at my head—or should I say, around my head—before snorting a little and looking away. What had he seen there, I wondered? What visions had his mind created for him? He had taken the drug, and far more than I had experimented with. I could see now that was why his eyes looked so dark—his pupils were hugely expanded.

"You must tell me why you are so fascinated with the Thames Killer," I said. "If you know something, you must share it with the police. They are poorly resourced and—"

"*Must?*" he said, cutting me off. "You follow me here and then tell me what I *must* do?" Again I heard the growl in his voice that made me think of Inspector Moore. They were both men cut from rougher cloth than I. "It is you who has the fascination, Doctor."

He glowered at me and it was my turn to be silent for a while. Eventually I said, "You are right. Perhaps I do. Others, they find this Jack the Ripper to be the most terrifying murderer on London's streets this year, but not I. And I do not understand that. I am a man of reason, of science, and yet . . . And yet, I am gripped by a fear that steals my sleep, and it is to do with this case, of that I am certain. If I could only find something—a clue, anything that might help the police to find him, then maybe my sleep and calm will return to me."

Although I had had no intention of holding back from the priest, I surprised myself with my candid words. My honesty must have had some effect, because the aggression drained out of the priest.

His shoulders slumped, and he cradled his withered arm in his strong one. Did it cause him discomfort?

"I can perhaps bring you something to help the pain if you—"

"Your police cannot find this killer." He spat the words out. "You do not even understand what you are looking for." He looked at me. "And you should not want to, for there is no return from that path."

"What do you know?" I leaned forward. "What is it you look for? Is it something in the visions?"

His leathered face cracked into a smile. "You sound like a madman. Are you a madman, Dr. Bond?"

"What do you look for?" I repeated. "If you do not tell me, then I shall have no choice but to bring the police here to question you." I had not wanted to make threats, but I could think of no other way to compel him to speak.

"You think I live here? You think I would allow you to follow me to my home?"

It was my turn to shrug. Perhaps these were not his rented rooms—and even if they were, he could vacate them quickly enough. "I would tell them about the opium dens—how you go there and study the dreamers—"

"I study everyone," he cut in, "everywhere."

"That might be true, but you need the dens in order to be able to have the visions. If I were to have the police watch them, then they would find you and take you in."

"I fear I would not make a very good murderer with this." He raised his crippled arm.

"But you might make a good accomplice. They're tired and desperate, and they will question you."

We studied each other, and I sensed a shift in him as we played out our game of cat and mouse. Some of his disdain was gone—not all, but some.

"I believe you are tired and desperate too," he said eventually, and I couldn't help but laugh.

"That I am, Father, that I am."

"Do not call me that."

"But you are a priest?" I pointed at his collar. "Unless that is some form of disguise? I must confess, I do not recognize the order, but—"

"You wouldn't. I am a Jesuit priest from Rome, a small group, picked and trained from youth for our calling. There is nothing more for you to know than that."

"And your calling brings you here, to find the man who is killing these women?"

He turned his head and stared into the fire, and I caught sight of a long, thick scar that ran down one side of his neck from behind his ear and disappeared under his dirty collar.

"The Jack they seek—this rabid killer of women—he is *nothing*. He is simply an effect. What I seek—the *thing* I seek—brings mayhem and wickedness in its wake, spreading it like this choking fog across the city. It runs in the water of the river, and it will destroy men's souls." The brutality in his voice was gone; his words were soft, and the foreign lilt was like music.

"You mean the man," I said. "Surely a monstrous man, but a man all the same. You think he hides in the opium dens?"

"You know nothing," he repeated. His head turned toward me suddenly, and his lips pulled back into a snarl. "You are blind." His good hand gestured wildly at my clothes. "You think you are clever; you think you know how to hide—this pathetic disguise? You are a fool. The creature I seek, the thing the people of the eastern lands call the *Upir*, it hides for years, decades even, sinking to the bottom of the river in the stagnant weeds until it is hungry once again. It is *endless*."

My heart was racing and although the fire was small, I could feel it burning my face. This nonsense was not what I had been expecting.

"I have tracked it across Europe," the priest continued. "I have barely rested. I have studied the damage it has left behind it, and now I am here, where it has chosen to stop, in the birth city of its host."

"Its host?" My spirits were sinking. I had followed this man of the Church in the hope that he would lead me to a madman—I had not expected him to be one. My expectations had been for nothing. Was he even a priest? Was this all part of some ridiculous delusion?

"It is attached to a man, of course," he said.

"Of course." I wondered if he could hear the weariness in my voice. I was in conversation with a lunatic. I itched to leave, and reached for my hat.

"But it is not visible to the naked eye—not unless, not unless—" He checked himself as his eyes met mine. "Not unless you have the gift of sight, and still you must use the opium to access the visions—or unless you are marked to die."

"Quite a creature," I said.

"You see?" He smiled. "And now you think I am mad, and that is as it should be. Get back to your cold, dead bodies, Doctor, and leave me to do what I have been trained to do."

I got to my feet, happy to have been given an opportunity to excuse myself. "I am sorry to have disturbed your evening," I said, giving him a curt nod.

He didn't get to his feet but tipped his head toward me, returning my gesture. His eyes still burned, and it disturbed me that he looked so sane. He had none of the tics and anxious movements one so often saw in the mentally afflicted. I wondered what had brought him to this—the drug Chi-Chi gave him to smoke? I would not be going back to the dens tonight. I found I no longer had a taste for opium. It was as if he had tainted it with his mad thoughts. I wanted the comfort of my own house and the safety of that familiarity, even if it meant staring at the ceiling while sleep was elsewhere.

"Dr. Bond," he said, just as I had pulled the door open, my mind already on where I could go to find a hansom, unsure as I was of the area. I had followed the priest without paying very much attention, and all I knew was that I was somewhere undesirable, near the river. I was also debating whether I should tell Inspector Moore about this incident—but how would I ever explain my finding him? Perhaps this disappointing encounter was something best kept to myself.

"Yes?"

"It'll be behind the man," he said, his voice once again level and soft. "Somewhere between him and his shadow—somewhere he can almost see, but not quite. And it will drive him mad. I guarantee you that."

We stared at each other for a moment longer, and then I turned my back to him and left. There was nothing more I could say. I wished the brandy decanter at home was full. If ever there was a night I needed a drink, it was this foul one.

17

The Daily Telegraph
Saturday, November 10, 1888

Another appalling murder was committed in the East-end yesterday morning. At a quarter to eleven, the body of a woman named Mary Jane Kelly was found dead in a room of the ground floor of 26 Dorset-street, the entrance to which is from Miller's-court. Her throat had been cut from ear to ear, and the body had been mutilated in the most revolting manner, the nature of the injuries leading the police to believe that the perpetrator is the man who recently committed the crimes of a similar character in the same neighbourhood. A post-mortem has been made, but the official results are not stated. The hour at which the deed was done can only be conjectured, as the last evidence of the woman being alive was at one o'clock in the morning, when she was heard singing. There is absolutely no clue to the murderer.

East London Observer
Saturday, November 10, 1888

THE WHITECHAPEL HORRORS
Another Horrible Tragedy.
The Head Cut Off.
Frightful Mutilation.
The Bloodhounds at Work.
Latest Details.

. . . that the work is that of the murderer of Tabram, Smith, Chapman, Eddowes, and Stride is only too evident. Quite apart from the extraordinary coincidence of the date—it being on the 8th of September that the Hanbury-street victim was murdered, and about the same period of the previous month that Tabram was also butchered—the similarity and ghastly nature of the wounds, and the class of women, all point to the same hand. Another curious coincidence is that although the window of the opposite house can almost be touched from that of the room in which the victim lies, no unusual noise or scream was heard by the occupants either of that room or of any of the adjoining houses.

The New York Times
November 10, 1888

"THE PARNELL INQUIRY AND ANOTHER BUTCHERY BY COMMERCIAL CABLE FROM OUR OWN CORRESPONDENT."

The discovery to-day of the seventh Whitechapel murder, this time believed to have been committed in broad daylight and involving the most terrible wholesale mutilation it is possible to imagine, overshadows all other topics in the London mind to-night. Bloodhounds are out, but I am unable to learn at this hour that they have discovered anything. The conclusion is now universal that the assassin is a periodic lunatic, who, unless detected at once, is likely to commit a fresh series of crimes within a few days before his frenzy passes away.

18

LONDON, NOVEMBER 9, 1888
DR. BOND

Whatever thoughts had been filling my mind, they vanished in an instant as I stared at the wreck of a human being who was lying so devastated on the cheap sodden mattress. I could not have recalled my own name, had it been demanded. It had rained heavily throughout the night and the stench of damp clung to me. I wondered if it would now forever be associated with this gory tableau in my sensory memory. I sincerely hoped not; it rained a lot in London, and I had no desire to be reminded of this more often than I could help in my future years.

"Inside?" I asked, eventually. It was the thought that disturbed me most. "He's working inside now?"

"They call it 'Do-as-you-please Street,' did you know that?" Bagster Philips said. "It seems Whitechapel Jack did just that."

"Who is she?" I asked. From what was left there was no way I could ascertain if she had been fine looking, or even if she were young or old. He might as well have cut her head clean off for what was left of her face, made her simply a collection of pieces of meat, as the Thames Killer did. But this was not the work of that man, and I did not want to think about him—there was madness enough on the bed in front of me without my mind wandering toward the priest and his words. I had been only once to the dens since that night, and I had chosen a tiny one, normally catering solely for Chinamen, lascars, and the like, and I had kept my eyes firmly shut as I lay on my cot. Since then, I had resorted to the laudanum from my cabinet when the need to sleep became too great. But try as I might, too often I found my thoughts turning to the wickedness gripping my city—wickedness such as these terrible deeds of Jack's.

"Her name is Mary Jane Kelly, apparently, and she has been renting this room a year or so. In her twenties or thereabouts."

"How long have you been here?" The inspectors on the scene, Beck and Abberline, had both been outside when I arrived, talking to a photographer who was no doubt waiting for us to be done before finishing up his own work. He had looked green, and now that I had seen what he had been faced with, I did not blame him in the least. Abberline had nodded me in, and we had not stopped to exchange pleasantries. He was a sensible chap and would let us work before asking questions—and he had his own hands full managing his men, who were gathering information from any witnesses and neighbors who might have heard or seen something or had some idea of the victim's last movements.

"I got here at quarter past eleven," Bagster said. "She was found at quarter to—behind on her rent to the sum of twenty-nine shillings, and the landlord sent his man to collect it. He peered through the broken pane"—he gestured in its direction—"and got quite a shock, I should imagine." He smiled at me from behind his mustaches. Dr. George Bagster Philips, the Police Surgeon for Whitechapel, was a strange character, I thought, and not for the first time in our association. He was popular with both the police and the public, and he was instantly recognizable from his somewhat old-fashioned choice of dress. He looked as if he had stepped out of a portrait from many decades past, and as he moved into middle age, he showed no sign of wishing to catch up with the present day—not that this mattered, however, for he was a charming fellow, and I had no doubts as to his professional skills.

"He ran back to get the landlord, a chap called McCarthy—owns a shop on Dorset Street—and he sent his man off to fetch the police, who called me in. I took a look through the window—any man could see there was nothing I could do for this poor creature, so we waited for those bloodhounds we were promised for the next of these terrible events." He laughed a little at his small joke. "As it transpired, the dogs had been sent on cases elsewhere and were no longer available. *Two hours* wasted. You can imagine how well that went down with our inspectors. Not that the dogs would have been much use after all the trampling around out there. I think everyone from a mile around us has been to see what's in this room." His voice grew soft. "Damned fools. Why would anyone want to see something like this if they didn't have to?"

"They should have asked for Jasper Waring and his dog," I muttered. This woman had little enough chance of justice if the lack of evidence from the previous murders was anything to go by; she certainly did not need any incompetence caused by too many levels of command to make things worse.

"Ah yes," Bagster said, "from your Torso boy? Found the limbs the police dogs missed, didn't he?" He looked at me and then sighed. "The city's the color of Claret this year, isn't it?"

The image made me think of the priest. Although I was quite sure he was a madman, I was finding him difficult to shake from my thoughts. Perhaps it was because in my mind he and the overwhelming darkness of men's deeds had become wrapped up together in my thoughts. I had hoped he would give me some answers, and now when I lay in my sleepless bed, I imagined him in the dens and walking the streets of the rougher parts of the city looking at the spaces around men's heads in order to find his "*Upir*," whatever that might be. I hoped that he never did, for the sake of whatever unfortunate man he decided was its host. The encounter would not end well for that stranger, I was sure of it.

"Thomas?" Bagster was watching me carefully. "You look a little off-color. Not this, I presume?"

"No." I could answer him quite truthfully. "It is a shocking sight, certainly, but I am too long in the tooth for it to make me ill. I have been slightly unwell myself—I am tired."

"I trust you are taking care of yourself?"

"I do my best." I looked again at our Mary Jane Kelly, who would no longer have to worry about her unpaid rent. Another wasted life. "How many of these have you done now?"

"I was at the scene for Stride and Chapman, and the autopsies for Chapman, Stride, and Eddowes. None of them were like this, however."

"No," I said. "Here he had time." The rage that had been taken out on Kelly's body disturbed me. It was frenzied, there was no doubt about that, and in sharp contrast to how her clothes—all aside from the chemise that clung to what remained of her form— had been neatly folded on a chair, no doubt only moments before he attacked her.

"Let's see what we can find out, shall we?" Bagster said. "And then we can let that poor photographer chap finish his job, if his guts have recovered. I doubt he's taken portraits like these before."

We set to work, and for a while my mind was wholly occupied with the science of analyzing the dead. At some point Inspector Abberline appeared in the corner of the room behind us, but he remained silent, allowing us to work without the interruption of questions. Bagster and I muttered quietly as we studied the mutilated remains, confirming each other's suggestions or observations as we tried to identify the wrecked human anatomy.

Only when we stepped back and looked up did Abberline come forward. "What can you tell me?" he said. His voice was calm and precise, as was the man himself. He could have been a bank manager or some such, with his manner and eye for precision. I respected him, as did Bagster Philips; they must have come to know each other quite well over the recent weeks.

"He's taken off the whole surface of her thighs and abdomen." I indicated the mangled flesh on the legs, that were spread slightly and bent at the knees a little, as if in mockery of the way she had earned her living in life. "Her abdominal cavity is empty, and as you can see, her intestines are there to her right. Both breasts have been removed, and he placed one under her head—along with her kidneys and uterus—and the other is there beside her right foot.

That is her liver between her feet. Her arms have several jagged cuts, and as for her face . . ."

"I can see that for myself," Abberline cut in. "Dear God, he really is a monster."

"No," I said. I was done with talk of monsters and creatures. "This is the work of a man—a monstrous one, perhaps, but a man all the same."

"Can you tell me how she died?"

In terror was the answer that rose up in my mind, but luckily Bagster was quicker to speak.

"I would say his normal method: he slashed her neck. Severed the carotid artery. Before he got to work on the rest of her."

"That would explain how no one seems to have heard anything." Abberline stared again at the body. "What about time of death?"

"I would say she was killed somewhere between two and eight this morning," I said. "Rigor mortis has started to set in. Although from the state of the grate, it looks like he had quite a fire going. The heat could put my assessment out slightly."

"Why did he light the fire?" Bagster asked.

"Light." Abberline sounded tired. I imagined he was as exhausted as I. "There was only one candle in here. He would have wanted to see properly as he did all this."

"Have you found out much about her?" I asked. After the anonymity of the river killer's victims, there was suddenly something comforting—if haunting—about having an identity to go with the corpse.

"We're getting there. It'll take a while to sift through all the information and get a clear sense of her movements. She was drunk in the Britannia last night at around eight or nine. The rest I'll need to piece together later."

"This is only two or three hundred yards from where the Nicholls murder happened, isn't it?" Bagster asked.

"That's right." Abberline sighed. "He's certainly partial to the streets of Whitechapel—but I know them well myself. I intend to scour them for him."

Our work done, we followed Abberline out into the small courtyard. A young policeman was talking to the photographer as we joined them.

"Remember, get pictures of her eyes," he was saying earnestly. "We might see the reflection of her killer in them."

"I thought you were supposed to be helping with the cordon, Detective Constable Dew?" Abberline said.

"I just thought . . ." the young man said, his eyes sparkling with excitement.

"Don't think. That's my job. Do as I tell you."

"And I can assure you, young man," Bagster added, "that I have looked into her eyes. There is nothing to help you there."

Only slightly cowed, but clearly irritated, the young man scurried back down the narrow arched alley that led from Miller's Court to Dorset Street.

"See the killer in their eyes," Bagster snorted. "What next?"

I smiled and shook my head, but something in the thought chilled my soul. Reflections. Shadows. Things just out of sight. Once again I was reminded of the priest and his urgent search for something supernatural.

"I heard him tell Beck he knew the girl," Abberline said. "Said he'd seen her often on the Commercial Road. Said she was a pretty thing, never wore a hat." He paused. "That detail was a nice touch."

"You don't believe him?" I said.

"Our young detective constable may well go far in the force. He's ambitious, determined to catch criminals—but he does like to embellish his role in these things." He glanced back through the broken window to where the photographer was now cautiously setting up his equipment. "I'll get the body over to you when I can. Probably an hour or so. Then we'll get this place boarded up, try and stop its becoming an exhibit before it has to."

"We should go and prepare for the postmortem," Bagster said.

I looked once more at the room behind us. I didn't need to peer in; I had seen enough for the image to stay with me for quite some time. "I wonder if you could let me see all your records on the others?" I asked.

"Of course," he answered. "But it won't make for pretty reading."

I didn't even attempt sleep that night. My head was full of wild thoughts of murder and blood, images no doubt fueled by my craving for opium, and I wondered if the distillation the priest was partial to was so much stronger that it had made my dependency worse. The visions were calling to me, I was sure of it. As much as the blank spaces it had left in my memory frightened me, the clarity of thought I had had during the experience was a lure in itself. It was only the lingering shock at the priest's madness that kept me away. Whatever illness the poor man suffered, the drug could only have made it worse, and I had no desire to follow into that fate myself. My anxiety attacks and insomnia were sometimes enough to lead me to half-believe myself mad already; I needed no further spurs into delusion.

As night gathered in, threatening to crush the light from the small lamp at my desk, I did the only thing I knew would calm me: I threw myself into analyzing the reports on the deaths of Jack's victims. There was a picture of the man to be found here, I was certain of it, hidden within the way he worked and the women he chose to murder.

I poured myself a glass of port and settled down to study the information I had gleaned from Bagster Philip's notes. The liquid shone like blood in the glass, and when I sipped it, I shuddered slightly as my imagination led me to expect a different flavor; something warm and metallic, rather than the fruity wine I swallowed. I pushed the thought away as I felt the first tingles of anxiety prickling on my face. I was a man of science. There were no monsters. No *Upirs*. There were simply wicked men who did terrible deeds. With that thought firmly fixed in the forefront of my mind, I set about building some kind of profile of one such person. A man was only ever a summary of his actions. It was time to see what kind of man "Jack" really was.

I was lost in my work for hours, the decanter forgotten beside me as I scribbled notes and questions until my desk was covered in an untidy jumble of papers. It was nearly dawn when I realized that my legs were stiff and my back aching from being hunched over for so long. As I finally felt a wash of sleepiness fall over me, I stumbled up to my bed where, still fully dressed and not even under the covers, I fell into a deep slumber for nearly four hours.

I was cold when I awoke, but my mind was clear, and sitting by the fire in the drawing room, I put my thoughts to paper. I would send them to Robert Anderson himself.

7 The Sanctuary,
Westminster Abbey
November 10ᵗʰ '88

Dear Sir,

Whitechapel Murders

I beg to report that I have read the notes of the four Whitechapel Murders viz:—

1. *Buck's Row*
2. *Hanbury Street*
3. *Berners Square*
4. *Mitre Square*

I have also made a Post Mortem Examination of the mutilated remains of a woman found yesterday in a small room in Dorset Street.

1. *All five murders were no doubt committed by the same hand. In the first four the throats appear to have been cut from left to right. In the last case, owing to the extensive mutilation, it is impossible to say in what direction the fatal cut was made, but arterial blood was found on the wall in splashes close to where the woman's head must have been lying.*
2. *All the circumstances surrounding the murders lead me to form the*

opinion that the women must have been lying down when murdered, and in every case the throat was first cut.

3.   In the four murders of which I have seen the notes only, I cannot form a very definite opinion as to the time that had elapsed between the murder and the discovery of the body. In one case, that of Berners Street, the discovery appears to have been immediately after the deed. In Buck's Row, Hanbury St., and Mitre Square, three or four hours only could have elapsed. In the Dorset Street case the body was lying on the bed at the time of my visit two o'clock, quite naked and mutilated as in the annexed report. Rigor Mortis had set in, but increased during the progress of the examination. From this it is difficult to say with any degree of certainty the exact time that had elapsed since death as the period varies from six to twelve hours before rigidity sets in. The body was comparatively cold at two o'clock, and the remains of a recently taken meal were found in the stomach and scattered about over the intestines. It is, therefore, pretty certain that the woman must have been dead about twelve hours, and the partly digested food would indicate that death took place about three or four hours after food was taken, so one or two o'clock in the morning would be the probable time of the murder.

4.   In all cases there appears to be no evidence of struggling, and the attacks were probably so sudden and made in such a position that the women could neither resist nor cry out. In the Dorset St. case the corner of the sheet to the right of the woman's head was much cut and saturated with blood, indicating that the face may have been covered with the sheet at the time of the attack.

5.   In the first four cases the murderer must have attacked from the right side of the victim. In the Dorset Street case, he must have attacked from the left, as there would be no room for him between the wall and the part of the bed on which the woman was lying. Again the blood had flowed down on the right side of the woman and spurted onto the wall.

6.   The murderer would not necessarily be splashed or deluged with blood, but his hands and arms must have been covered, and parts of his clothing must certainly have been smeared with blood.

7.   The mutilations in each case excepting the Berners Street one were all of the same character and showed clearly that in all the murders the object was mutilation.

8.   In each case the mutilation was inflicted by a person who had no scientific nor anatomical knowledge. In my opinion he does not even possess the technical knowledge of a butcher or horse slaughterer or any person accustomed to cut up dead animals.

9.   The instrument must have been a strong knife at least six inches long, very sharp, pointed at the top and about an inch in width. It may have been a clasp knife, a butcher's knife, or a surgeon's knife. I think it was no doubt a straight knife.

10.   The murderer must have been a man of physical strength and of great coolness and daring. There is no evidence that he had an accomplice. He must in my opinion be a man subject to periodical attacks of Homicidal and erotic mania. The character of the mutilations indicate that the man may be in a condition sexually, that may be called Satyriasis. It is of course possible that the Homicidal impulse may have developed from a revengeful or brooding condition of the mind, or that religious mania may have been the original disease, but I do not think either hypothesis is likely. The murderer in external appearance is quite likely to be a quiet, inoffensive-looking man probably middle-aged and neatly and respectably dressed. I think he must be in the habit of wearing a cloak or overcoat, or he could hardly have escaped notice in the streets if the blood on his hands or clothes were visible.

11.   Assuming the murderer to be such a person as I have just described, he would be solitary and eccentric in his habits. Also, he is most likely to be a man without regular occupation, but with some small income or pension. He is possibly living among respectable persons who have some knowledge of his character and habits and who may have grounds for suspicion that he isn't quite right in the mind at times. Such persons would probably be unwilling to communicate suspicions to the police for fear of trouble or notoriety, whereas if there were prospect of reward, it might overcome their scruples.

Dr. Thomas Bond

19

MURDER.—PARDON.—Whereas on November 8 or 9, in Miller's Court, Dorset Street, Spitalfields, Mary Janet [sic] Kelly was murdered by some person or persons unknown: the Secretary of State will advise the grant of Her Majesty's gracious pardon to any accomplice, not being a person who contrived or actually committed the murder, who shall give such information and evidence as shall lead to the discovery and conviction of the person or persons who committed the murder.

CHARLES WARREN, the Commissioner of Police of the Metropolis
Metropolitan Police Office, 4 Whitehall Place,
S.W., Nov. 10, 1888

From Queen Victoria to the Home Secretary, Henry Matthews:

The Queen fears that the detective department is not so efficient as it might be.

No doubt the recent murders in Whitechapel were committed in circumstances which made detection very difficult; still, the Queen thinks that, in the small area where these horrible crimes have been perpetrated a great number of detectives might be employed and that every possible suggestion might be carefully examined, and, if practicable, followed.

Have the cattle boats and passenger boats been examined?

Has any investigation been made as to the number of single men occupying rooms to themselves?

The murderer's clothes must be saturated with blood and kept somewhere.

Is there sufficient surveillance at night?

These are some of the questions that occur to the Queen on reading the accounts of these horrible crimes.

20

LONDON, NOVEMBER 1888
INSPECTOR MOORE

Inspector Moore pulled on his overcoat and joined Inspector Andrews in the busy throng outside his office. Another day over, and still no end in sight.

"Let's get out of here before some bastard pulls us back in," he said. "I've already been here an hour longer than I should have and I do not see tomorrow being any less chaotic."

"Nor do I," Andrews said, carving a path for them through the corridor toward the main entrance. "Abberline's got orders to question anyone who appeared at all suspicious during the house-to-house last month."

"Suspicious? In Whitechapel?" Moore snorted. "We'll be here till hell freezes over."

"O'Brien's already back out. He should have gone home."

"What about the man he brought in?" Moore asked, standing aside to allow past a beleaguered constable dragging a scruffy man behind him who had several teeth missing. The man was loudly protesting his lispy innocence. "Did they get him to hospital?"

"Yes—he was lucky though. That mob would have beaten him to death in another few minutes."

"They were *all* lucky they were so close to the station." Moore nodded good-night to the officer manning the entrance desk, but he was too focused on his paperwork to notice. They were all too busy for polite formalities this week. "Mobs don't think straight."

He pulled open the door, and they stepped out into the street. Night had fallen heavily, and the air was bitter, but the street was still busy. Wives, mothers, and sisters were waiting for their menfolk to be released, and several constables had been charged with keeping the entrance to the building clear so the inspectors could get in and out freely without being further assaulted, either verbally or physically. Sometimes Moore felt as if the public thought the police knew who Jack was and were willfully not sharing the information, just to terrify the people of Whitechapel some more.

"What kind of fool claims to be Jack in the middle of a crowd? It's beyond comprehension."

"A fool or a madman." Moore lit his pipe. "Or both." He looked across at Andrews. "You can't fathom those minds, so don't try. For my own part, I'm too tired to remember my own name, let alone all those I've questioned today. I'll sleep like the dead tonight."

"Ah, there he is." Andrews gestured at a man climbing down from a hansom cab.

"Dr. Bond?" Moore frowned. "Don't tell me there's been another."

"No, I'm dining with him. If there's any man who can fathom those minds, I believe it's the good doctor."

"You may well be right. His report made for interesting reading." He raised his hand in a hello as the doctor made his way toward them. "Apart from that shit about the killer having no medical skills—but we can forgive him that defense of his profession, I think."

"He works hard," Andrews said, "as hard as we do. I think it's taking its toll."

Moore studied the doctor as he joined them. Andrews was right: Thomas Bond looked thinner and older than he had at the beginning of the year—but then, no doubt they all did. It had been one of those years. *No*, he corrected himself, *notoneofthoseyears*. There hadn't been a year like this before, not during his time with the force, he was sure of that. This year was something altogether different.

"I've kept the cab waiting," Bond said. "It's too miserable a night to walk and I fear I'd like to be out of this area with some speed. It feels too much like work, if you understand me."

"Oh, we do," Moore said. "Enjoy your dinner, gentlemen. I shall see you tomorrow, Andrews—maybe at some point we'll be able to do some work on our own case."

He was about to head down the steps when the doors flew open behind them and a scruffy, wide-eyed man was thrown out into the street.

"Go home!" a constable—Brown, Moore thought his name was—growled. "We've done with you for the day. What's the matter with you?"

The young man was thin, and although not overly poorly dressed, he was unwashed, even by the standards of this dire area of London, and odors both stale and fresh carried from him to the clutch of men, who'd stepped backward automatically.

"You don't understand!" the man said. His accent was thick, Polish, perhaps, as so many in the poorer parts of the city were. "It won't be the man you need to see. It will be what's behind him— it's hiding behind him! *In his shadow!* Don't you understand? I've seen—in my dreams. The water. The *Upir.*" He said the last word softly and shuddered slightly, scratching at himself as if trying to wipe something away.

A madman, Moore concluded. The streets were filled with them. The Pole stumbled off, still muttering to himself. No one went near him, and Moore didn't blame them.

"Everything all right, Constable?" he asked.

The man in the doorway nodded. "Lunatic. And he stinks."

"Who was that man?" Bond asked. Moore wasn't sure if it was simply the effect of the light pouring from the open doorway, but the doctor appeared to have paled.

"No one for you to worry about, sir," the constable said.

"But what was his name? Do you know his name?"

"Of course: he's just been interviewed. A waste of time, given that drivel he was spouting. Kosminski, Aaron. A hairdresser—or was, when he last worked, which hasn't been in a fair while. Lives with his sister, poor woman."

"Is everything all right?" Andrews asked.

"Yes, yes," Bond murmured. "He just looked familiar, that's all."

"Have you treated him at some time, perhaps?"

"Maybe that's it—where does he live?"

The constable pulled a small notebook from his pocket and scanned the page. "Greenfield Street, sir."

"You know him?" Moore said. He was tired, but if this was something that might lead them somewhere, he'd be back in the station like a shot.

"No," Bond said, after a moment. "No, I must have been mistaken."

"There can't be too many around like that," Andrews said.

"You'd be surprised. From my experience in the Westminster I can guarantee you that destitution, illness and madness are three who are very happy in each other's company." He smiled, a flash of expression beneath his mustaches. "Shall we?"

"Yes, of course," Andrews answered.

"Goodnight, Inspector Moore, and I hope you sleep better than I have been of late."

"Oh, I will, Doctor. A brandy or two will see to that."

He watched the two men climbing back into the cab. The doctor was tired and slightly on edge—it didn't take a detective to see that. Moore hoped it would pass. They needed Dr. Bond—if he was going to have some kind of nervous collapse, then he needed to wait until all this was over.

PART TWO

21

VENICE, CHRISTMAS DAY, 1885
JAMES HARRINGTON'S DIARY

It must be said that I have rarely seen so much beauty in one place as I have in Venice. Even in the crisp cold, which I'm told is rare for this part of Italy, there is something magical about the watery city. Edward Kane, my new friend and drinking companion, might say that my excitement was more to do with the wine and good food we've enjoyed rather than anything the sinking city has to offer. Perhaps he would be partly right; he does, after all, have a very different way of looking at the world.

Tonight, after all the other guests had drifted away to their beds, we lay on the couches in the library and talked until we were almost sober. Once more, I have to say how glad I am to have met Edward. Like the other Americans, he is so full of energy. He also has that enviable confidence that comes from being exceptionally wealthy— new money, of course, like my father's own, but earned in far greater sums from the railroads of America.

"You won't find me in an office, though, Jim, when you come to visit, which you will and I won't hear an argument against it," he said, his feet up over the antique arm of the chaise. "I'll be in an artist's studio, painting the finest female forms New York can provide. Naked."

I laughed along with him, my head still buzzing pleasantly. He fitted so well with the group of artists and poets who had gathered for the festivities in the Palazzo Barbaro. They fascinated me, but I still felt stiff around them—too English. They laughed freely. They were warm. There was no overpoliteness to be observed. If I were honest, I would say they reminded me of *her*. I had been so absorbed in my travels so far that as much as I had vowed not to have her out of my mind for a single second, that had proved not to be the case. My parents had been right: the world was vast, and there were many distractions in it. The further I had traveled into Europe the more she faded, even as I had been determined to cling to her, but now that I was here, in this strange enclave of wealth and libertarianism, she was back in my thoughts.

"It was a girl, wasn't it?" he said. "It was a girl with me—several of them."

I laughed again at that. My natural reserve eased around Edward; though I still felt middle-aged around him and his set, I was slowly relaxing with them.

"Come on, it's always a girl—or some kind of trouble. The 'Grand Tour' is no longer the done thing. It's too easy."

"It was a girl," I admitted.

"In trouble, was she?" He sat up and poured us more wine.

"No, nothing like that." My face flushed. I imagined that Edward had left many girls in trouble in his wake. "But I loved her." And I had, truly. However much my travels had gripped my imagination, and made London seem so far away, I knew that what I had felt—what I am sure I probably still felt—was real.

"Love, eh?" He frowned, and then smiled in triumph. "Ah, the wrong sort of girl!"

"Something like that."

"No wonder your parents sent you away," he snorted from behind his wine glass. "Love is a dangerous emotion in the young. They want it beaten out of us so we can be as cold and dead as they are."

For the first time I saw something other than good humor in his eyes and I wondered at his upbringing. Had it been particularly hard for him? Was that why he was so wild now?

"I do believe that my parents love each other," I said, "in their own way. They just want . . . well, I suppose they just want the best for me. My studies were going badly, and then they found out about . . ." Now that I had started, I couldn't stop. "They thought this would be a good idea for me. I was ready to start in the family business and they said no, they wanted me to see more of the world before I limited myself to one aspect of it." As I listened to my own words, I felt quite ashamed at some of the darker thoughts I had had toward them in the early days of their discovery of my secret and as I had set off for Calais. They were good people. They were kind. They probably would fit much better into this artistic Venetian palace than I did.

"Then I apologize," Edward said, and he raised his glass. "To your family. To kind hearts."

We sat in silence for a while, both tired, him drunk and me definitely merry, and both lost in our own thoughts, no doubt of people far away. I thought of my bed a few floors up, but could not muster the energy to find it. It was the end of Christmas Day, and it had been a fine one. Despite my thoughts of home, my heart was content.

"Of course," Edward said, lying back once more on the chaise and staring up the painted ceiling far above us, "you have seen nothing thus far on your trip, nothing of any real import."

I sat up, my tiredness forgotten, and immediately began to protest. I had seen Rome for one thing, and the remains of Pompeii—how could he—?

"Enough, my friend!" He held one hand up to silence my protest as he smiled. "Yes, of course you've seen beautiful things—the famous arts, the work of the Renaissance. Culture, buildings, all built by dead men—all just relics. What of life, Jim? What of that?"

"What do you mean?" I said, taking a long sip of my own wine. My head spun slightly, but I didn't mind. I was glad of it. I wanted to be more like Edward. He had adventures. He had confidence. I wanted both of these things. I wanted his courage. "I'm here with you and all these glorious people. Surely that is life?"

"We are like the arts, though. We are wealthy; our lives are easy. They are what we want them to be. I talk of painting beautiful women, and maybe I shall, but in my heart I know I'll end up with a stiff collar, a sensible wife and working with my father in the railway business." He smiled. "Oh, I shall be comforted by my fortune, and I shall holiday in the finest places and live in a beautiful home, but will I *live*? Will I know the struggles of day-to-day existence? I doubt it, and that haunts me. That's what I came to see. And that's what you must see too."

"I do not understand."

"Where were you planning to go next?" he asked.

"Vienna." I was looking forward to the cultural city of learning.

"Then that is good. That's on the way."

"On the way to where?" I frowned. Where would he have me go?

"Poland—but don't go to the cities. Go to the heart of it; see the *people*." He waved his wine at me as he spoke.

"But surely not?" I said. "There is so much unrest . . ."

"That, my English friend, is the point." He shrugged. "For what is life, if it is not struggle, pain and death?" He got to his feet and swayed slightly. "And as much as I have no desire to experience these things for myself, not really, we must *see* them, surely?"

He leaned forward and slapped me hard on the shoulder. "And now I must find my bed. Or somebody's bed. Any bed." He turned and wandered off toward the stairs, his footsteps echoing on the stone floor.

I sat there for a while longer before finally venturing to my own room. I haven't stopped thinking about what he said though. Even in the gray light of dawn, with my head throbbing from an excess of wine and good cheer, more than I am accustomed to, my heart is racing with excitement. For I shall do what Edward suggested: I shall go to Poland. My mind is set. I shall have an adventure!

22

LONDON, NOVEMBER 1888
AARON KOSMINSKI

He had come out early, before dawn, and he walked aimlessly in the quiet, his feet carrying him through the miserable streets that made up so much of Whitechapel. He had thought perhaps if he immersed himself in wickedness, then the evil that haunted him would get lost there, but it was not to be, of course. At four o'clock in the morning, even in the overcrowded houses of Flower and Dean Street, most people slept, whether an honest sleep or the stupor of the drunk. But not Aaron: he'd awakened gasping for air once again, only just managing to contain the scream that threatened to burst from his chest.

Matilda and Morris were no longer sympathetic to his night terrors—not that Morris had ever done more than tolerate them. Matilda gave him no practical comfort when they struck; she was barely able to contain her anger and irritation. He woke the children and scared them, and even though they knew he could not control the workings of his sleeping mind, his panicked screaming allowed his relatives to vent their frustrations with everything else, all the things they felt he could control if he put his mind to it: his fear of water and his subsequent filthiness; his strange nervous tics and irrational behavior; and of course, most of all, the financial burden he'd become to all of them over the years he'd been unable to work.

Could he blame them for any of that? No. It was all true. If he were Matilda—sensible, practical Matilda—he would think himself a madman too.

He had tried to fight the night terrors by staying awake as long as possible, and once he managed a whole twenty-four hours before exhaustion got him, but the constant pacing and slapping his own face in the last hours infuriated and worried his sister and her husband more than the screams in the night. They had started to whisper about him when they thought he could not hear, and he found himself wondering if, in their own darkest moments, they too suspected him of foul deeds. He had noticed the change, ever since the police had come back for him—although Matilda must surely have realized he was too weak to have committed those terrible atrocities. And where would he have hidden the tools required? And he had not washed himself in a long time, so if he were Jack, then he would be covered in dried blood.

Still, fear and worry could make people have the strangest thoughts—he knew that better than most. And the city was infected with the darkness that came in the creature's wake—the *mayhem*—and it was filled with suspicion and intolerance.

He was infected in a different way: he had the visions—the scent. He was the unwilling hunter in this game that had been played out so many times over the ages. The creature had found its way out of the river, and now the pieces had been reset; they would hunt each other until one was the victor. He knew these things, though without knowing how. He'd tried to explain the visions to Matilda—it was not so very long ago that his dreams had saved all their lives—but she did not want to listen. She had no time for the old ways now. She had no time for *him*.

So when the dreams had awakened him once again, he'd wrapped his thin coat around his sweat-soaked, stinking carcass and come out into the graveyard of the night, walking with no real sense of purpose but looking all the while for the man with the devil on his back who plagued his dreams. How could he hope to recognize him? There was never a face visible—in the main, he viewed the visions as if from within the man looking out; sometimes they came in an abstract flurry of images, like pieces of a puzzle. None of it made sense. He wondered if perhaps he had started to fear the dreams as much as the creature itself.

He had walked the streets for perhaps two hours, and now his thin legs ached, and his feet were numb with cold. Sometimes he circled through the narrower alleys, which were so dark it could still be midnight there, and sometimes he wandered along the main thoroughfares. His body shook from expending so much energy. He rarely left their home for so long these days; even when the visions forced him out, he would be back within the hour.

Slowly, the city around him came back to life. How many of those were waking with more than a touch of excitement, wondering whether Jack had struck once more while they slept? Perhaps he'd even been wandering the same streets as Aaron, a few moments behind or before him—it was possible; for all the efforts of the police, he had seen not a single constable during the past hours. He felt quite alone, and suddenly, wanting to cry, could not stop a small sob escaping him. It was all madness, of course, he knew that—not the madness his sister thought he suffered but the madness that came from knowing that so many around you were living in an illusion, believing that the solidity of the world was all there was. They would never see or understand the wickedness that had taken up residence in their city. He alone carried the weight of the truth, and he wasn't up to that burden. He could taste the stagnant river water in his mouth from the visions; it was more real to him than the sooty air he breathed. Where was the creature now? Was it watching him, laughing at him? And what of the man it clung to—was he yet aware of what he had become? Perhaps he was now as tortured as Aaron himself, for they were all victims in different ways.

He walked up Church Street, licking at the snot that dribbled from his running nose. Only when a woman crossed to the other side to avoid him did he realize that he was also muttering to himself. A fine sight he must be, he thought: a filthy, scrawny lunatic, twitching and stumbling through the streets. *A monster*. He was a monster seeking a monster. He almost laughed at that.

He stopped outside the church and stared up at the magnificent pillars, admiring the beauty of its Romanesque strength of shape. If only he could take comfort from it—but no place of human worship, no synagogue, mosque, or church could help him. It took lost souls to fight the devil—for that was what the *Upir* was, he was sure of it: a devil by a different name, a tormentor of souls. How he wished for faith.

"Stand back and let me through."

The gruff voice coming from somewhere to the side of the building made him jump, and suddenly he was very much back in the real world of the dark morning. He sniffed to clear his nose and rubbed his face with the back of his cold hand. From around the corner he could hear more voices, and suddenly in need of human company, he walked in their direction.

Metal rattled against metal: somewhere ahead, a man was unlocking the gates to the small cemetery attached to the church, but Aaron could not see whoever it was through the gathering of figures shuffling for places nearest the front. There must have been twenty or thirty of them, all of a type: roughly dressed, with worn coats and threadbare gloves. They kept their heads down, and those who did glance at him looked at him with mild curiosity only, not disgust or disdain. Poverty and filth stripped them of their sex, and Aaron found it hard to distinguish men from women. As he stood there, the gates ahead finally swung open, and more figures emerged from the gloom behind him, seeking out the entrance. The weariness in their trudging walk echoed in Aaron's soul.

Caught up with the tide, he moved into the graveyard, where those ahead were already claiming benches and places beneath trees, curling up with their knees tight under their chins, trying in vain to fend off the cold.

Sleep, Aaron thought, *they've come here to sleep*. Exhaustion flooded through him. He found he felt safe here among the destitute, lost in their midst. Maybe, if there was a God, he was smiling a little on him after all. He sat down at the base of a stone mound topped by a crucifix and watched the shadows drift in. He would rest for a few minutes, he decided, just sit here for a while and watch those who were as lost as he was, maybe even let his troubled soul calm itself. The stones were rough on his spine, but he didn't mind. *Just a few minutes*, he thought again, as his eyes drifted closed. *Just a few minutes.*

It was daylight when he opened his eyes, and his back screamed from where the hard stone had dug into him as he'd slept. He was frozen, even though there were two other bodies huddled close to him and he had somehow managed to pull his coat tightly round him and tucked his hands into his stinking armpits. One man had actually fallen into his lap, and another, with barely a tooth left in his fetid mouth, was leaning against his shoulder and snoring soundly. As Aaron pushed him away, the man fell backward, revealing open sores on his face and neck. Aaron looked down. The elderly man who was either sleeping or dead on his lap was also covered in some kind of skin disease: his face and hands were flaking away, and sores oozed foul pus from the edges. He shivered in disgust and wriggled his aching body free.

The cemetery had filled considerably over the however many hours he'd slept, and now people were strewn across the grass and benches, but even where areas were crowded, none other than these two, the lowest of the low, had come close to him. It was as if an invisible circle had been drawn around the small monument he'd slept against, and no one with any soul left would come inside it.

A woman stared at him from a bench opposite. Her look was feral. Aaron dropped his gaze and hurried for the gates. He did not look back. Whatever comfort he had believed he had found had disappeared; he did not belong here. Most people saw him as a stinking man in ill-fitting clothing, a tramp, but perhaps these vagrants recognized him as something other than one of their own. His teeth chattered violently as he headed home, weaving his way through the busy streets of Whitechapel, where Londoners were well into their day. Filth squelched through the gaps in his shoes where the stitching had frayed and he hadn't yet repaired them. Matilda would not like that. He must remember to take them off when he got through the door.

"There's someone here to see you."

He wasn't expecting those to be his sister's first words. Nor was he expecting the rather tight expression on her face.

"Who?"

Matilda's eyes glanced down at his boots, and he crouched to remove them and his soaking socks. His fingers shook as he worked at the laces. Who would come and see him? He had no friends; those acquaintances from his hairdressing days no longer spoke to him, Matilda and Morris's friends left him well alone, and even the rabbis ignored him.

From behind a closed door came the chatter of children. Matilda must have shut them away. His heart thumped. Was it someone from the asylum? Had she finally decided that enough was enough?

"He says he's a friend of a friend of yours. He wants to ask you some questions. He talks like a gentleman, but his clothes are poor." She frowned angrily, a sure sign she was worried. "What have you *done*, Aaron?" she whispered. "Where have you been?"

"I haven't done anything." He took his coat off and tried to smooth down his shirt below. Black lines of dirt ran under his fingernails. He should wash his hands, he knew that, but he couldn't bring himself to, not now. A gentleman? A friend of a friend . . . He didn't move. If it wasn't someone from the asylum, could it be—? He couldn't bring himself to think it, but he must: could the *Upir* have found him?

"Well, come on," Matilda snapped at him. "I've already lost an hour to him. I have washing to do!"

Aaron shuffled forward. On some level he was still as scared of his big sister as he was of the monsters who tormented his dreams.

In the small room that served as the family's living space, a man was standing at the window and looking out. He could see what Matilda meant: although the jacket he wore was of cheap fabric, even with his back turned, Aaron could see that his hair was well cut. When he turned, his skin was clean and his mustache shaped and trimmed.

The man didn't flinch at Aaron's unkempt appearance but looked him straight in the eye.

"I'm sorry to disturb your day, Mr. Kosminksi, but I wanted to ask you something," he began.

Matilda was right: he wasn't from this part of London. Aaron had his own heavy accent, and he could recognize the different tones in others' voices.

"Who are you?" Aaron stayed where he was in the doorway until, from behind, Matilda shuffled him forward and then closed the door, sealing them in. Although his bones were still freezing and their rooms were never entirely warm, fresh sweat prickled his itching scalp.

"I mean you no harm." The man looked awkward. "It has taken me a few days to track you down. I saw you outside the Police Station the other night—"

"I've done nothing wrong!" Aaron started, and the man raised his hands in supplication until Aaron quietened.

"I am not a policeman, and truly, I was not suggesting you had. It was something you said as you came out—a word I have heard before, from a priest. I wondered if you knew him?"

There was a long moment of silence, and Aaron fought to think clearly. What was it that he had said? He knew no priests, so what was this, some kind of trick?

"I don't understand," he said at last.

"Neither do I," the man said, "and I am hoping you can help me." He came closer and sat down in the worn chair next to the unlit fire. "You see—I thought he was mad. And now I'm not so sure."

For the first time, Aaron noticed the dark rings that rimmed the man's eyes. He had placed him at perhaps fifty, but now saw he was probably several years younger. Aaron Kosminksi wasn't the only one having difficulty sleeping.

"Who are you?" he asked again, more softly this time as his fear abated. This man was almost as troubled as he was; he could sense it.

"I was on the steps," the man said, ignoring his question, "and I heard what you said. You talked of not needing to find the man, but what was behind the man. 'In his shadow,' you said. You mentioned the river." His eyes searched Aaron's. "You said '*Upir.*' I need to know what it means."

Aaron flinched at the word, and one dirty hand started rising to tear nervously at the dry skin of his lips. His head twitched, and he stared down at the carpet. It was a trick. It had to be.

"The priest told me of these things, and I thought him mad. I want to know if he spoke to you too."

"Who are you?" Aaron muttered again. "Who *are* you? It sent you—it is trying to trick me. I don't know any priest. Who are you?" His anxiety was rising, and his head twitched. The river tasted strong in his mouth, and he wanted to spit it out. He wanted to get all the liquid in his body out. It was contaminated—that must have drawn him here. His breath came in sharp pants— And then suddenly the man leaned forward and gripped his knee, and the shock of such voluntary human contact stopped his panic in its tracks, and Aaron looked up, his eyes wide.

"I do not mean to upset you," the man said. "My name is Doctor Thomas Bond. I have been examining the remains of the women found in Rainham and Whitehall—the body parts pulled from the river. I am not here about Jack, and I do not believe you are Jack. I just want to know if you have been to the opium dens or spoken to this Italian priest."

This was all too much to absorb. What opium dens? And someone else knew of the darkness roaming the city? Could it be a trick? He rocked forward and back for a moment, but the doctor kept his hand on Aaron's leg. There was kindness in his touch, and it was calming.

"I don't know the priest," he said, eventually. "An Italian priest?"

Dr. Bond nodded. "I didn't recognize the clothes of his order, but he was a priest, I don't doubt that. He said he was a Jesuit. From a special order."

Aaron looked up, cool relief spreading through him like balm. He was not alone. If Fate was at work, then Fate had found him and this man and the priest. They would stand together.

"We must find this priest," he said, simply. It was all there was to say.

23

LONDON, MAY 1887
ELIZABETH JACKSON

She had just about reached the third floor with the two pails of fresh water when Mrs. Hastings appeared on the landing below and called up to her, "You're needed. In the drawing room. Straight away." Her eyes were suspicious; maids did not get summoned to the drawing room.

Elizabeth's stomach plummeted. What had she done wrong?

"But I was changing the basins," she said. "Should I finish? I can't just—"

"*Immediately*, girl," Mrs. Hastings said.

Her muscles aching from having carried them this far—she didn't think she would *ever* get used to that! Elizabeth placed the buckets against the wall and kept her head down as she scurried past the housekeeper and made her way back to the ground floor. She could feel Mrs. Hastings' eyes burning into her back. What had happened? She'd been distracted and she wasn't sleeping well, but she didn't think it had affected her work. She'd always taken pride in her job, no matter how backbreaking and thankless it was. She'd been at this Chelsea house for a long time now, and aside from *that* time, she'd never been in any trouble—and even then, her mistress hadn't known about it—so what could it be?

She paused outside the door and smoothed her uniform down over her full figure, checked that her golden-red hair was tucked neatly into her hat, as it should be, took a deep breath and knocked.

"Come in."

For a moment she stood in the doorway and stared, before collecting herself and bobbing a curtsey, her head lowered. Her heart was racing. Was she about to lose her position? Was that why *his* mother was here? He was back now, so perhaps she had decided she wasn't going to risk a scandal of any sort and had told their secret first?

"Mrs. Harrington wants to speak to you." Mrs. Blythe stood by the fire, and while her tone was not unpleasant, it echoed the look that Elizabeth had seen in Mrs. Hastings's eyes: suspicion, wariness. "She assures me that it is nothing of concern to me, so I shall leave you to it."

"Yes, ma'am," Elizabeth said, bobbing again.

"Thank you." Mrs. Harrington stayed where she was, sitting next to an untouched cup of tea.

Fabric rustled as the stout, middle-aged woman exited, and it was only when she had gone that Elizabeth looked up. Mrs. Harrington's silk dress was a deep maroon, and the tapered sleeve and small bustle were elegantly fashionable. How Elizabeth ached to wear a dress like that one day. Her own "best" dress was well worn; it had been her sister's before her . . . But Mrs. Harrington belonged in a different world, and so did James.

"Sit down, child," Mrs. Harrington said, waving her toward the chair opposite. "And don't look so afraid. I haven't told her about your unfortunate affair."

Elizabeth blushed slightly and took the seat, perching awkwardly on the edge. It wasn't right to be seated in this room, and she couldn't help but wonder if there'd be punishment for it later.

"You know James is back, of course. And that he has been ill?"

"Yes, ma'am, I had heard it."

"Has he attempted to see you?" Her voice was soft, and Elizabeth noticed how tired she looked. There were shadows around her eyes and lines on her face that had not been there before. She hesitated over her answer. Should she lie? Would she be getting James in trouble? She didn't know what to say, because in truth she didn't know what to think. She had been so excited when she'd heard of his return, but her feelings had changed, and she couldn't explain it. There was something different about him.

"Yes," she said eventually, because it was the truth and she was at heart an honest girl. "When he was first home, I saw him outside my mother's house. He was waiting for me."

"Was he ill then?"

"No—he said he had been but that he had recovered."

"He did." Mrs. Harrington's eyes drifted to some unknown point. "But of late he has suffered a relapse. His chest is weak again, and his color is wrong."

"Is it the consumption?" The question came out even though Elizabeth knew she should be sitting quietly and waiting to be asked questions herself.

Mrs. Harrington appeared not to notice, or perhaps she did not care. "The doctors are not yet sure; he certainly has some of the symptoms they would expect to see from the condition."

There was a moment's silence as she continued her sad stare into a place Elizabeth couldn't see. She gathered her own thoughts: he was ill again? The old love she'd had for him surged to the fore as she considered that perhaps it was the sickness that had made him different. How ill was he—did he need her?

"Tell me," Mrs. Harrington said, coming back to the present and watching Elizabeth thoughtfully, "did you find him strange?"

Elizabeth's heart quickened. It wasn't just she who had noticed the changes, then. She had wondered if it was simply that his feelings had changed or that his experiences abroad had roughened him, but perhaps not.

"A little," she answered, cautiously. "He was not as . . ." She searched for the right word. "He was not as *kind* as I remembered him. His smile was different."

"Yes," Mrs. Harrington said. "I am finding the same. His good humor, his gentleness: they are harder to see. Sometimes I feel almost as if my son is a stranger to me. How long ago did he visit you?"

"There were two occasions," Elizabeth answered. "The last perhaps a month ago." She didn't tell her of the times she'd seen him watching both her mother's house and this one. She didn't want to think about how he'd looked at those times, so unlike himself—so *hungry*, almost fevered. Maybe he had been, if this illness had returned.

"Do you still love him?"

The question was so direct that it startled her. Throughout the whole discovery of their closeness, neither of James's parents had mentioned that word—"infatuation," yes, and "fleeting attraction," "folly of youth." But not love. As they sat opposite each other, no doubt examining the reflections of their own tiredness, Elizabeth wondered whether for Mrs. Harrington they were now simply two women, their places in society temporarily suspended. Elizabeth wished she could feel that way, but the chair felt wrong underneath her, and she wasn't used to seeing the room from this level or angle. She kneeled in front of the fire to clean and set it; that was it.

The blush crept further up her pale face. Her instinct was to say yes, but for some reason the word wouldn't come.

"I don't know." It was the closest to the truth she could get, but it seemed to satisfy Mrs. Harrington, who let out a soft sigh.

"Neither do I, my dear." Her lips trembled and her eyes watered.

"Are you all right, ma'am?" Elizabeth asked.

"I don't believe I will be." She leaned forward and touched Elizabeth's knee. "Something is wrong with him, and it's not sickness—unless the sickness is in his soul. Don't let him near you, my dear. *Run* from him." Where her touch had been gentle, she now gripped Elizabeth's knee so tightly it was almost painful. "*Run from him.*" The words came out in a terrified hiss.

"Ma'am—"

"Promise me." Her eyes burned into Elizabeth's. "Do not let him near you!"

"I promise," Elizabeth whispered. She was starting to cry, as much from confusion and Mrs. Harrington's upset as from her own. She didn't understand what had made her so afraid, but her terror was now obvious.

"Good." She released Elizabeth's knee and sat up straighter. "I truly could not bear that on my conscience."

She rose, and Elizabeth did the same, relieved to be standing again. The water upstairs needed changing and the buckets she'd taken up would be cold now. Mrs. Hastings would not be best pleased if she didn't get it done by lunchtime, regardless of this unheard-of visit. She looked forward to getting back to her work, even if her back ached constantly and her knees were raw: it was simple, honest, not this madness that was plaguing Mrs. Harrington. It wasn't all the things she'd seen in James's fevered eyes that she didn't want to think about.

"Perhaps I should have just let him marry you," Mrs. Harrington said, softly. "We should never have sent him away. A stranger has returned in his place, and I don't believe he likes us very much."

Elizabeth said nothing but stood there, her head bowed, until the lady had left.

The rest of the day passed quietly, although Elizabeth could feel the tension coming from Mrs. Hastings, whose suspicion had metamorphosed into curiosity, but who was too proud to come out and ask why on earth the lady from next door would want to talk to the housemaid. It wasn't as if the two households were particular friends; the Harringtons were new money, from trade—quite different.

Elizabeth had ignored the questioning looks and gone about her endless labors, for once happy to be so exhausted that she had no energy for thought. She'd been happy in service here for the last six years. She fervently hoped that within a week this visit would be forgotten by both the housekeeper and their mistress and she could get back to being diligent and relatively invisible, just as someone in her position should be.

She finally left at half-past ten. The air was mild as the city moved from spring toward summer. Though she was tired, she looked forward to the walk home. One of her sisters would invariably be awake, and they would talk about the mundane irritations of their day before at least trying to sleep.

She had been determined that she wouldn't even look up at James's house as she passed—it had been smiles through the window that had started all this trouble, after all—but as it was, the shouting caught her attention. She stopped on the pavement and looked up at the large white house beyond the railings. Lights still blazed from the front room and the curtains and one window were open. The raised voice came again, though the words were indiscernible, and shadows danced against the wall as someone gestured angrily inside. Even though it was muted, she knew it wasn't James's voice; it had to be his father's. But what could have infuriated him so? James had always told her his father was a gentle man; kind and liberal, who approached every situation with understanding—he certainly had with theirs, even though he had insisted that their relationship end.

Someone moved in front of the glass, too suddenly for Elizabeth to move away or even duck her head: she recognized the stout figure of Mr. Harrington, and as their eyes met briefly, she saw that he was as terrified as his wife. But why? A taller figure appeared behind him and stared out: James. Even if she couldn't have seen his face, she would always know the shape of him. Over his father's shoulder he smiled at her, an unpleasant expression, and her breath caught in her chest. She froze like a rabbit caught by lamplight in the middle of the hunt. For a moment she thought there was something else— something *behind* him, a dark shape that clung to his shoulder as if it had crawled up his back and was peering around his neck to look at her. And it was filled with awfulness.

Her hand clutched at her mouth to stifle a scream, even though the shadowy *thing* had disappeared as quickly as she'd seen it, and it was just James and his terrible smile and Mr. Harrington and his fear. An icy chill gripped her stomach and spread outward, threatening to freeze her heart and lungs where she stood until, finally, Mr. Harrington pulled the curtains closed, leaving her in the blessed darkness of the ordinary night.

Her breath came out in a gasp. What had that been? What was going on in that house? She felt as if she had peered into someone else's nightmare, but it was not so much what she had seen but what she had felt: this awful dread.

Mrs. Harrington would have no need to convince her to stay away from James anymore. She ran all the way home, but still she could feel her ex-lover smiling at her, all that unnatural hunger in his eyes.

By the time the early morning came round, Elizabeth had almost convinced herself that she had simply been spooked by Mrs. Harrington's conversation; that all she had witnessed through the window was the interaction between an angry father and an unrepentant son. Yes, James had changed; she had known that the moment she had seen him again, but he had been traveling for two years, and such experiences were bound to change a person. In his case, perhaps, it had not for the better, but she *knew* James; she had no doubt he would return to being the diligent, reserved young man he had been when he left.

As she passed by the Harrington house, just before half-past five, she saw it was still closed up. She chided herself for her flight of fancy the previous night. She was a sensible girl—a practical girl; such imaginings were not part of her personality.

She had laid the fires and lit them, and the family was breakfasting by the time anyone noticed the strange activity going on outside: a doctor arrived and was hurried in the front door. A little later, another carriage pulled up, a bigger one, and several men rushed in. By this time, the other inhabitants of the polite Chelsea street could no longer contain their curiosity, and masters dispatched servants to quietly inquire about what had occurred, and was there anything anyone could do to help?

Slowly the story rippled outward. Elizabeth was in the kitchen when Tom, the boot boy from halfway down the road, told them, wide-eyed, that the whole Harrington family had been taken sick in the night. "It came on 'em sudden-like," he explained, obviously enjoying his moment of glory. "Mister 'arrington, 'e was found by the maid on the bedroom floor with foam all round 'is mouth and 'is body twisted up, most unnatural-like in its position, with 'is nightclothes almost up to 'is waist. The doctor reckoned as 'ow 'e'd been dead most of the night—bin trying to crawl out of the room to get 'elp, that's what the doctor reckons."

As Elizabeth listened, the chill in her stomach returned and she shivered, despite the heat of the oven beside her.

"As for the missus"—Tom was a natural showman, playing to the crowd—"she's a goner too, but she was in 'er bed, and still with that awful foam round 'er mouth—and still looking like she went in agony."

"And what about the son?" Elizabeth asked the question, and Mrs. Hastings fired her an irritated look. Even down here in the kitchen, there were strict rules of precedence: these might be exceptional circumstances, but it was not Elizabeth's place to ask the questions.

"What about the son?" Mrs. Hastings repeated.

"'e's the lucky one: sick as a pig, 'e is, but still breathing. The doctor's seeing what 'e c'n do for him now; I says best pray, that's what everyone's reckoning."

"But what *was* it?" Mrs. Hasting said. "Sounds pretty rum to me."

"They don't know, not as yet, but the doctors, they fink it was somefink wot they ate at supper. Master 'arrington, 'e brung some chutneys back from 'is trip and they 'ad 'em with their supper. And there was somefink with mushrooms in too, some kind of potted paste."

"Never trust a foreign cook," Mrs. Hastings muttered, shaking her head. "You never know what they use. And *mushrooms* too."

Elizabeth swallowed hard, fighting the urge to vomit. She felt dizzy and cold, and she was sweating. She leaned on the kitchen table, hoping no one had noticed, as she let the rest of the conversation turn into a hum around her. Her brain felt as if it

were on fire. By some miracle James had survived—but she knew
that wasn't true, though her heart would not accept it: somehow,
James had killed his parents. *Her* James. Her quiet, studious James.
There was a pit of dread at the core of her that knew the truth—but
why? And how?

She thought of the way he had looked at her through the glass,
the awfulness of his smile, and her fear turned inward. He had seen
her watching them—what if he came for her?

Finally, Tom the boot boy left, and the day continued in some
semblance of normality, even though those upstairs and downstairs
alike were gossiping about the events next door. Elizabeth felt their
eyes burning into her: after all, Mrs. Harrington had spoken to
her just the previous day, so surely she must know something. She
kept her head down and continued with her work, but inside her
mind raced. What was she to do—what *could* she do? She didn't
have any evidence against James, only her own suspicions—and if
she said anything, then who would ever believe a jilted maid over
a gentleman? All she would do would bring suspicion on herself.

Her days passed in a cloud of anxiety. As news reached them that
James Harrington was mending she lost weight and her shining hair
grew dull. He was very lucky, they said; the doctors had given him
little chance of surviving, but after knocking at death's door a few
times, he finally turned the corner.

She watched from the window the day that the funeral cortège
arrived, and she saw him leave the house in his mourning clothes. He
was thinner, pale, and his face was ridden with grief. His shoulders
were hunched and every movement seemed like an effort. Rain
streaked the glass, smearing the departing carriage into a smudge
of black. Elizabeth was a whirl of mixed emotions. Seeing him as he
was, she could believe he was devastated, but always in the back of
her mind was the memory of him at the window, standing behind
his father and surrounded by wickedness, the only way she could
describe it.

She lay awake at night wondering how long she could live
like this, until two weeks after the funeral, and there he was,

five o'clock in the morning, waiting for her at the corner of her mother's street.

She stopped in her tracks when she saw him and let out a small cry she couldn't contain—shock, fear, surprise—and she turned to rush in the other direction.

"Wait," he said, "Elizabeth, please wait—I only want to talk to you for a moment. I *have* to talk to you. It's important."

It was the sadness in his voice that made her turn. This was her James who was speaking, not the stranger who had returned from his great adventure.

"What?" She kept a few feet between them. Whatever her heart might still feel for him, her gut knew what he had done in that house and it horrified her. "I have to get to work."

"I'm leaving," he said. "I can't stay here. I shall rent the house and take rooms elsewhere."

Elizabeth wasn't sure what she felt most: relief or heartache. "Why are you telling me?"

"I love you," he said, simply. His eyes darkened slightly. "But I can't be around you. I don't . . . I don't *trust* myself. Something is—" His face twisted a little as if some internal torment gripped him. "Something is different." He reached forward and held her arms.

"I need you to promise me something."

"James, you're hurting me." For a man who had so recently been ill, his hands were strong, and Elizabeth just wanted them off her. "You're scaring me."

"Good," he said, "*good*. You should be scared of me—*I'm* scared of me." He leaned forward and looked deep into her eyes. "Promise me that if you ever see me back here, you'll leave—just get your things and go, anywhere—but nowhere I can find you."

"But why—?" she started. His breath on her face smelled rancid and sickly, as if he were still battling this disease, as if it were still determined to claim him.

His eyes hardened, and his next words almost stopped her heart. "You know why, Elizabeth," he hissed at her. "*You know why.*"

He released her with such energy that she stumbled backward, her mouth agape.

"Promise me," he repeated. His face was flushed, blotches of sickly purple stark against the pale of his cheeks. "Promise me you'll run."

"I promise," she whispered.

He turned and strode away from her without another word. He didn't look back. She waited where she was for a long five minutes before finally continuing her journey to work on shaking legs.

He left with his suitcases at lunchtime, and this time Elizabeth felt no sadness at all, only an overwhelming sense of relief. It was over. He was gone.

24

LONDON, NOVEMBER 1888
DR. BOND

We made a strange pair, the little hairdresser and I, on our nightly rendezvous searching the streets of London, he with his filthy skin and I with my stiff back, which gave me away no matter what I chose to wear. Kosminski's sister, although obviously wary of me, not knowing what interest I might have in her brother's well-being, had gone some way to smartening him up, forcing him into clean clothes and insisting that he at least washed his most intimate parts and his armpits. I too made these a condition of his assisting me in my search—I did not wish to draw any more attention to us than was absolutely necessary. I could only imagine what Inspector Moore would make of my association with one of his suspects, should it be discovered.

It was four days before we found the priest. I could not remember the route to his rooms, much to my dismay, and instead I had taken the little Polish hairdresser to the various opium dens, hoping that my visit hadn't scared the priest away from them. I doubted that, though: the priest was not afraid of anything *I* could do to him. Kosminski did not speak much, perhaps because his English was poor, or maybe because he was clearly uncomfortable in the company of others, and I found that suited me. Curious as I was about how he and the priest could have spoken such similar words,

I could not help but feel I was allowing myself to be dragged into a whirlpool of madness. I had been convinced the priest was insane, and everything in Kosminski's behavior implied the same about him—so what of me, I wondered? Here I was, wanting answers from them; what did that say about my own sanity?

On the fourth night, while we were loitering outside the opium dens of Bluegate Fields, my cravings overtook me, and I led Kosminski inside. I told myself I would have just the smallest of pipes—not enough to make me sleep. As soon as the sweet smell of the poppy hit me my mouth started watering—but I was also repulsed, perhaps fear of the lost time I had suffered previously. Since meeting the priest, I had broken my own rule on self-medicating, taking laudanum when the urges became too strong, but it was not the same as the bliss of drifting on one of the cots. Chi-Chi was serving another customer, so we sat on a low bed and waited.

Kosminski was fascinated by the den—perhaps because those around us were in such a relaxed state. I thought it had been a long time since he had experienced that sort of relaxation.

"And the priest—he does this?" he asked quietly.

"Not like this. He takes something stronger. This makes you dream, but that . . ." I remembered the sensation. The clarity. "It gives you visions."

"Visions?" Kosminksi leaned in, alert. "I have visions—my grandmother's visions." He paused. "My grandmother's curse."

"What kind of visions?" I asked. He had alluded to these before, but only in passing, and I had never been exactly sure what he meant. For once, he sounded entirely focused.

"Things that are true but that I cannot possibly know: my father's death, events far away that I do not understand. And then there are . . . there are the *others*—the river. The *Upir*. All so dark. So awful." He shivered, and I knew I had to stop him from drifting away from me.

"Perhaps you should try it," I said.

"I don't want to see more clearly." He flinched at the very suggestion, drawing away from me.

"It will make you more confident."

I did not know why I suddenly wanted Kosminski to take the drug I was nervous of taking myself—perhaps because on some level I already thought him mad, so I had no worry for his sanity, but I also was curious to see its effect on someone else.

Chi-Chi scurried over to us and I placed our order with him. He returned with the pipe and the opium and as he carefully prepared it, I smiled at Kosminski, who looked afraid—but that had been his natural expression since we'd met.

"Breathe it in, just like a pipe."

He looked at me the way an infant does a parent, nervous and yet trusting, and did as he was told. As he took several puffs, I, for my part, found my curiosity had quashed my own desire for the drug. Instead, I sat and watched him, waiting for the effects to take hold. Would they be the same as they were for me?

For ten minutes or so, he simply sat there, looking around, nonplussed. He did not speak, but neither did he gasp or proclaim any strangeness in what he saw. I felt a vague disappointment. The room was warm and my collar itched. It was strange to be here in the den and entirely in control of my senses. Normally, my arrival would be all about the need and my departure would be in the echo of the haze. I had never had time or inclination to notice how rundown the building was, although in that regard it suited its clientele, including me. It did not judge.

Suddenly I felt maudlin, exhaustion overwhelming me. This was pointless. It was madness. It was—

"The priest," Kosminski said urgently, "we must find the priest." He reached forward and grabbed my arm, dragging me to my feet, and then he rocked backward on his heels, his balance gone. He gasped as I fought to keep him steady.

"Are you all right?"

No one around us so much as glanced our way as I led him to the door, for they were all lost in their own versions of the dreams. This reality had faded into insignificance for an hour or two.

"You followed him," Kosminski said as we stepped back out into the bitter night. His eyes darted this way and that in the gloom, but they were looking at something beyond my capability to see. His hands no longer twitched, but he kept one gripping my arm even though he was stable once again.

"Yes, yes, that's right."

"Through the fog," he continued, pulling me forward, almost dragging me through the dangerous alleyways. "He was ahead of you—he knew you were there. He was leading you."

I said nothing as I followed him. This was like no vision I had ever had with the drug. Was he truly seeing my experience—my past? Was this because he held my arm? How could that be? His English was improved, and his accent had faded—was this because he had somehow accessed my memories? Was he partly inside my own mind? The thought was enough to drive me to the brink of madness myself. Promising myself laudanum when we reached wherever Kosminski was leading me, I went with him.

He said very little more, just muttered now and again as we grew closer to the river. The priest's rooms had been near the wharves, of that I was certain, but nothing looked familiar. It was a wild goose chase—it had to be. There was no possibility that Kosminski could be "seeing" my journey from the past; this was just the drug's dream, and as the fool who had made him try it, I felt I had no choice but to see him through it, even though my hands and feet were now freezing.

But then there it was, right in front of me: the building with the door hanging loose on its hinges. The squalid tenement looked ready to give up and crumple in on itself, should the wind rise.

"He went up first," Kosminski said. "You waited a few minutes and then followed."

Just as I had before, I now stood on the street and looked up to where a grainy light shone through the filthy glass. When a few minutes had passed, Kosminski pulled me forward, and I did not resist—how could I? This was beyond my comprehension. The solid foundation of my beliefs was shaking. This was no color, no fish darting around a man's head; this was no flight of fancy.

When Kosminski finally released my arm as we reached the priest's door, it was my hand that was shaking, not his. I knocked gently, with none of my previous arrogance. Beside me, the hairdresser slumped against the wall.

"What happened?" he said. One hand rose to his mouth and he picked at his lips. "I don't understand."

He had returned to his normal nervous state, worry settling back into his tired eyes.

I didn't have time to answer. The door opened, and there he was.

25

POLAND, JUNE 1886
JAMES HARRINGTON'S DIARY

June 15, 1886

This is the first day I have been well enough to write in what feels like years, although my guide reassures me that it has been only just over two weeks. Two weeks lost to delirium, when time passed in a vague haze of images and dreams I cannot quite remember. It is very strange to have part of your life lost to you. If it were not for my body being so weak and emaciated—having been kept alive through being force-fed vegetable broth and water, and in my more lucid moments, some strong-tasting potato-based stews—I would not have believed it.

I am somewhat regretting my bold adventure into the Polish countryside. I am not Edward, I have realized, admittedly a little late. I do not think that my nature and adventures go hand in hand as his must do. I doubt very much that Edward would have fallen as ill as I have. All I want now is to recover enough to return home as soon as possible.

I am not sure what sickness it is that I have contracted, but I am concerned that it has left me with symptoms of consumption. Although my entire body feels wretched, my lungs are the worst. My breathing is labored, and I have had two coughing fits since waking, both lasting some time and both strong enough to make me think I was choking. Not only does my upper body ache awfully from the strain, I noticed after the second that there was blood on my hand. I asked my guide to fetch the mirror from my small trunk, and after the shock of seeing myself so much thinner, looking as if I had aged ten years in these two weeks, I studied my complexion. Spots of blotchy purple sat high on my pale cheeks. The water in my eyes was tinged pink. My heart sank, and has stayed there, for I know that the consumption carries these signs too. However, I am glad to be finally free of the fever that had claimed me.

I long for London. Happy as I am that I am recovering, and as grateful for the kindness the villagers have shown me, when they are all clearly living a very basic existence, I just want to be well enough to go home. I have done with adventures.

June 16, 1886

I slept well, despite the heat and the buzz of flies and biting insects that had found their way through the gaps in the shuttered windows. I had always imagined Poland cold, which of course it is when in the grip of winter, but I had not expected this damp summer heat. It started in May, just when I had decided I had seen enough of the grim cities and wanted to explore the countryside. I had announced my decision with hearty vigor, as if I wanted *more* adventure than the cities with their universal problems could show me, but in honesty I felt I was done with the gray harshness of life that surrounded me. I wanted to see something more beautiful, and if that could not be found in humanity, then I would hope to find it in nature, and those who chose to work with it. The young men whose acquaintances I had met on the train into Poland heartily approved, and although they did not join me (I fear they were far more political in their stances than I, and I must confess that their intense conversations often both confused and bored me), they helped me find a guide who would take me to see some of the villages. This was to have been my last sojourn before making the trek back to England.

The heat wave had hit, and I was glad to be leaving the stinking city. Now I wish I had stayed. I am feeling quite unsettled.

This afternoon, two old men from the village visited me, in the company of my guide. Until then, the only human contact I had had was with an old woman who brought me soup and a hunk of bread. While I ate it, she brought a bucket in the corner of the room and put a chipped ceramic jug of water on the wooden drawers next to the window. I tried to engage her in conversation, but she barely looked up and in the end I could only nod and smile my appreciation as she took my empty dish away. She did not return the expression. In fact, she did not even look me in the eye.

I fell asleep after that, awaking only when the three men came into my room. Through the window I could see the sun was sinking into a lazy late afternoon. The heat was fading, and a light breeze worked its way through the room, making me feel better than I had. I smiled and pushed myself up on my pillows and looked at my guide, Josep—a man in his thirties who did not say much but at the same time had an air of affability about him that had made him an easy traveling companion for the past few weeks.

"Please tell these gentlemen how grateful I am for their village's hospitality. I will of course reimburse them for everything they have done for me."

Josep nodded, but he did not speak to them, instead tugging at his cap with his hands as he spoke in English to me.

"They want to know how you got sick."

I looked at the two men with him. It was hard to place their ages. Their skin was weather-beaten and leathered from working the fields, and their beards were gray. They watched me intently.

"Are others ill? Like me?" I felt a growing dread. In the short time that I had recovered my senses I had not considered that my illness might be contagious or that I might have brought a plague on those who had been kind enough to take care of me.

"No," Josep said, "but—" He hesitated, then went on. "Some animals have sickened. Cows aren't milking."

"Perhaps it is this awful heat," I said.

"Perhaps. But they want to know when you started feeling unwell. And if you remember exactly what you were doing beforehand."

"You know this already, Josep. We had been traveling for several hours and were both hot and tired. We stopped for a rest." My eyes moved from him to those beside him as he repeated my words in this unfamiliar language of which I am ashamed to say I have learned only a phrase or two. I regretted that now. There is nothing worse than relying entirely on others for your communication. So much can be lost in the space between the words and the meaning that comes with the delivery.

"You fell asleep under the tree, and after I had finished my lunch—bread and dried meat—I went for a walk. I was very hot and sweaty, and walked until I found the river. You had told me we were not far from one. I crouched by it and soaked my face and hair. Though it was freezing cold—far colder than I expected—I would have stripped and swum in it, but the bank dropped away steeply and I couldn't see the bottom. Judging from the temperature, I thought it must be deep, and I did not want to get tangled in any weeds at the bottom." As I spoke I thought of Edward. Had Edward been with me, he would have leapt into the water without even considering its depth. In his company I probably would have too. I thought once again that perhaps it had been folly to amend my travel plans and move away from the well-tried routes of the Grand Tours of the past.

"I sat there for a while," I continued, "and then before I turned back, I leaned over the side and drank some of the water. It was later that afternoon that I started to feel odd." A thought struck me at that point. "Do they feed the animals from that river? Perhaps that is the cause of their illness and mine? Some kind of parasite in the river?"

Josep, his hand gesturing as he spoke, once again relayed my words to the two somber men beside him. They turned away and spoke rapidly and quietly between themselves. I could see Josep getting confused trying to catch their words.

"But actually," I said, leaning forward slightly, a memory of that afternoon suddenly hitting me, "I am not sure it was the river water—I think I might have been running a slight fever before that but not realized it. Perhaps it was an insect bite that has made me ill."

"Why?" Josep looked almost relieved, and I wondered if the animals were sicker than they were telling me. "What makes you say that?"

"It was something that happened when I was drinking the water," I said. "I had forgotten all about it until now—I suppose with the fever and everything, I have barely known who I am myself."

"What happened?" His tone was sharp.

I felt slightly defensive as I explained, "I must have had a fever because I had a momentary hallucination—ridiculous, when I think about it—but as I knelt on the bank and leaned forward to drink, I was sure that I saw something rushing up toward me, from the bottom of the river. A dark shape." I laughed slightly, but the warmth had gone out of the room with the memory. "It gave me quite a fright. I can see it still: something on the other side of the ripples, moving incredibly fast, and with such intent I almost thought I drank it in. I leapt right back from the edge, I can tell you."

Josep swallowed, his Adam's apple bobbing nervously in his throat, before translating my words.

"Of course," I continued, "it was probably a reflection of a cloud or some such, but it must have been some precursor of the fever that gripped me later in the afternoon."

Josep almost tore his cap in two as he relayed my last sentences, and for the first time I saw emotion on the two men's faces: dread, fear, anger. I had no idea what I had said, but as I looked dumbly around me, they got to their feet and stormed out. At the door, one spat out a word so vehemently, I knew it had to be a swearword of some kind. The old woman peered through for a moment, and then the door closed.

"What?" I asked Josep. "What is it? I don't understand."

He said nothing but stared at the floor, his cap now a twisted wreck in his hands. I had to repeat his name three times before he looked up.

"It is just a stupid superstition," he said. "Don't worry about it. Just get better. I will talk to them."

"What kind of superstition?"

"Just sleep." He got to his feet. "I shall be in the other room."

If he had been trying to reassure me, well, he hadn't been successful. What did those men think I had brought to their village?

About an hour ago, the old lady brought me another bowl of soup, but this time one of the men accompanied her. He waited in the doorway, watching me, as she put it on the table by my bed.

I reached up weakly to take it, and she grabbed me suddenly, holding my face tightly in her gnarled hands. She stared into my eyes with such intensity that I almost cried out.

After thirty long seconds or so she released me and stepped backward, her face a mixture of revulsion and more than a little fear. I tried to speak to her, but she would have none of it, instead muttering under her breath—some kind of incantation or prayer—as she returned to her companion in the doorway. She said one word to him—I heard it clearly, even though I had no idea what it meant.

They closed the door and this time I heard the key turn heavily. They had locked me in.

It is dark now, and I should be sleeping. I am still exhausted and the small candle is nearly burned out. However, I cannot relax; I keep thinking about how the man's face had changed when the old woman had spoken that word:

Upir.

June 18, 1886

Yesterday I was left alone for the whole day, except for two bowls of soup being shoved through the briefly opened door. I was forced to rise from my sickbed to retrieve them. My legs were weak, but I was pleased to find that I could stand now, and make it across the room and back without dropping my food. I could not afford to waste any potential energy.

The coughing fits are still gripping me. At one point, after leaving a bloom of blood on my pillow, I tried calling out for help, but none came. Instead, once my breathing was restored, I had to fetch the jug of water to ease my throat myself. To say that I felt uneasy would be an understatement. Not even Josep had visited me. I felt entirely abandoned and more than a little afraid.

What had I done to offend these people so? If they did not want me here, why not just send me on my way? I tried the door several times, but it would not open. During the previous night's fitful sleep, I had been awoken by the sound of nails hammering into the wooden window frame, and when day came, the room was patterned in streaks of sunlight and gloom, and full of shadows. They had sealed me in. The window had been my only means of escape, and I had failed to use it while I had the chance. As I lay there in that strange half-light, I wondered what they had done to my guide. The poor man had wanted to provide for his wife and child by leading me into the countryside and then setting me on a course for home; he had no bond with me. I hoped I had brought no ill fate onto him.

My stomach churned, my anxiety fighting with my hunger as my recovering body cried out for nourishment, and slowly the hours passed, one bleeding into another until night fell once again. I felt calmer in the darkness though I am not entirely sure why. Perhaps it was the thought that these people who were both my saviors and my captors were asleep. I also felt oddly stronger, as if the cooler air were energizing me.

I was fully in the grip of the night when I heard the key turning in the door. It was a cautious sound, and I sat bolt-upright in my bed, my heart hammering in my weak chest. In the darkness I could make out only a dark shape as a man stepped inside.

"Who is it?" I hissed.

The man raised his hand to his mouth to silence me and to my great relief I realized that it was Josep. He hurried over to me.

"We have not much time," he whispered, and he handed me a small bundle of clothes—those I had arrived in. "Get dressed. We have to leave now."

"What is happening? I don't understand what I have done to these people."

"They have called for a holy man. Quickly!" He snapped the word; his urgency was obviously driven by fear.

My questions could wait. I was as eager as he was to leave.

Josep carried my small trunk, which had been in the room with me, and I paused only to leave a few coins on the table for the old woman who had fed and looked after me. Whatever had happened to make them hate me so, this was not an affluent village and I wanted to pay my debt to them.

It was dark outside, the ground only a shade lighter than the sky, but here and there were torches marking the ends of the roads and placed around chicken coops, no doubt to fend off any hungry foxes. It was bright enough that I paused to stare at the wooden doors of the villagers' ramshackle homes: every one had a strange sign daubed on it, and some had trinkets and crucifixes crudely affixed to the wood.

"What is that?" I whispered. "That sign on all the doors?" In the still air I could still smell the acrid fumes of the paint: this work was fresh.

Josep said nothing for a moment, but my refusal to move finally prompted an answer. "It is to protect against evil. They want to stay safe until the holy man comes." He walked on ahead and I followed, my curiosity overwhelming my desire for safety.

It was only when we had retrieved our horses and cart and quietly left the village for the safety of the woods that Josep spoke again.

"We will move quickly through the night. We will be safe—they will not come after us. I will take you as far as the next railway, and from there you must travel alone." He did not look at me.

"Thank you," I said. "For what you've done. I was worried that perhaps they had harmed you, or that you believed whatever madness has gripped them about my illness."

"It is not madness," Josep said, "but if I helped them, then the holy man would kill you and cast the devil back into the river." He kept his eyes on the barely visible black track ahead. "And that would mean the devil would still be in my country." He hawked and spat. "This way, it will be gone. You are strong enough to last until you are home, and then it will be your England's problem."

I was starting to tire and I shivered. I pulled the cart's rough blanket round my shoulders, finding comfort in the smell of horses ingrained in its fiber. It was a natural smell. Earthy.

"What devil?" I said, wearily. He was making no sense to me. Was this some old superstition? These people were more backward than the more civilized European countries like England and France, and their beliefs in folklore and legend had persisted longer than ours, especially out here, in the middle of nowhere.

"I think I have the consumption, nothing more," I said, as if that weren't a worry enough in itself. "I have always been prone to illness in my chest."

"That is not the consumption," Josep said. The horses' hooves beat a steady rhythm on the uneven track. "That is the *Upir*. You woke it in the river. And now it has you."

It was the word the old woman had used, and I refused to acknowledge the dread I felt on hearing it. "I don't know what this *Upir* is," I said, "but I assure you, I am simply ill. These are modern times—there is no place for silly superstitions." I looked at him. "You live in the city—surely you know that."

"I know many things," he answered, "and I know, just as the old lady did, that you are cursed. I should never have told you the river was there. I shall pray for you."

"It is going to kill me, is that what you are saying? This devil—this *Upir*?" My patience was wearing thin. I wanted to be home, or at least in civilization somewhere. In the dark, with the trees hanging over us as if reaching down to tear me limb from limb with their jagged branches, it was hard to believe in my own logic. I had seen the symbols painted on the doors. I had seen the fear. If I were not careful, I could get sucked into believing their ridiculous legends, especially if even Josep was refusing to see reason.

"Oh no," he said, "it will not kill you. It will be far, far worse than that."

And then he told me.

It is now past dawn, and even in the sunlight I shiver while writing down his words. I scoffed at him, of course I did, but my heart is filled with dread. It was awful, and I wish I had never heard a word of it.

26

LONDON, NOVEMBER 1888
DR. BOND

"So, these *are* your rooms," I said, as the priest moved out of the way to allow us entry. "You do not live elsewhere."

"I had a feeling that the only way you would return was like this." He looked at Kosminski, who was shaking and shivering the doorway. "Unless the members of the Metropolitan Police Force have lowered their standards."

"He is not well," I said. "He has taken some of the drug you use. It helped him . . ." I did not know whether I wanted validate my next words by speaking them aloud, but I had no choice, for it was the truth. "It helped him to lead us here." I took Kosminski's arm and gently led him inside, seating him on the wooden chair next to the blazing fire.

"I have something that will calm him." From within his robes, the priest pulled a small bottle and held it out. "Drink this. One swallow."

"Liquid?" Kosminski's eyes narrowed. "Where from? Is it from the river—?"

"Do as I say," the priest growled. He was a forbidding presence and the little hairdresser took a swallow before hastily giving the bottle back. The effect was almost immediate. He became calmer, quieter, and now I could understand how the priest could remain so in control when under the influence of the strange drug. When he had seen enough, he must have trained himself to take some of this liquid—but what was it? Another drug, of course. How could anything any man said be relied upon when he was so often not himself? But here I was anyway, searching out one madman because of the words of another.

I looked around the small room that was so bare of possessions. "You do not have a Bible?" I said, frowning. I had expected to see one beside the bed, or at least on the table—I would expect as much in most gentlemen's houses, let alone a priest's rooms.

"The Lord and I do not need words." He grunted and sat on the bed, forcing a groan from it as it took his heavy weight. "I am trained by the Church. I am part of an order of the Church—but the Church is not my home."

"I do not understand—you are a priest?" I sat on the other end of the mattress and turned inward, so that the three of us were quite huddled together with the stranger at our center.

"I come from the gray area between good and evil, born with an unnatural gift. Perhaps this gift came from God, or perhaps from the devil. For my part, I choose to serve the Lord with it, to join the order and fight the old evils that hide among us. But wicked deeds must sometimes be done in God's name. I would not speak to the Lord and share these with him; the guilt is mine alone. If I must forego my place in Heaven for the work I've done in this world, then I will make that sacrifice."

He cut a strange figure in the flickering firelight. It was as if the flames of hell were already burning around him. I did not wish to know more of the deeds of which he spoke. I was already more than slightly concerned that I might find out firsthand.

"What unnatural gift?" I asked.

"The gifts come in many guises," he said. "Mine comes as visions." He nodded at Kosminksi, who was watching the priest with his mouth slightly open, as if he could not quite believe his own eyes. "Not like his," the priest continued. "I could not see into your head and lead you here. What I see—I see what is *really* there. I see creatures and people as they really are. I can sometimes *manage* them, bend them to my will for short bursts of time. At first, as a child, they all thought me mad, but then the priests came, and when they saw what burdened me, they took me and trained me. Now, like my brothers, I travel to where I am called, to hunt the evils that ordinary men find so hard to see."

He stared into the flames for a while before carrying on, "Each one of us is different. But each brother has a skill; something that connects us with evil. That is why our souls are no doubt damned."

"I have to admit, I find it all very hard to believe," I said honestly. "Even with what I have witnessed tonight—how I got here. I am a man of science first and foremost. I believe in logic and reason."

"And yet, still you are here, with us." He smiled, his white teeth bared and sharp. "I think you are touched with the gift too: a damned soul."

"I am afraid I do not share your visions," I said. I felt suddenly defensive, and fought the urge to loosen my collar in the heat.

"No, perhaps not, but you do not sleep, and you have become restless. You suffer anxiety. You know that it is among us."

"I have always suffered with bouts of insomnia," I protested, but he held a hand up to stop me.

"This one is different. I know these things. I have seen you in the dens. More than all this, though, is your obsession with this killer. Everyone else seeks this flamboyant 'Jack,' but not you. Somewhere inside, you recognize the work of true evil."

"Are you saying Jack is not evil?" I wanted to transfer the focus away from me. There was a limit to what I was prepared to believe in one go. My anxiety was simply a condition, as was my insomnia. I was not the first to suffer from either, and I would not be the last.

"I think Jack is a result of this older evil—another like us, perhaps, who can sense the presence. Someone with a wickedness locked deep inside that has been set free. But Jack is human evil, and there will be others like him in the city who are pulled into the mayhem. The city is full of anger and crime this year, yes? More than others? The creature that has drawn we three together is not human evil."

"There were stories of your order," Kosminski said, quietly. I had almost forgotten the hairdresser was there. "The Roman one—the men of God who had no God. My grandmother told me, before she died, when I was very small. She had visions, and her grandmother before her also. It should only be in the women." His nervous tics had faded and he looked saner than he had in our entire acquaintance. I wondered again what was in the bottle the priest had given him. I also found myself wondering if it would help me sleep.

"You two have never met before?" I asked, even though I knew what the answer would be. There had been no recognition from the priest when we had arrived, and I could think of no good reason for them to concoct such an elaborate ruse.

"Never." The priest shook his head.

"Tell me more about this 'Upir,'" I said. "You spoke about it before."

"It is so old," Kosminksi muttered, his eyes lost in something only he could see, "and it stinks of the river. It is in the *liquid.*" He spat at the flames suddenly as if terrified of his own saliva. "And there is so much blood. I can *feel* it." A trembling beset his body, and even though he was sitting close to the fire, it did not abate.

"It is a parasite," the priest said. "An ancient wickedness. Something from a legend almost forgotten. It is *rotten*. Old, earthy—but it is sentient; it wants our reactions to it. It wants us to hunt it. It enjoys the game."

"I do not understand." I felt myself sinking deeper into the mire between what was real and what wasn't. "What is it? What does it *do*?"

"It *feeds* on us. When it is weak, it sleeps on the bottom of the rivers. It will not be far from one, in case it needs to flee there. It cannot live without a host for long."

"A host?" He had said this the last time I had been in this room, but I had barely listened then, so focused as I was on my own disappointment. Now, even as I fought the suggestion that I was being sucked into their madness, I wanted to know.

"It attaches itself to a host—someone unsuspecting. It either moves to another when that host dies, or takes refuge in the water to regain its strength." His eyes burned like dark coals. "It lives in the space between the host and its shadow. Its presence, forever just out of sight, eventually drives the host mad. It will control him when it wants to."

"Control him to do what?" Once again I knew the answer even as I asked the question. I had seen the limbs dragged from the Thames, the emptied and ruined torso in the vault at Whitehall.

"To *feed*," the priest said. "It wants the soft flesh. The organs."

"And the river," Kosminski muttered, "it has to feed the river. It has to make the river its own."

"What do you mean, 'its own'?"

"In case it needs to escape there."

In the hazy warmth of the room in the middle of the night, it all made a strange kind of sense. Part of me still screamed madness, but I was fascinated by what both men were saying.

"But why leave the torso in the Scotland Yard building? Why would it draw attention to itself like that? Or does it not have thoughts?"

"Dark mischief," the priest said, "just like all the other devils that my order hunts down. It wants to taunt us."

"It brings chaos," Kosminski added, nodding just a little bit too fast. His tics would be returning soon. "Mayhem."

"And the strange opium allows you to see it?" I asked.

"Normally it is only visible in the moment it moves from one host to another." His eyes looked directly into mine. "Or when it is about to kill you."

"You know a lot about this creature, given that it seems a little shy," I said, but neither of them rose to my bait. Part of me had hoped to get some reaction out of them that would allow me to leave here, to storm away. *Ancient demons?* I was still not sure my belief could stretch that far.

"There is a lot written, and there are myths and legends. The country people understand, those who live side by side with nature. I was sent by the order to a village in Poland, where an English traveler was believed to have inadvertently freed the beast from the riverbed. He had escaped by the time I got there. I tracked him through Europe."

"How do you intend we find him in this heaving city if the police are having no luck?"

"The host will have been sick after the *Upir* attached itself to him. The illness will still come in bouts between killings. The villagers also said he was a young gentleman—perhaps you can use your medical connections to see if any strange illnesses in such a man had been treated before the first of these murders that now plague you."

"I can try," I said, "but I must be honest with you. I am not sure I can believe in your story. However much I might see truth in it here, in the middle of the night, by morning I know my reason will be restored." I *hoped* it would, at any rate, though I could not help but remember how Kosminski had led me here. There was nothing natural about *that*.

The priest smiled at me. "You search for the *man*, in that case, Dr. Bond. You do not have to believe in the *Upir*. As long as we find the killer, that is surely all that matters?"

I had no argument to that.

27

LONDON, NOVEMBER 1888
ELIZABETH JACKSON

"It's none of your business, Annie!" she shouted at her sister before turning and half-walking, half-running down Turks Row. Her golden-red hair hung tangled down her back where it had come free from her bonnet.

"You're a disgrace!" Annie fired at her back. "A shameful disgrace."

Annie always did have to have the last word, and if it could be a hurtful one, then all the better. Elizabeth's cheeks burned, and she swallowed angry tears. At least having to run after the unexpected argument had chased away the freezing cold, for a few minutes. She rounded the corner and leaned against the wall, her shoulders slumping slightly. Why did she have to go and bump into Annie, of all people? She let the tears flow, rubbing her cheeks with a grubby hand.

Her family did not understand—of course not; who would? Why would she leave a perfectly good job to work the streets, give up a nice warm attic room to doss down in a flea-filled lodging house? What could she tell them? Certainly not the truth.

She couldn't tell them James had come back, that he was getting married and moving back into the house where his parents had died, because they wouldn't understand why that would matter. And she certainly couldn't tell them what he had done to her in the streets between her house and his. She rubbed her belly and the ruination growing inside and as she remembered the terror of that moment when he had *changed* from one person to another, the tears fell heavier and she started sobbing. He would come for her again if he could find her; she knew that. But this time it would not be her body he would want—it would be her blood.

Promise me you'll run.

She needed to leave Chelsea; the ease with which Annie had found her proved that.

She wondered if she would ever be able to run far enough.

28

LONDON, FEBRUARY 1889
DR. BOND

If 1888 had been a lion of a year for crime, then 1889 was starting as a lamb, and I was not the only one relieved at that. The search for Jack had thus far been fruitless, but at least he had not killed again, and slowly, life in Whitechapel and across London was returning to normal. Jack was silent, and there had been no more dismembered bodies pulled from the river either. We were in a hushed lull of hopefulness.

Inspector Moore, who, along with the rest of the force, was finally being able to return to his normal duties, called it right when he said that they were all praying that both killers—if they were indeed separate—had either died or moved on. If they could not be caught, then they could at least go and plague someone else's city.

I hoped he was right; I hoped we could finally put all this madness behind us, but my continued sleeplessness and bouts of anxiety made it hard for me to relax or let go. I almost regretted my alliance with the priest and the strange little hairdresser—for one, should Moore ever find out that I was meeting secretly with a man once considered a murder suspect, this would not bode well for my career, and possibly even my liberty. And as long as there were no fresh murders around, it was easy to start considering their ideas madness once again.

All the same, every fortnight or so I would find one or the other waiting for me outside my home or at the hospital, or there would be a letter through my door, arranging a time, and we would go to the dens, take the strange opium and walk the streets of London together until dawn broke. Then the priest would share his elixir, and we would return to our homes. I knew they were frustrated at my relative inaction, but first we had had Christmas, and then, in late January, Juliana and James had wed, and there had been a fine celebration. I had been distracted—I had *wanted* to be distracted.

Yet here I was, finally sending letters to colleagues asking of any travelers who might be presenting strange symptoms after visiting Poland. I had already checked the records in my own hospital and found nothing. I told myself I was carrying out the searches simply because I had promised the two madmen I would, but that was not entirely true; my own behavior told me otherwise, and I was something of an expert in analyzing human action. I could hardly ignore my own.

I no longer walked by the river if I could avoid it.

Even with only laudanum to bolster me, I would look first around the heads of those I met before I looked into their eyes. I avoided shadows, and I never walked in those left by others.

When night came, I could still feel that awful disquiet. I remembered how Kosminski had reached into my mind and led us to the priest. I felt the dead women gathering around me in a throng, demanding I comply.

Inspector Moore was wrong: the killers had not moved on, nor had they died. There was still something not quite right in the air of London. Perhaps they were sleeping or resting, replete after such a bountiful previous year.

In the dark, I believed in the *Upir*, and my sleepless hours were so much longer and lonelier than those of the day. During the days, when the night's thoughts would linger, I wondered if madness were infectious. I decided that, if anything, I was doing the research because I wanted to *disprove* the story the priest had told me, however convincingly he had relayed those awful facts. This would make me sit taller at my desk. But still I wrote the letters, and still I found my heart beating excitedly when I received replies, only to feel bitter disappointment when there were no names to further the chase.

As the weather turned from miserable to crisp and frozen, I returned to the hunt. It had always been my passion, but now I found it vital to my well-being, regardless of the exhaustion that had become my constant companion. The freedom of riding out relieved both my anxiety and my frustration, and for a few hours at least I could become lost in the thrill of the chase, a hunt that had far more chance of success than those with which I was professionally engaged.

I gathered up the next batch of completed letters and smiled as I pulled on my coat to go and post them. I would hunt again tomorrow, and the very thought lifted my spirits. I smiled. I couldn't help myself.

Juliana joined me occasionally, and she had agreed to come along the next day. Her new husband encouraged her in it; he was not a huntsman himself, and there was obviously nothing improper in our friendship, so he declared himself glad that she had found something she enjoyed so thoroughly, that was good for both her spirits and her constitution. He was busy with both work and the renovations to the house in Chelsea, and Juliana was not a woman to occupy herself with visiting ladies and sewing alone. Although he had promised she could do some bookkeeping for him, this had not as yet happened, and I often sensed that I was not alone in taking out my frustrations with the world around me through the ride.

Still, if I could provide that for her, then I was happy. There was very little in my life of thrills or excitement; both the hunt and Juliana's company offered me those.

She was always flushed and smiling on the way home: truly radiant. I was not the only one to notice; I had seen several of the gentlemen of the hunt looking her way approvingly, and not only for her skill on a horse. She was a beauty, even if she failed to realize it herself. I wondered if young Harrington knew how lucky he was to have her. I hoped he would not let his affections slide now that they were married. Her loneliness still worried me, and that was how our conversation started that afternoon.

"And how are you finding married life?" I leaned back on the seat. It was a personal question, but our friendship had settled into something beyond the bounds of polite formalities and we were relaxed in each other's company.

"Very good," she said, then added, "Well, James is very busy and he has made so many plans for changes to the house that I think we shall be living at my father's for the best part of a year, but I am glad he decided that we should move there. I'm sure his parents would have wanted it."

"How did you and he meet? I can't recall you ever told me."

"I'm not sure I did tell you," she said, smiling at the memory. "We met in the park—I was out walking, and there was a sudden downpour." She smiled. "We stood under the same tree together for a while until the rain passed, and then he walked me home. As it happened, the rooms he had rented were only a few doors down from our house."

"It sounds very romantic." It was so easy for the young— chance meetings, with all the possibilities of the future wrapped up in a shy smile and a first hello. I wondered why that changed as we got older—perhaps we no longer saw the potential for good experience in others, only the possibilities for complications and trouble. The idea of upsetting the routine balance of our lives no longer feels appealing. The young, of course, know no different.

"I cannot remember the last time I took a walk in the park simply for its own sake," I said, a little wistfully, "and I can safely say I have never sheltered under a tree with a stranger and have it lead to love at first sight."

She laughed aloud at that. "I never took you for a romantic, Thomas—but I must correct you, for it wasn't love at first sight. We were simply friends at first. I don't think he felt any immediate attraction to me, not in that way."

"I find that hard to believe," I said. "I imagine he was just shy. He seems a reserved kind of chap."

"That might be true," she said, "but it was only after meeting my father that he began to court me properly. I noticed a distinct change in his behavior." She smiled at me, her eyes all warmth and intelligence, and once again I was struck by this young woman's depths. In many ways she was far older than her years. "I think after the loss of his own parents he wanted to find a new family of his own—parents he could love as well as a wife."

"He has certainly done that."

"Yes, he has—although both he and my father work too hard." She looked at me more closely. "As, I think, do you."

I shrugged in acknowledgment. "It is the nature of the beast," I said, meaning that medicine in itself did not allow for much relaxation, but as the words came out I found myself thinking of the priest and Kosminski and the *Upir* they hunted. What would Juliana think of me if she knew of my involvement with such men—if she knew that I was hunting something not quite man and not quite devil, and telling neither her father nor the police what I was doing?

We turned into Juliana's Chelsea street and I rapped my stick on the roof of the hansom to get the driver to stop.

"Thank you, Thomas," she said, and she kissed me on the cheek before climbing down. "We must arrange a dinner at my father's. We'll be back there again soon, once the wallpaper arrives."

"That would be lovely." I could still feel the softness of her lips on my skin, and I did my best to ignore the effect that had on me.

I watched her walk away toward the house. Her shadow was stretched out against the pale steps as she reached the front door. It was just a shadow, an empty space denied light—how could anything exist between her and it?

The *Upir*. My rational brain was taking charge after the ride in the brisk fresh air and once again the whole thing seemed ridiculous. I sat back against the seat as the cab moved on.

I knew exactly what Juliana would think if she knew of my secret activities.

She would think I was mad.

29

Paris, November 1886
James Harrington's Diary

I am not myself. The illness that plagued me in Poland lingers, and I am exhausted from lack of sleep. I have barely rested since the morning I awoke, two days after our flight from the village, and found Josep dead. Since then my journey has been swift and constant, as if I could somehow run from the memory. And maybe I have managed it, in part at least, for the immediate horror I felt on seeing him like that beside me in the cart—with no mark of malice on his body but his eyes wide and mouth stretched open in a silent scream of terror—has faded. I still think of the dream I had that night, however, and I cannot help but shiver, especially now.

I dreamed I was leaning over him while he slept—it was so vivid; even now I can see the images as clearly as ever. His mouth was hanging slack and he was snoring, lost in a deep sleep. I could hear animals rustling through the leaves as they hunted in the dark. There was a slight prickle on my skin from the cool air. I noticed that the strange little talisman he carried with him—the same symbol that had been painted on the village doors—had rolled to the floor from his pocket. I felt a weight on my back and something caught my eye, just beyond my left shoulder. In my dream I twisted round this way and that, but whatever it was remained constantly just out of sight, though I could feel its weight, a heaviness from the base of my neck to the bottom of my spine. I reached behind, but there was nothing to touch. I shook myself, but still the sensation remained. The weight pushed me forward, until I was once again leaning over my traveling companion. I could feel his breath on my face. And then his eyes suddenly opened.

After that, the dream must have ended, for I have no recollection of anything but slumber. I did not report my companion's death—who would I tell, out there in the wilderness?—but instead dragged his body deeper into the woods and left him there. In truth, I feared that if I found someone to tell, I might never get home.

By the time I had reached France, although I was getting sick again, I had begun to convince myself that Josep's death and my dream were linked: we had both been through the ordeal in the village, and their superstitions had taken their toll on us. Perhaps Josep's heart gave out with his own fear in the night—that would be understandable. Even younger men than he died when their hearts failed suddenly. And my dream was most likely my own subconscious working through the past few days' events. That Josep's death and my dream occurred on the same night was not that much of a coincidence; it had been only two days since we'd left the village, after all.

I arrived in Paris in quite good spirits, glad to be nearly home. Since my chest was weakening again and the strange blotches were appearing upon my skin once again, I decided to check into a hotel for three or four days to get some proper rest before heading home. I sent a telegram to my father to let him know my plans and to request that he wire enough money to cover my stay, my last few pounds having been spent on some respectable clothing on my arrival in the city. Then I settled into comparative luxury and tried to put my ordeal behind me.

At first it was easy. Sleeping in a comfortable bed and eating fine food made the village in Poland feel like a bad dream.

But I cannot shake this dreadful hunger that plagues me, and I awoke this morning with the weight on my back returned, and something dark and awful filling a spot at the edge of my left

eye, as if there were something creeping over my shoulder. I spent
a long hour in front of the hotel mirror, but no matter which way
I twisted, I could see nothing there. I wondered if there might be
something wrong with my spine, something that was making me
feel this way, or perhaps it might be a symptom of this strange
illness that I was suffering? Despite the knocking of my heart, I
convinced myself both of these things were causing my discomfort,
and promised myself that I would go to the finest doctors in London
when I got home. There would be a cure for this, I had no doubt,
and within weeks I would be laughing at the dark fears that were
starting to creep in on me.

But there was no explanation for where I found myself this
afternoon. I was in a workshop in a place called Montrouge, far
from my hotel and hitherto unknown to me. I was also wearing
my traveling clothes, not one of the new suits I had bought so I
would not embarrass myself among my fellow guests at the hotel.
There were instruments laid out on a table on one side, butchers'
and doctors' tools, all designed for cutting or hacking. As I looked
at them, my mouth watered and I tasted river water. Red flooded
the shadows behind my eyes and I felt an *eagerness* that I was sure
did not belong to me. My neck felt wet, as if a long tongue were
somehow wrapping itself around my throat. I was sure there was
something staring out from behind my head.

I left the place and returned to the hotel. I was shaking—I am *still*
shaking. The hunger is worse than before, and the blotches on my
skin are now so purple that one of the hotel staff asked if I wished
to see a physician.

I will cut my rest here short and return to England. First thing in
the morning I shall set off for Calais. Perhaps this is just madness—
perhaps the ridiculous superstitions of the villagers have combined
with Josep's death to somehow infect my consciousness: perhaps
my mind is playing games with me.

I had planned to stay in my room tonight, to lock the doors and
try to sleep, but my mind will not rest. Rereading my words, I no

longer know what to make of all this. I think I shall go out, find some wine and people and life and laughter, and distract myself from my own dark thoughts.

My horror at Josep's death has been replaced by a more sinister thought: *What if he and the villagers were right?* What if something terrible did come out of the river and attach itself to me?

What if I am now the *Upir*?

30

LONDON, APRIL 1889
ELIZABETH JACKSON

"I'll get you the money," she said, "honestly. He'll come back. He's working away—he's coming back with the rent, I promise."

"He's not coming back and you know it." Mrs. Paine's arms were folded firmly across her chest. "And in your condition you're better off without him. If you're going to take up with a man, don't pick one who beats you when he's drunk—you'll be beaten all your life."

"Please," Elizabeth said, her eyes filling with tears, "please, just one more night. I'll get the money. I'll—"

"It's been a week. Enough's enough."

Even as Elizabeth continued to plead, she began to gather up her few possessions. Mrs. Paine was not going to change her mind. She had never liked them much in the first place, and it wasn't as if she was short of people looking for somewhere cheap and safe to rest their heads for a night or two; her rooming house was always full.

Her stomach felt heavy; the baby growing inside was five months old now. Over the past few months with John Faircloth, she had found herself hoping his violence would kill the child—such a wish would send her straight to hell, but she couldn't help it. If she had been braver, she would have tried to get it out herself. It was a monster's child.

The moment she had collected her possessions, Mrs. Paine followed her to the front door and closed it firmly in her face. Night was coming, and the air was damp from the rain that had fallen all day. She cried some more, although no one paid any attention, and that made her feel invisible. She wished she *were* invisible. Ever since she had got back to London a month before, the dreams had become worse: dark dreams of something coming for her. She should have gone to Croydon with John, instead of fighting with him and telling him to go without her.

She had thought John a savior when he asked her to go north with him to find work. She almost cried with happiness when he'd suggested it: off the streets and away from the city. But the work was hard to come by, and he showed himself to be not the kindest of men. After Ipswich came Colchester, and more failure, and finally he announced that they would walk back to London: better the devil you know.

It had been clear to Elizabeth then that she had been fooling herself, thinking she could run from her fate. She wished for sunshine, for some brightness to fight the awful dread that filled her soul, but she knew that would never happen now. Her carefree days were done.

Her feet ached as she trudged through the mud, heading down to the nearby docks. She had nowhere to go, but if she stayed still the cold would eat into her quickly and the longer she walked, the longer she could delay the inevitable. Even at five months pregnant there would be men who would pay, but the thought of rough hands and rough walls and foul breath just made her want to cry some more. After the familiarity of just one man—however violent he was when the mood took him—the thought of doing *that* once again was almost too much to bear.

She looked out over the water. Perhaps she should find a bridge and throw herself from it. She had told John that she was going back to her mother's, but the darkness that hounded her had reached out to her family too; when she went to visit her mother a few days ago, swallowing her pride and hoping to borrow a few pennies, she found her family no longer there. When the new resident told

Elizabeth that her mother was in the workhouse, she felt almost weighed down by the guilt. It was the *wickedness* looking for her, she was sure of it, and now it had tainted her mother's life too.

The water called out to her, suggesting it was somewhere she could hide forever. She wondered if it would be so bad to die in there—how filthy was it really? Would anyone ever find her body and fish it out? It would be a way to win, for *he* would not have found her. She was so lost in her bitter reverie that she did not see the three men rounding the corner until the tallest had collided with her, sending her crashing to the ground. Her head spun as the moment broke, and she was back in the London chill and the river was just the river, as it always had been. She did not want to die. She did not want this life, but she did not want to die. She sobbed and coughed in one.

"I'm so sorry." A man crouched beside her, and took her hands to pull her back onto her tired feet. "Are you all right, madam?"

His voice did not belong with his scruffy clothes. His eyes dropped to her swollen belly. "Are you in any pain? I'm a doctor."

Elizabeth shook her head. She had no time for kindness. It would break her. "I'm fine, thank you." She wiped her eyes.

"Leave her," the tall man said. His eyes were dark and his accent foreign. The other man with them stared at her, picking at his face as his eyes darted to the river. She tugged her arms free and began to walk away.

"Wait."

She turned. The man who had helped her held out a few coins. "Take this," he said. "We've dirtied your dress."

She hesitated for a moment, a pretense at thought for the sake of her pride, and then took the money. "Thank you," she said.

And then they moved on.

The money was warm in her cold palm. At least she would eat tonight, and sleep somewhere safe. She turned her back on the river. She would not end up in its grasp. She *would not*.

31

LONDON, APRIL 1889
DR. BOND

I was impatient to get home. I had to change and be at dinner with the Hebberts within two hours. Our investigations had once again proven fruitless. My research had revealed lists of those who had been treated for various strange illnesses, but often the details were vague, especially as to whether the patients had traveled in Europe, and if so, where, prior to becoming sick.

The man we had come to see tonight—a cloth manufacturer, as it turned out—had been dead for more than a year, as his poor wife told us. What she made of us I could not tell; we were normally greeted with some form of suspicion, and I could not blame them for that. Even the poor young woman the priest had knocked over looked at us strangely. I thought perhaps I should start wearing smarter clothes—at least that way one of us would look respectable.

"I had hopes for this man," the priest muttered. "He lived and worked close to the river. He had traveled."

"Well, unless he is killing from beyond the grave, I think we can cross him from our list." I tried to keep the irritation out of my voice but failed. The police were having no better luck, but at least they were trying to follow traditional leads, not ones founded on superstition.

"I feel it so much more when I'm around you, Dr. Bond," Kosminski said, watching me. His pupils were still wide with the effects of the drug, even if his tics and odd mannerisms were returning. "It is almost as if you carry a little of it on you."

I shivered slightly at that. "Perhaps it is because I have examined the victims?"

"Maybe." The hairdresser did not sound convinced. There was something about his manner when he was under the influence of the opium that gave the nature of our hunt, the *insanity* of it, credibility. He *made* me believe, and I could not help myself. He *saw* things.

The priest, who still refused to share his name, paused in his stride, bringing the three of us to a halt. If we were a small army in this mad search, then he was our general.

"What?" I asked as he studied me, leaning in so close I could see the wide pores and deep wrinkles on his worn face. He ignored me and glanced at Kosminksi.

"You say you feel the presence more? Near the doctor?"

"Yes." Kosminski's thin fingers worked at his wrecked top lip, peeling more skin away as he nodded vigorously. "Yes, don't you?"

"I see differently than you."

"I can assure you," I said, indignantly interrupting their moment, "that I am not the killer you seek." Heat rushed to my face. This was ridiculous. Could they really be suggesting such a thing? What about the visions? The auras? Surely—

"Calm yourself, Doctor." The priest gripped my arm with his good hand. "Of course you are not."

"So what has made you look at me in that way? So suspiciously?" I was still disgruntled, and I was also tired. I wanted to go home, to wash and make myself look like a decent human being who did not spend his life secretly hunting for a monster.

"The *Upir* likes to be around blood and death. The stronger it gets, it will become more aware of us, those who wish to cast it into death or the river. It is a wicked and mischievous creature and it will seek us out—perhaps it already has, or perhaps it has found us by accident, through its host."

"What are you trying to say?" I had no energy for more superstitions. I missed the days when my anxiety and insomnia had led me to seek refuge in the opium dens and the priest was just a stranger with a withered arm. It might not have been a perfect life, but it had been simpler. Now my exhaustion was worse, my housekeeper had started to mutter about my odd hours and erratic behavior, and if the police were to see me with my current companions, we would either all be arrested or incarcerated in Colney Hatch before you could strike a match. My patience had worn so thin it was tearing.

"He's saying that perhaps we should look closer to home," Kosminski said, softly. "That's it, isn't it?"

"No," the priest said, "I don't think *we* should."

I looked from one to the other as the priest's words sank into my tired mind. "You think I *know* the killer? Is that it?"

The answer hung in the silence between us.

"That is *madness*."

I almost laughed at my own words. *Of course* it was madness— all of this was madness: three unstable, drug-addled men feeding each others' wild fantasies of ancient beasts and possessed men.

"You think he is lurking among my friends and colleagues? Perhaps it is Inspector Moore, or Inspector Andrews, hmm?" I was aware that my voice had risen and that other pedestrians were picking up their pace, not wanting to be part of any trouble that might arise, but I could not stop myself.

"Or maybe it is my housekeeper? She carves meat well enough!"

"Dr. Bond—" Kosminski cut in, trying to calm me, but I shook him away and stepped backward, away from the pair of them.

"I have had enough," I said, and in that moment I meant it. "Stay away from me. And stay away from my acquaintances. If I see you near my house I shall call the police. Do you understand?"

We all stared at each other as my breathing calmed. Neither of the other two spoke, and that suited me. I had no more argument in me. I straightened my cheap jacket. "Now, if you will excuse me, gentlemen, I have a dinner to go to." I tipped my hat to them as if we were passing strangers sharing words in a busy street, and I made off in search of a cab.

I was finished with them, this I swore.

At first I thought it was simply an echo of my earlier evening, but dinner was a strange affair. Still resolute in my decision to give no more credence to the priest and Kosminski and instead focus on my work and regain some form of sane sleeping routine, not only did I wash and change when I got home but I also burned the clothes I used on my trips to the dens. I had crouched so close to the fire in my study, watching the flames consume the cloth, that as I took my place at the Hebberts' table I could still smell the soot clinging to me.

The dining room, normally so full of hearty laughter, seemed darker than usual, the candles in the chandelier above flickering every now and then, casting sudden shadows across the table. Our knives and forks chattered to each other as they clinked against china in quiet mockery of the lack of conversation and humor amongst the dinner companions. We did not sit in silence, but there was an unusual restraint in our talk, an emptiness in the subject matter, as if questions were being asked with no desire for any answer, simply because that was what one did at dinner.

I was surprised at the vast amount of food that had been prepared. Charles was always a generous host, but this time the quantities were almost obscene. As well as a brace of hares jugged in port wine, there was a boiled ham and a pigeon pie, and a fine array of potatoes and vegetables, after a thick fish bouillabaisse to commence the meal.

So much good food was at odds with the tension in the air. I looked around me as both Charles and James refilled their plates, and I decided that it was not tension; it was more as if each of us were dining alone. We were lost in our own thoughts, all except perhaps for Mary, who kept some semblance of interaction going with her questioning and recitation of the day's events.

"Do have some more, Thomas," she said, a tic of a smile touching her face, looking as if it were slightly embarrassed to be there.

I shook my head and leaned back in my chair. "It is all delicious, but I fear if I eat any more I might not move from this chair—in fact, I strongly suspect I might break it."

She laughed louder than my small joke deserved. "As long as you have enjoyed it. I know it might look somewhat excessive for a simple supper, but James is unwell, and his illness makes him hungry, all the time." Her eyes flitted across to her son-in-law, and I could see the worry in them. "As you can see, he has lost weight." She looked over to her husband and added, "And his hunger seems to be catching."

Charles looked up and smiled as he lifted another forkful of pie, but I had the impression that he had only half-heard her; he gave no witty reply. I glanced at Juliana. Her mouth was pursed and she was pushing food around her plate, making a pretense of eating. Small lines furrowed her brow, and although they relaxed when she lifted her head, they did not disappear.

"If only they could find the cause of it," she said.

"I'm fine." James put his knife down and wiped some gravy from his chin. "It will pass. It always does."

"It's strange," I said, "for an illness to cause both hunger and weight loss, but it's not unheard of, is it, Charles? It could be that a parasite has found its way into your body."

"How revolting." The lines returned to Juliana's head.

"It sounds worse than it is." I smiled at her. "It would explain his hunger." I was glad to have some focus for our conversation at last and I looked over at her husband. He certainly had lost weight, and his blond hair no longer shone, almost as if it did not have the energy. "These things are often found in water," I continued. "You haven't been in the river, at all, have you, James?"

"The river?" His head snapped upward. "Why on earth would I have been in the river?" I had never heard him speak so sharply, and it even drew Charles's attention from his food.

"I say, son," he said, "Thomas is just trying to help."

"But who in their right mind would go into the river?"

I realized this was the first time I had had a good look at young Harrington since I had arrived, and I was shocked by his appearance. Mottled blotches covered his face and neck, and his skin had shifted beyond pale and into that slightly blue hue that I would more normally associate with a chilled corpse.

"You do work at the wharves." Juliana's voice was small; tonight she was not the confident young woman I had come to care for. "Perhaps the water splashed you?"

"It's not the river," Harrington said. The edge had gone from his voice. "I was ill before I took up my father's business—you know that. I'm sorry, Dr. Bond; I did not intend to sound rude. I'm just rather tired, and my chest is weak."

"He's going to start coughing up blood soon." Juliana looked at me, her eyes unhappy.

"It always passes," James said. "You should worry less."

"I wonder if the paint fumes at the house might have brought it on," Juliana said. She looked across at her mother. "Or perhaps the dust. I think we should move back here again."

"Someone needs to be in the house to supervise," Charles cut in. He looked somewhat disturbed. "I love you dearly, Juliana, you know that. But you cannot leave your house in the hands of laborers."

"We wouldn't—of course not. But—"

"Of course you can come here if you want," Mary said, and as their words faded out to a hum around me, I stared at my plate, not really seeing the grease sitting on the surface. There was a rushing in my ears, as if it were I who had fallen in the river. My head was filled with the priest who, despite my resolve, still occupied a constant space in my thoughts. My words had been an echo of his.

A parasite. From the river.

I looked once more at James as I replayed in my head the conversation from that afternoon. Perhaps the *Upir* was someone that I knew. My mouth dried, and as I instinctively reached for my wine, my hand trembled. The warmth in my throat did nothing to soothe me; I needed something stronger.

But surely this was just a coincidence? So young Harrington was ill—it didn't mean anything. The hospitals were filled with sick people. I was sure that if I asked any of the people in my small circle of friends and colleagues, they could each describe a similar ailment to me.

I swallowed more wine, and then I asked, "When did you first become sick?" I imagined that he was going to say it was something he had suffered from since childhood, and then I would be able to laugh at my own flights of fancy.

"James did the Grand Tour," Juliana said, "all around Europe."

"I can talk for myself," Harrington muttered. "I'm not that sick." He looked warily my way, and I wasn't sure if it was the dim light, but the edge of one of his eyes was flecked with an angry red. "It was something I caught in Europe, yes. But it never lasts long." He leaned back in his chair. "However, I am feeling rather tired. I am sorry to be such a terrible guest, but I think perhaps Juliana and I should go home. I should have stayed in bed—I have work to do tomorrow."

"You should rest, darling." Juliana squeezed his thin hand. "You shouldn't be working like this. Between the company and the house it's no wonder you're sick again."

"Maybe you would like to stay here?" Mary asked. "There's always a room ready."

"No, but thank you." James smiled, giving a hint of his usual kindness. "Again, I apologize." He got to his feet and Juliana took his arm, steadying him. I rose too, but Charles waved me down.

"Stay here with me, Thomas. We don't stand on ceremony, you know that—we're all family, after all."

After Juliana and James had said their good-byes, Mary also bade us goodnight, leaving Charles to pour us both a brandy. I fought to steady my thoughts. So James had traveled in Europe—but where? There was so much more I needed to know, if only to stop this dread rising in my blood. My head rushed, and my palms were clammy. I struggled for breath as my anxiety rose.

I tugged at my collar as Charles handed me a glass.

"Are you all right, Thomas?" His eyes were on my shaking hand.

"I think perhaps James is not the only one who is unwell," I said. My words sounded as if they were coming from far away, and my vision shimmered as if I were separated by glass from the world. I knew these sensations. My anxiety was getting the better of me. I struggled to control it. I took a deep breath, and then a long swallow of the liquor—that would help. "I can't shake this slight fever."

I made the effort to smile at him, but it was wasted; Charles was looking down at his plate again, and there was not a trace of his normal good humor.

"I'm sorry, Thomas."

"What for?"

"This evening—we are not quite ourselves, I fear. James is ill, Juliana is worried about him, Mary is worried about her"—he shrugged slightly—"and I . . . well, I have been having these awful dreams."

I wanted to ask him about Harrington's travels—I *itched* to do so—but this was not the time for it. Charles was obviously distracted.

"Sometimes I can't breathe for the wickedness in them," he whispered, and I had never seen him look so desolate. I was reminded of the time he spoke of evil at his windows. This was not my friend Charles I saw before me; Charles was a blustering man, firmly rooted in the present and full of life, even when surrounded by death. Something was most definitely plaguing him.

He stared into his glass.

"I see things in them." He did not look up. "I scare myself with what I see."

"They will pass, Charles," I said gently. It was all I could say. However, I wondered about the gifts the priest had spoken of. If I could sense something, then maybe Charles could too? And if Harrington truly was the *Upir* . . .

I couldn't bring myself to carry that line of thought through. It surely could not be possible . . .

I excused myself not long after the young couple had left, and Charles put up no argument. We were all exhausted from our individual internal battles. By the time I got home, the bracing air had chased away the remnants of my anxiety attack, and although I was tired from its effects, I poured myself another brandy and stared out of the drawing room window at the gloomy night. The road was empty: no strange priest, no mad hairdresser. My reflection looked back at me, light and ghostly, the edges refusing to remain firm. It was like looking at myself in a river, with the night outside as black as the murky depths, and the glass the only slight surface between me and whatever might be hiding there. I shivered.

I told myself I would stick with my resolution to free myself of this madness; I would not seek out the priest. However, I needed to prove the foolishness of my mad thoughts, and I could do that only by dispelling any doubts my unruly mind had: I *would* look more deeply into James Harrington and his travels.

My reflection refused to stop studying me, and I knew that I would need more than brandy if I were to make even a pretense at sleep that night. I turned and reached for the laudanum.

32

LONDON, JUNE 3, 1889
ELIZABETH JACKSON

The days were warmer, but the nights were still cold, and Elizabeth could find no better shelter than under the bridges by the river. As the afternoon was turning to evening, she had found a place, and she had pressed up against the wall, and in the hour or so since, more people had gathered around her. At least there was company here, although even among the destitute and lost there were hunters, those who would think nothing of taking what they wanted and throwing the original owner into the water.

She had become an expert in reading prey and predators, learning to recognize them: there was a silent growl in the way the predators walked, a snarl in every tilt of their heads. But none of them could match the one who was after her. She was nearly always left untroubled, almost as if those feral men realized that she was marked by something far beyond any evil they could conceive.

There were others here, though, young and old, men and women, the waste products of the ruthless city. They huddled in groups, barely speaking but still needing some sort of human company to make their grim, isolated existences bearable, and Elizabeth felt safe joining them. Her once-nice clothes, bought by John Faircloth for their fruitless search for work, were now dirty and ragged, and in the furtive glances, the others recognized her as one of their own. Elizabeth found a small comfort in the false sense of security they gave her, even though she knew in her heart that nothing could keep her safe, not even in her dreams, where she was endlessly running for a patch of light somewhere in the distance, for the darkness had started to overwhelm her.

The wall was damp, and she could feel the chill creeping through her coat, but she did not care; she was glad to be off her feet. She was seven months gone now, and the baby sat low and heavy. Her thin frame was struggling with the weight; she was weak, and often dizzy, and it felt like this had been her life forever. Everything that had gone before was inconsequential.

And here she was, back in Chelsea: all that running, and she had just come full circle.

Elizabeth sighed. She had always known she would end up back here, ever since she saw him on the Embankment, looking—*hunting*. Time had melted into one long, endless moment of survival, but she was sure it had to be at least two weeks ago, maybe even longer. It was before she had seen Mrs. Minter in the street—when the kind woman, an old family friend, had taken pity on her and given her the Ulster coat she now wore.

It had been very late, in the silent hours, when she had seen the tall figure moving through the sleeping bodies, but she had known instantly it was him. She would always recognize him, the way his shoulders moved, his gait, even if he had lost his natural shy stiffness to whatever unnatural instinct now drove him.

She had pressed her face into the ground, and he had walked past her. She knew then that it was only a matter of time; he *would* find her. She was sure he could smell himself as he grew inside her, and he would not let that go, just as whatever was growing inside her wanted to be near him and the river—it was the reason she was here; it had drawn her back. It sounded like madness, even in the confines of her own thoughts, but she knew it was true. She had been living in Purgatory since the night he had violated her. All that was waiting for her in the future was hell. She had lost the will to keep running from the devil.

Even when she and John had been on the road north, she had known that Chelsea would drag her back. Finally, after John

Faircloth was gone and she was back on the streets, she had walked into its clutches. She had gone to her mother first. Her pride was gone—it had not taken many nights out in the open in London for that to happen. She was ready to beg to be able to stay, if only her mother would give her the chance, but the woman who answered the door was a stranger who brusquely told Elizabeth that her mother was in the workhouse, and she did not know, or care, where her sisters were. Elizabeth had cried then. The wickedness that had marked her out was touching them all.

She went to his street—the street where she had worked for six happy years—and watched both houses with an aching heart. She looked at them for so long that she could see their reflections as shadows behind her eyes when she closed her eyelids. She peered around corners and tried to stay out of sight. It was all so painfully familiar that for a while she wondered if perhaps she had just gone mad; that she had never seen anything the night his family fell ill—maybe his mother had been sick already when she came to Elizabeth with her worries.

When she saw the woman coming from his house, her fingers gripped the wall so hard that two nails snapped. The woman was tall and elegantly dressed, but she was not much more than a girl, really—she might have been younger than Elizabeth. Her shining hair was a deep red, and thick, curled neatly under her hat. She existed in another world, one of warmth and security and comfort. As she stared more intently, Elizabeth saw that the redheaded girl's mouth was tugging down in a frown that aged her, and the sight of it closed the divide between them. She understood the cause of that worry, probably far better than the girl did. A shape moved behind the window and there he was, looking out, his pale, thin face a contrast with the dark shadows behind him. Even from a distance and through the glass, Elizabeth felt a wave of revulsion, looking at the man who was now a stranger to her.

She gagged as the night he had filled her belly came flooding back. She had been with rougher men since, but she had never experienced anything so inhuman, so cold, so utterly terrifying. The girl on the pavement glanced back, as if she too could sense his presence. Elizabeth wanted to run to her and pull her away, wanted to tell her to save herself; to leave and never look back.

She felt his eyes on her. Her breath hitched and she turned her head back to the window. His lips were curled in an unpleasant smile, and she felt herself, huddled against the wall and trying to stay out of sight, exactly where he had expected her to be.

All thoughts of the finely dressed lady were devoured by dread. She tore her eyes away from his gaze and ran, her exhausted legs somehow finding the energy as she pressed her filthy hand into her mouth to stop from crying out. He was coming for her; she knew that. It was only a matter of when.

And now here he was. She looked up at him, and although she felt that awful dread, it was mixed with a resigned calm: this was Fate at work, and there was nothing she could do about it. The wall was rough, even through the coat, and several strands of matted hair fell across her face. The river gurgled, and somewhere a few feet away, a baby cried. Inside, her own infant squirmed, perhaps aware of its father's presence, desperate to be free of her body. She felt no urge to protect it—but then, she felt no urge to protect herself.

She thought idly that he might not recognize her now. She was thinner, even pregnant, her hair was no longer spun gold, and it had been a very long time since she had smiled in the way he had claimed to have fallen in love with. Her shoulders were hunched. There was nothing beautiful about a broken woman, and that's what she was, broken beyond redemption. He strode toward her, and even in the fading light of the evening she could see the mottled blotches on his cheeks. She shuddered, but she did not move. Where would she go?

He stood in front of her and reached out his hand. A tear slid down her cheek. She was glad she had seen her mother, two days past—perhaps that meeting, purely by chance, bumping into each other in the street, had been Fate's work too. They might not have talked for long, but they parted friends, and she was happy about that, for her mother's sake. It would help her with what was to come. She reached out. His fingers were cool.

33

Evening Star—Washington, D.C.

JACK THE RIPPER
A Belief that He Has Resumed
His Bloody Work

London, June 4.

The denizens of Horsleydown, on the southern side of the
Thames, were thrown into a fever of excitement this morning,
by the discovery in the river of the lower portions of a woman's
body cut into pieces. The rest of the body and the legs were no
where to be seen. These ghastly objects were tied in a parcel
with a stout cord. Shortly afterward a parcel of female clothing
was found at Battersea. Both the fragments of the body and
the clothes were wrapped in pieces of cloth, which together had
comprised a pair of woman's drawers.

At Battersea were also found the thighs of a female, showing
conclusive evidences of having been cut from the trunk found
at Horsleydown. They too were wrapped in pieces of the pair
of drawers.

The Times of London
June 5, 1889

Early yesterday morning, almost simultaneously, two packages
containing portions of a woman's body were discovered on the
foreshore of the Thames . . .

The Times of London
June 7, 1889

In fact, the entire makeup of the ghastly parcel was exactly similar to the others, and the work was evidently done by the same hands.

The Times of London
June 8, 1889

A most careful search for the portions of the body still missing is being maintained. All along the foreshore of the Thames experienced watchers have been engaged, and every likely hiding place, such as the shrubbery of Battersea Park, where one of Thursday's discoveries took place, is being inspected.

34

LONDON, JUNE 13, 1889
DR. BOND

As winter had passed into spring and with no further killings, London had relaxed slightly. Jack was gone, the people whispered—either he was dead, or he had moved on to become some other place's problem.

For my own part, however, although the days were lightening, my mood was not. I did not analyze the amount of laudanum I was taking, nor the frequency, nor the fact that sometimes my urge to visit the dens was so overwhelming that I paced and paced around my house through the night until my legs ached. My anxiety attacks were increasing, so I did my best to battle them and my perpetual exhaustion by hunting more often, embracing nature and fresh air and putting all thoughts of creatures existing in men's shadows out of my mind, if only for a few short hours. Juliana rode with me, and rather guiltily, I used these opportunities to question her about Harrington's travels in Europe.

It appeared that most of his stories were focused on a rather eccentric American he had met in Venice, a person to whom he now spent long hours writing; it was this gentleman who had apparently prompted James to be more adventurous. Juliana told me Harrington's stories of his travels had become more vague after he and the American split up in Venice, although she thought he had become ill for the first time in Poland.

After hearing this, I could not settle. That very night I had found my way to the priest's rooms, determined to share this with him—if only to relieve my own anxiety. There was no light on, and no answer to my knock on the door, so I headed to Whitechapel to find Kosminski. His sister told me that he was in the grip of one of his "fits" and could not receive visitors, doctor or no, but the expression on her face suggested that no matter her verbal assurances, she would not be passing on my message, asking him to contact me. Perhaps she saw a little of her brother's madness in my own eyes, and I found I could not blame her for that.

Afterward, when I had returned home and my nerves had calmed, I was glad I had not reached either man, for I had no actual proof against young Harrington, who had grown weaker and sicker over the weeks. He was still just about managing to go about his business, but he was not capable of much else, and this in turn worried Juliana enormously. My suspicions of her husband felt like a betrayal of her. I needed to remain as rational as possible.

And yet here we were: another death—another woman—and in the brief, snatched moments of sleep I had managed over the past few days, I had been haunted by something awful in the shadows: something watching me, something that I could not quite see. I had woken sweaty and breathless, and more exhausted than I had been before. The last piece—a right arm folded at the elbow and tied with string—had been recovered this very morning and brought to us at Battersea Morgue, to add to our gruesome collection.

"Let's put her back together then, shall we?" Charles had been eager to start from the moment he had arrived, and immediately started removing the preserved body parts and laying them out for our study. There was something about the intensity of his enthusiasm that unnerved me slightly. I did not know if it was simply my own dark imaginings of late echoing into this situation, but there was an eagerness there that differed from his normal cheerfulness. "I think we have nearly all of her," he said.

"Apart from the head," I added.

He nodded and smiled, but was already lost in his work, making notes as he examined the brutalized remains. Once again I was glad that I had distanced myself from the priest and the hairdresser, for I found Charles's mood swings disturbing enough. Some evenings he was so gripped with melancholy I was sure he was going to do some harm to himself, and at others he was bouncing with fevered overenthusiasm, as he was now. Although I still went for dinner frequently, I did so mainly for Juliana's sake. Harrington rarely came himself—he was too ill—but he insisted Juliana did, for the company, as he was too weak to provide much at home. I did not know if I was flattering myself, but I sometimes thought that given her father's strange moods, she too was there primarily to see me.

"How is James?" I asked as we studied each of the severed pieces. The top portion of the trunk had been separated from the missing head at the sixth vertebra, cut off with several relatively clean cuts. "A fine-toothed saw, perhaps?" The chest had been opened up at its central point, the sternum cut through and the lungs and heart removed to God only knew where.

"I would say so," Charles agreed. "And a sharp knife through the skin. The separation of the arms and legs would definitely suggest a saw." He shrugged at me, calmer now that he was working. "He's certainly adept at dismemberment. Oh, and I meant to say earlier, but with all this"—he gestured toward the gory display—"anyway, thank you for asking, but young James appears to be on the mend. Juliana says that he's become much more himself over the past week. He's certainly got his color back—quite a relief, I can tell you. They're going back to Bath for a few days, and then when they return, they'll come and stay with us while the house is finished." His face twitched slightly as he spoke, an involuntary action, betraying an underlying distaste or worry at that thought that was at odds with his next words. "Mary and I are looking forward to it tremendously."

For my part, although my hands continued with their work, my mind was racing elsewhere. Harrington was recovering. There had been another death, and Harrington was now regaining his strength. What about the other bouts of sickness—had he got better around the time of the previous killings?

"Glad to hear it," I said. I leaned in toward the torso section. "The lower part of the vagina is still within the pelvis, the same with the rectum." I tilted my head slightly. "And the front part of the bladder." I stood back and looked at the wreckage of the woman. Could James Harrington really have done this? James, who slept at night with the lovely Juliana—did the hands that touched her so gently, so lovingly, also commit this atrocity?

It was quite late by the time we had compiled our report and replaced the body parts in alcohol, and I was relieved that Charles did not suggest I return and dine with him and Mary. His behavior had returned to normal over the course of the day, but that did not mean his melancholy of previous evenings might not return, and my mood was black enough with thoughts of monsters and madness and Juliana. I needed to speak to her, to get some clear idea of Harrington's movements over the past year, when he had recovered from his various bouts of illness, but until she had returned from Bath I would have to wait.

When I arrived home, I paid the driver, and as I did so, I felt the hairs on my neck prickle. I turned and looked behind me, my eyes peering through the fading evening light for evidence of someone watching. I found him in the flash of waxy black cloth in a corner opposite. Knowing I had spotted him, the priest stepped out onto the pavement. Our eyes met, his as full of fiery purpose as always—and he must have seen something in my own because he began walking toward me. Despite my last words to him, my heart thumped with relief: I could talk to him about Harrington, and he would understand. The newspapers had been filled with the gruesome details of each new part pulled from the river or the park, so the priest knew his *Upir* was back at work. If I could just talk to him about it, then perhaps I would feel better, maybe my anxiety would lessen—at the very least, thoughts of my own madness would dissipate. I took a step forward, toward him.

"Dr. Bond!"

The words came from somewhere to my right, and I jumped slightly, then turned swiftly—I had been so focused on the priest that I had not looked for anyone else I might know.

"Inspector Andrews," I said with a smile. "You startled me."

"I'm sorry. You looked distracted."

Andrews had as keen an eye for detail as I did, and he was already looking across the road, but there was nothing where I had been staring; the priest had gone.

"I wondered if perhaps you would care to join me at my club for dinner?" Andrews asked. "I know you've had a busy day, but I thought you might want to discuss some of your findings. It can be hard to unwind at the end of the day, and sometimes reviewing the information can help. I am always impressed by your thoughts, you know that, and I would enjoy your conversation."

I smiled again, this time a more natural expression than my first had been. I too had grown to enjoy Andrews's company and his rational thinking. We had, perhaps without noticing it, become friends of a sort, and it was a friendship I hoped would grow—it might have done so already, if I had never met the priest and become so entwined in his hunt. I could never share this with the inspector, of course, but I found that the idea of a quiet dinner of rational conversation was entirely what I did need.

"Shall we walk?" I asked.

"Certainly," he said.

The priest could wait—he *would* wait; I was sure of that. Deep in the pit of my stomach, I knew the priest was always waiting.

35

London, June 1889
Inspector Moore

Henry Moore watched as Smoker emerged from the thick undergrowth. With his nose pressed to the ground, the little dog ran briefly in one direction and then circled back on himself. Moore had never been one to give beasts human attributes, but if ever a hound could wear an expression of frustrated confusion, it was this terrier. Jasper Waring egged the dog on, making noises of encouragement around the cigarette clamped between his teeth, but Moore held out no hope that Smoker would find a trail. It had been several days since the gardener had pulled the wrapped torso from the bushes, and hundreds of people had traipsed through here since then.

"I take it we're having no luck?" Andrews came alongside him, Dr. Bond in tow.

"He's doing better than the bloodhounds," Moore answered, tipping his hat to the doctor. "At least he's in the right bush." They watched the dog for a moment before Moore turned away. The others followed. The dog would find nothing; there was no point in their watching him doing it.

"Thank you for your report, Dr. Bond. Very thorough, as usual."

"To be fair, Charles Hebbert did most of it. I would not be at all surprised to discover he was preparing for a paper of some kind."

"Strange how there is always some benefit to tragedy," Andrews said. There was no accusation in his voice, just observation. "I hope you don't mind my bringing Thomas along. Just in case something was found."

"Not at all," Moore said, and meant it. "You have a good eye, Dr. Bond. Any observations you would care to share with us?"

"From here?" Dr. Bond looked around at the mêlée of people in the park. "I don't think you'll find anything here—most of her went in the river. A dog can't scent a trail from water. But he would not have wanted to carry her far."

"We think the site of the murder was probably here in Battersea somewhere, or maybe Chelsea, so that would fit," Moore said. "We do know that despite the name in the clothes she is not the missing barmaid, who has been found safe and well in Ramsgate."

"No one has come forward for her?" Bond asked.

"There is no one missing who matches her description," Andrews said, then added, "Not listed, anyway."

"And as the bosses think we should not yet publish your findings, or the details of her death," Moore said, "it's not bloody likely that more will come forward. As if there isn't enough already splashed all over the newspapers." He shook his head in despair; sometimes the stupidity of his superiors made him want to walk out of Division headquarters and never look back. "As if someone would imitate this murder just from your report—if someone wishes to kill like this, then they will go right ahead and do just that. And if it was a one-time-only accidental death, then your report will make no difference, will it?"

"Accidental death?" Dr. Bond asked.

"There is a suggestion that she might have been trying to get rid of the baby; that she died while trying, and her friends then cut her body up to hide the evidence."

"Highly unlikely," Dr. Bond said, frowning. "She was about seven months pregnant—that is very late. In my experience, women at that stage will either kill themselves, or abandon the child after giving birth to it."

"I agree," Moore said. He liked the doctor's analytical mind. He could see why he and Andrews had become friends. "However, the bastards above me seem to have aborted their own brains at times."

He glanced back over his shoulder. The dog continued to run up and down the short trail it had found, desperately seeking the next lead, but finding nothing. He knew how Smoker felt.

"If only we knew how he killed them," he muttered. "At least that would give us *something* to go on."

"I'm sorry I cannot give you more," Dr. Bond said. His gaze was shifting from one place to another, but he never looked straight at Moore, and the inspector wondered if he was feeling guilty, if the police were applying too much pressure for answers.

"You can only give us the facts, Doctor," Andrews said. "And we're very grateful for them."

"For what good they do us," Moore added. "At least we had six months off—and at least it's not bloody Jack. That bastard can stay wherever he's gone to ground—although under it would be my preferred choice." He looked again at the doctor. "Tell me, Bond: you've got the kind of mind for it. Why the river, do you think?"

"I don't understand." The doctor looked startled. Moore wondered if perhaps he had spoken too abruptly. His patience was thin at the best of times, and although his preferred outcome would have been to catch the killer, this period of calm leading to the man's simply disappearing would have been an acceptable second-best. It didn't look like he would be getting either.

He looked at Dr. Bond and explained, "I mean, why is he dumping so many of the parts in the river, where we can—and are—finding them? We don't have the heads because he doesn't want them found—he is either burning them or burying them, I would reckon. He leaves other parts in places he knows we will find them—that damned torso at Scotland Yard, and the one in the bush there—but the rest goes in the water—so why? Why is the *river* so important?" He could hear his own frustration, and he stared at the doctor, almost willing him to have an answer.

Not that he could, of course; the only person who really knew was the killer himself.

For a long moment, Dr. Bond said nothing. His eyes turned toward the River Thames, out of sight, but ever present. "Perhaps," he said eventually, "perhaps it is some kind of sacrifice: a gift to the water. Man or monster, we all have our gods."

"You think he's worshipping the river?" Andrews asked.

"Or feeding it," Bond finished.

"A madman, then," Moore concluded. "As if that weren't clear enough."

Jasper Waring was heading toward them. Moore sighed: his turn to buy the beer—and to be fair, the little dog had done its best. After that, he'd go back to the station and tell them in no uncertain terms that he was going to need the public's help if they wanted any chance of finding out who this body belonged to. God help them all, and God help him, but they needed all the information out there.

"Sometimes I think we are all mad, Inspector, in our own ways."

Dr. Bond had spoken so quietly that his words barely carried, but there was something heavy in his tone that gave Inspector Moore pause. He looked again at the surgeon. He had become so used to his gaunt, tired appearance that he had failed to notice that his cheeks had grown even more sunken, his shoulders hunched. He hoped the doctor was not speaking too much from his own experience. He needed sane and rational men around him.

"Not me, Doctor Bond," he said. "That you can always rely on."

He walked over to join Waring. Slapping the reporter on the back, he announced, "The dog's done his best. Let's call it a day."

"If you say so." Even Waring had had enough of hunting for dismembered bodies, juicy stories or not. "Dr. Bond looks tired," he commented, as if following the inspector's own train of thought.

"We're all bloody tired," Moore said, "Dr. Bond as much as the rest of us."

"Hebbert's more tired than Bond, I reckon," Waring said, and whistled for his dog. "Unless my eyes were deceiving me and it weren't him I saw in the East End, dressed all untidy."

"What are you talking about?"

"I told you: I saw him, last year, out on the streets. More than once."

"You must be mistaken."

"My Smoker's got the nose, Inspector," Waring said, patting the dog, "but it's me with the eyes. Now, let's get that beer."

36

The Times of London
June 13, 1889

The remains are those of a woman, age from 24 to 26 years, height 5 ft. 4 in. to 5 ft. 6 in., well built and fleshy, very fair skin, hair light brown or sandy, well-shaped hands and feet, bruise on ring finger probably caused by wearing a ring; nails on both hands bitten down to the quick; four good vaccination marks, about the size of a three-pence piece [5 cents U.S. or Canadian] on left arm; skin on palms does not indicate that deceased did hard work; considerably advanced (probably about seven months) in pregnancy. The articles in which the remains were enclosed are as follows:—The skirt of an old brown linsey dress, red sleevage, two flounces round bottom, waistband made of small blue-and-white check material similar to duster cloth, a piece of canvas roughly sewn on end of band, a large brass pin in skirt, and a black dress button (about size of a three-penny piece) with lines across in pocket; a piece of the right front, two pieces of the back, the right sleeve and collar (about 4 1/2 in. wide) of a lady's ulster, gray ground, with narrow cross stripes of a darker colour, forming a check of about three-quarters of an inch square; ticket pocket with outside lap on cuff, upon which there is also sewn a large black button; the material of good quality but much worn; a light blue flannelette bag, about 13 in. square, top edge unhemmed; a pair of women's drawers (old); square patched on both knees, originally of a good material, band formed of several pieces joined; "L. E. Fisher" in black ink at right end of band; a piece of tape sewn on with black cotton to each end of band to tie round body. The various parcels tied up with black mohair bootlaces, pieces of venetian blind cord, and ordinary string. The various articles described can be seen between 10 A.M. and 4 P.M. daily at Battersea Station by persons who have missing female relatives. The clothes may not have been worn by the deceased.

Decatur Saturday *Herald*—Illinois, U.S.A.

ENGLAND
THE VICTIM OF LONDON'S LATEST BUTCHERY IDENTIFIED.
London, June 25

The identity of the woman whose body was recently taken piecemeal out of the Thames has been established, several persons having recognised her by the clothing in which parts of her body were wrapped and by the peculiar scars upon the arms. She was Elizabeth Jackson, a frequenter of the common lodging houses in Chelsea and virtually a prostitute. She was known to be alive on May 31.

PART THREE

37

LONDON, JUNE 1889
DR. BOND

Finally, I had a name to haunt me: Elizabeth Jackson. Inspector Moore's insistence had paid off, and although he and his colleagues had been swamped with both the genuine and the ghoulish wishing to see the remnants of clothing that had been found with her, eventually the police had managed to put the more difficult pieces together.

I had been at the mortuary when Annie Jackson had come to identify her daughter. She was not long out of the workhouse and clearly not faring well in life herself, but the sight of her child, headless and identifiable only by scars on her arms, was enough to break her.

After that, Moore and Andrews had been able to work more quickly, piecing together the fragments of her life in much the same way Charles and I had done with her physical remains. I had arranged an early dinner with Andrews, as was becoming our habit, knowing that he would think nothing of sharing any information with me. I kept myself calm, telling myself that this might finally bring an end to my mad suspicions of Juliana's husband. In the days since the first inquest I had veered wildly from one extreme thought to the other; indeed, I had at times locked myself into my own house to avoid searching out the priest. I wondered why they had not come for me—surely they would be fired up over the fate of the poor discovered woman? I had to admit, to myself at least, that some small part of me hoped that some awful fatal accident had befallen the priest, freeing me of their grip.

But nothing Andrews told me allayed my suspicions. I fear my hand trembled slightly as I forced food into my mouth, chewing methodically as I listened. My mouth was dry, and what little hunger I might have had had vanished. Elizabeth Jackson had come from Chelsea. She had fallen on hard times, not an unusual story—although in her case, her employer knew of no reason for her sudden departure from a secure place as a housemaid in a good household—and then taken up with a disreputable man. She had spent some time in Whitechapel (which, Andrews pointed out, had caused some excitement amongst those who were determined that our Thames Killer and Jack were one and the same) before returning, heavily pregnant, to her native streets. She had been seen sleeping by the Thames; we could only assume the child's body had gone into the river too.

It was a maudlin tale, and I could see the lack of any real leads was taking its toll on my friend, but for my own part, I felt a *frisson* of excitement. This woman had a name now, and that gave me a far greater chance to disprove any possible link to young Harrington. Then I could put this madness to one side at least, even if not entirely out of my head.

I elicited Elizabeth Jackson's place of work from Andrews, and now here I was, standing in the late-evening gloom and staring at the familiar houses opposite. Of course they were familiar: I had collected Juliana for the hunt and dropped her off here too, on several occasions.

Dread curled in my stomach, knotting like a snake in slick, perpetual movement, slippery coils twisting this way and that. I looked up at the empty house brooding in the middle of the street. Even the pale stone of its walls seemed darker than those around, as if the dirty air were drawn to smear its residue across its surfaces. Juliana and James were still in Bath, and so all the lights were out, but still the windows glinted, as if daring me to challenge the wickedness held inside. Did he leave an echo here, whispering through the empty rooms when he wasn't there? Had it seeped into the very fibers of the building? Was that why they were giving it so complete a renovation that they might better have sold it and moved to a different property?

A streetlamp flickered momentarily, sending a flight of shadows across the pavement. I shivered at the thought of my own shadow, and I twisted to see it. It moved with me, and I fought the idea of something existing in that space, of always being just out of sight. I pulled a bottle of laudanum from my pocket and took a long swallow to steady my nerves. I was becoming as twitchy as Kosminski, and he, that poor tormented man, was only a few breaths away from an asylum. I looked back at the houses—at the one close to Harrington's where lights blazed out. It was perhaps a little late for a house call, but not so much that it would cause undue alarm. I needed to do what I had come here for.

I turned my back on Harrington's house and crossed the street.

"If you are a newsman, then you can leave right now. We have nothing to say to you. The family are all at dinner and cannot be disturbed." The housekeeper had barely opened the door; even through that narrow gap I could tell she was a formidable woman. Her eyes were suspicious, but alert, and I knew that if there were secrets in this house, this woman would know them.

I held my hat between my hands.

"I am very sorry to disturb you so late. My name is Dr. Bond. I am the Police Surgeon. I . . ." I hesitated around the words, and then managed, "I examined Elizabeth. I just have a few questions."

She stared at me for a long moment, but I had seen a flicker of pain and care cross her stern face at the mention of the dead girl.

"You 'ad better come in."

I was shown into the drawing room, and after a few moments an elegant woman in her forties appeared, with the housekeeper alongside her.

"Dr. Bond?" she said, and she gestured to a seat, which I took. She remained standing. "I am Mrs. Blythe. I am afraid my husband is not at home. This is about Elizabeth Jackson?" She was elegant and polite, but there was a distaste in her voice, as if the whole business of Elizabeth's demise was, while undeniably unfortunate, intensely irritating for the scandal it had brought to her door. "Mrs. Hastings will be best able to answer your questions. She manages the staff. She spoke to the inspector. I will say that we had no trouble with Elizabeth—none of which I am aware."

I thanked her, and she drifted gracefully out the door and back to her family and their polite dinner, leaving the housekeeper and I to discuss the brutal facts of murder as if they might stain her hands like coal dust. Elizabeth Jackson had been in her service for several years, and yet I doubt she had given her more than a few minutes' thought since finding out about her death. I was equally certain that Mrs. Hastings, however, had given her considerably more thought than that.

"Was she a good girl?" I asked, when we were alone.

"Yes, she was. Very good." The defensiveness I had seen in her eyes at the door was still there, but now I could see that she was protecting Elizabeth. I thought perhaps she felt a little guilt and sadness for how badly the maid's life had ended.

"And yet she ran away?" I saw Mrs. Hastings's mouth tighten. "I am not looking to add to any supposed shame on her name, Mrs. Hastings," I said, quickly. "I have seen what happened to her—the violations of her body. I more than most am aware of what she must have suffered. I wish to help lay her to rest."

"But—if you don't mind me saying, sir, you're a surgeon, not a policeman—"

"The police trust me," I said—and that was true, even if neither of the inspectors knew I was here. "I have a natural leaning to understanding human motivations. I want to get to know her life." As I spoke, I realized how true my words were. I wanted to know—I *had* to know—if Elizabeth had known the Harringtons. Of course, even if she hadn't spoken to him, James could have known her. He could have—

"She was a pretty little thing, you know," Mrs. Hastings said suddenly. "I don't think many people told her that—*I* didn't—but she was pretty. And she was quiet, did her work well, no backchat—not a complainer."

"Was she courting at all? Did she have someone?"

"No, not then, but there was a young man a year or so before she ran off—she was giddier than usual, smiling and laughing downstairs." She sighed a little. "I'm not so old that I don't remember what causes that in young girls."

"What happened?" I asked.

"Oh, one day the smiles stopped. She settled back into her work, but she was quieter—for a few months at least. I presumed he had found another girl, or he had moved away—you know what young men are like. But there was no scandal. She was a good girl."

"Tell me," I asked, my mind turning over her reiteration of Elizabeth's "good girl" qualities, "why would she run away? A man again—the same one, perhaps?"

Mrs. Hastings went to speak and then stopped, though her mouth moved silently for a second as she rethought her initial response. "That's what I told the officers, yes: I thought there was a man, and I thought that something unfortunate had happened. She had changed. She wasn't getting enough sleep. Her eyes had dark hollows around them"—she looked at me pointedly—"much like your own. She was troubled. Yes, I think there was a man involved."

"But there is something else?" I said gently.

"Elizabeth was afraid." The statement was matter-of-fact. "I believe she was terrified. I've seen girls who've got themselves in a shameful mess before—I've been in service a lot of years, and there are a lot of silly girls out there—but their fear wasn't like hers. I've seen shame, yes, but this was *terror*."

"What—or who—could terrify her so, I wonder?" I thought of shadows behind men's backs; I thought of a young man who had gone off traveling and come back sick and haunted.

"I am afraid I do not get involved in the personal lives of the staff." This time the defensiveness in her tone was entirely for her own benefit, and I smiled and nodded, and, needing her to open up again, said, "Exactly as it should be. Did she have visitors, or anyone waiting for her after work?"

"No, as I—" She stopped abruptly. "Actually, she did have a rather unusual visitor—not just before she ran off, though. That must be why I did not recall it when the police inspector asked. It was a while before that—but I remember the day well, for it was the day before she died."

"Who died?" I was confused, but despite the laudanum calming me, my heart began to pound with excitement.

"Mrs. Harrington."

It took all my self-control not to jump in my seat, but still my faced burned with a sudden rush of blood and my fingertips tingled.

"Who was Mrs. Harrington?" I feigned only mild interest, but found myself leaning forward, as if I could somehow suck the information out of her more quickly that way.

"They lived in this road, she and her husband, until they died— some awful poisoning from some foodstuff their son brought back from his travels abroad. He nearly died himself, but his youth saved him. It was that night, after she had come here to speak to Elizabeth. The son moved away for a while, but he's back now, and with a new young wife. They're having all sorts done to the house." She spoke the last with some disapproval.

"This young man"—I tried to keep the eagerness from my voice— "could he have known Elizabeth, do you think? Is that possible?"

"You would have to ask him, sir." The barriers had come up; Mrs. Hastings doubtless disapproved of gossip, and yet here she was, tattling to me about the goings-on behind the baize—that would be how it appeared to her, of course, although she was in fact providing valuable information in a murder case.

"Of course," I said. "Perhaps I shall." I got to my feet. I needed to absorb the pieces of the puzzle she had given me, and as much as I loathed myself for it, I needed to see the priest too. By rights I should go to Inspector Moore, or Andrews—but what could I tell them? That I suspected Dr. Hebbert's son-in-law of these awful crimes? In truth, the only evidence I had was that he might once have known one of the victims. The rest of my "evidence" was founded on the supernatural. I could never repeat any of it to Henry Moore; he would think my insomnia had finally got the better of me.

I did not look at Harringtons' house as I passed it, but as I walked away, I was sure the ghosts of his dead parents were screaming at me from behind the dark sockets of the windows.

I shivered and pulled my coat tight around me and tried not to jitter at the sound of my own footsteps echoing on the pavement.

This time I did not struggle to find the crumbling building where the priest had made his home. Perhaps Kosminski's strange delve into my mind had somehow fixed the route more clearly in me, or perhaps it was a more basic drive, the instinct for survival, that led me there. I needed to see them—I needed to be with others who *believed*, as I now had to admit to myself, the last doubter, I did.

"I knew you were coming," Kosminski said. He smiled, with no evidence of his usual tics and twitches. His filthy body was calm and his eyes were orbs of darkness. He had taken the drug, that was clear.

Heat engulfed me as I stepped into the room, for the fire was blazing and the windows were shut.

"I saw you walking," Kosminski said. "You went to the dead girl's house, the last sacrifice, the last *feed*, and then you needed to see us: I could *feel* it, the shift. The *change*. It led you to us."

The priest was on his knees in front of the fire. He had removed his shirt and robes, leaving his torso bare. His back was slick with sweat, and the once-smooth canvas of skin below his muscular shoulders was lacerated with a pattern of sliced cuts. Even by just the glow of the fire I could see that under the fresh wounds were years of scars. Beside him on the floor lay the birch with which he had been flagellating himself.

"What are you doing?" I asked.

He picked up his shirt with his good hand and dressed while getting to his feet, deft, swift movements that belied his deformity.

"Preparing," he said. "Making my peace with what must come."
He pointed at the bed and I sat as he took the other end. Kosminski
dropped into a cross-legged position on the floor.

I thought of our madness, and the madness of how we must
look, but I still found comfort in being around them. Kosminski
had *known* I was coming—he had *seen* it. Such visions were not
madness; they were surely a gift.

"Do you think this is truly God's work?" I asked. The question
came from nowhere, but I found it was important. In all of this
I had never considered what would happen when or if we found
the *Upir* and its host. But after seeing the priest punishing himself
so, the answer was becoming clear to me. "Or are we becoming
playthings of the devil?" The object of our hunt was no longer a
stranger: it was James Harrington. He had a face and a name—and
a wife. What was to become of him?

"I believe in my calling," the priest said, simply. "Beyond that, I
cannot answer you. Your soul must speak for itself."

I looked from the priest to strange little Kosminski and felt a wave
of tired, irrational anger toward them. What had they been doing all
this time anyway? I was the one who had found Harrington. They
had simply lurked in the shadows.

"We had to wait for you to believe," Kosminski said, answering
my unspoken question as if plucking it direct from my mind. "Three,
the power of three. Two is nothing, three is everything." His words
were so much clearer than his normal broken English, coming out
sharply in fast bursts. "The Father, the Son, and the Holy Ghost—
three—I could see you—your fears. Someone who had been sick,
someone who had traveled, and someone else, someone you love."
He plucked a few hairs from his head and laid them out on the dusty
floor. "Pieces: all the pieces, coming into place. He didn't know." His
voice was wistful. "He didn't know, not for a long time, not in Paris,
maybe not in Rainham. But now he does. Now the *Upir* is stronger
than he is."

"Aaron sees you in his visions," the priest said, "and I have
watched you."

"You are very good at watching," I said, "but thus far, that is all you have done. If you are so sure the creature is among my friends, then why have you not hunted it down yourself?" The flames cast dancing shadows across the walls, and the priest sat in the middle of them, a dark lord in a dark, cold fire.

"The police have taken in the hairdresser twice more for questioning, did you know that? His strange ways, his agitations, make them think he might be Jack the Ripper. I have made him stay at home most evenings. Tonight, two hours ago, he just turned up. He was terrified—upset and irrational—but still he came. I had to give him the drug to calm him. I think perhaps he must be the bravest of us three. We do not have to *see* what he sees. He said you were coming. He said you had found the *Upir*."

I was shocked. There was, of course, no reason for me to know of the arrests, or for anyone to have told me—none knew of my acquaintance with Kosminski—and yet I was disturbed by the idea that there were cogs and wheels turning that touched on our hunt unknown to me. I had to try and distract the investigation from him; I would speak to Andrews—or perhaps Moore. But how to steer such a conversation in that direction? That was another question.

"Have you?" the priest asked, leaning forward to look at me more closely.

"Have I what?" I had been so focused upon the first half of his statement that I had paid no attention to the rest.

"Found the *Upir*?"

For a moment I said nothing. Kosminski rocked slightly backward and forward, muttering under his breath, the words barely more than a whisper, but I heard them clearly enough: "Yes he has, yes he has, yes he has . . ."

I wondered what he saw in his dark moments. Had he seen Harrington? I doubted it—if he had, they would surely have told me. They would not have been here and waiting. They would have come to my house. Or even bypassed me completely and attacked James. Maybe Kosminski only had glimpses and emotions. Parts of the whole, just as I was presented with the parts of those the monster had killed. Enough to know something without knowing everything.

"What will we do with him?" I asked.

"So you *have* found him," the priest said, turning to face me, and leaning forward until he was only inches away. His eyes blazed with dark excitement. I fought the urge to pull away from him as an irrational fear gripped me. I had forgotten that under his calm words he was a zealot: this was his life's work, and he would die if he had to, rather than let the creature he hunted escape. I, on the other hand, was just an ordinary man who had been caught up in events beyond his control—a man who doubted his own sanity because of these same events. This man, this priest, had no doubt sustained the injury to his arm in some other hunt such as this one.

"What will we do with him?" I asked again.

"We shall try to destroy the *Upir*," he answered. "Separate it from the host and starve it."

"How do we separate it from the host?" I asked.

"You know the answer to that," the priest said. "We kill him."

I stared into the fire for a long time after that, the heat barely warming the chill that was settling into my veins. I thought of the dead women we were unable to identify. I thought of the rotting torso in the vault at Scotland Yard, found so many months ago. And I thought of poor Elizabeth Jackson, a good girl who was so afraid that she ran to a miserable end she could not escape. I thought of Juliana and James. Would that be her body, laid out in the mortuary one day for her father and me to examine? Where would this all end if we did not end it first?

I told them everything I knew. That was why I had come here, after all: to share the madness, to speak my suspicions and evidence aloud.

When I had finished, it was the priest's turn to speak, and he did so calmly and softly: a quiet explanation of what I must do.

Juliana was pregnant, and this news stopped me in my tracks, for all I had been so committed to my undertaking. They had returned from Bath a week after I had seen the priest, and I had thought myself ready to take the next step.

Although June had moved into July and the heat and stench were stifling in London, the days had been cold and dark for me, haunted by thoughts of Elizabeth Jackson and her misfortune at meeting James Harrington.

I had contacted the Harrington family doctor, under the guise of research into a disease I had come across at the hospital, and I had learned more about James's affliction. During our subsequent conversation, I heard the story of his parents' painful death. I put out inquiries on murders similar to ours, and I discovered one similar had taken place in Paris, at the very time that James Harrington was traveling through France on his way back to London.

None of this filled me with any comfort. I was ready for some kind of confrontation, if only because I could no longer stand the bleak tension building inside me.

I had been invited to dinner the next day at the Hebberts'— James and Juliana had once again taken up residence there, while the top floor of their Chelsea house was completed. I had intended to take the strange opium and confront Harrington over his connection with Elizabeth Jackson, to see if I could see the *Upir*. I tried to convince myself that the latter was less important than the former; for all the priest's talk of the monster possessing Harrington, I was more concerned with finding some trace of suspicious behavior in the man himself, believing that if I abandoned the rational entirely, then I would have lost myself entirely too.

My plans came undone, however, by a chance meeting while I was returning from an inquest. London is a large city, but there they were, on the pavement in front of me, laughing happily together. My initial disquiet was forced aside by their effervescence and it was clear that although they had intended to keep their news until the next day, they could not hold it in.

"We are expecting our first child," Juliana exclaimed, reaching out and gripping my arm. "Isn't it wonderful?"

I almost recoiled with the impact of the words. My mouth dropped open as I fought to find some emotional footing. Thankfully, they were both so wrapped up in it themselves, they did not notice nor give me time to respond.

"We were going to tell you tomorrow," James said. His eyes danced merrily and his skin looked healthy. "But as you can see, we cannot contain ourselves—a new arrival for our new house. And we would like you to be Godfather."

"Oh, I could not—" I was still reeling from the news—and then this. *Godfather?*

"Of course you can," Juliana said, "and you must—we insist. We would not want anyone else. You have been so kind to us."

"We shall celebrate at dinner tomorrow," Harrington said, "but now, we must get on, or we shall be late for our appointment."

"Of course, of course," I said, finally gathering myself. "And my heartiest congratulations to you both."

I did not take the opium with me the next night—how could I? Juliana had looked so happy; how could I spoil that? She glowed as we all laughed and ate and drank, and for the first time in a long time, it felt as if life were normal. Charles was in fine form as we toasted all of our soon-to-be new roles in the life of the unborn child, and although it was high summer, there was a feeling of Christmas to the night: an expectation of better things to come. I could not ruin that by asking questions about cold, dead girls, however much I felt their ghosts watching me and waiting for justice. I could not bear to be the one who destroyed Juliana's joy that way.

I studied James. Every now and then he would absently touch Juliana's hand, a gesture of love and affection that she would return. I saw no sign of madness in him. He was a gentle man; quiet and studious—could I really believe that he had a secret life in which he carved up women and threw them, bit by bit, into the river? For *Upir* or not, that is what I had convinced myself of. Even if I *had* taken the drug, how could I be sure it would not show me just what I expected to see—how would *that* be proof of anything at all?

I could not see how I could trust myself, and suddenly, I was full of doubt. For the next few days, I threw myself into work, forcing all thought of James Harrington from my mind. I discussed the cases with Moore and Andrews and drew out the names of Ripper suspects from them. The priest had not lied to me; Kosminski was indeed a "favorite" of one of Moore's superiors. I suggested that the killer they sought would probably be far more contained and controlled than the little hairdresser. The madness would not be apparent but would come to the fore only in the frenzied bouts during which he had murdered those unfortunate women. In short, he would appear quite normal, to all intents and purposes.

I knew that Moore respected my opinions and would pass this on, and hopefully, it would help Kosminski—the man was tortured enough without being suspected of being a monster. I felt very little guilt because my evaluation was entirely honest: I *did* believe the Ripper walked among polite gentlemen, unnoticed as the madman he was.

Despite myself, I could not help but apply the same logic to my own suspicions of Harrington: he *had* known Elizabeth Jackson, after all, and yet he had not mentioned it—why was that? He would surely know she was a victim. Juliana was always abreast of her father's cases and my own, and even if we had not discussed it, she would have seen it reported in the newspapers. My head was filled with questions, and I could not empty it.

38

LONDON, JULY 1889
DR. BOND

As the days passed, my thoughts grew increasingly dark and all pretense at sleep left me. I took too much laudanum and paced the house through the long hours of the night. I felt like a ghost; an echo of the man who used to live here.

One late afternoon I found myself in church. Like all good Englishmen, I am a Christian, and I have faith in the Lord, but my belief was more a habit, an effect of my upbringing, than something I felt in the core of my being. The study of science can be at odds with matters of the spirit, but now that so much of my thinking concerned the existence of the supernatural, I wondered if perhaps I could find some comfort in God's house.

As it was, I found the empty silence of the austere building oppressive. I tried to pray, but my mind wandered and my tired eyes rested on the figures stained in glass who looked down on me. Was that pity or revulsion? Was I working for God, or against him? My mind was dulled by exhaustion and laudanum and I longed for the quieter times of years past. Eventually I got up, my knees aching, and turned to leave. There was no peace for me here. I wondered if hell was eating me up from the inside in a mass of doubts and wavering commitment.

"It will feed again."

The words came so suddenly out of nowhere that I gasped aloud, my heart almost stopping in my chest.

"You cannot hide from what you know—what you *need* to know." The priest stepped out of the shadows by the vestry. I had felt unwelcome here, but he was truly an interloper. He might be a man of the cloth, but there was no place for him in the public face of the Church.

"I am not sure I have the right man," I said. The words sounded feeble, even to me, and I moved quickly, wanting to scurry past him and back out into the throb of the city. I kept my head down.

"Then make sure," he growled. He grabbed my arm, and I was aware of how thin and weak it felt in his tight grip. The past year had taken its toll on me physically, and while those around me might not have noticed the gradual changes, when I faced myself naked in the mirror it was clear how much this had literally eaten away at me.

"He will kill again. And we must stop him."

I could not help but meet his resolute gaze. "I will not do anything without proof. I cannot—it goes against everything I am. I must have more solid evidence against him."

The priest hissed in disgust and cast my arm aside, sending me twisting awkwardly into the stone wall. "Always there must be a doubter," he said, "a half-believer."

We stared at each other as I nursed my arm. *Always?* How many times had he done this? Were there always a Kosminski and a me involved?

"Perhaps," I said, straightening myself up and remembering the sacred nature of the building in which we stood, "I am here to serve as your conscience."

There was the slightest slump in his shoulders at that. I had hit a nerve of truth.

"You need to trust your instincts," he said. His words were quieter now. "I will not wait forever. Find your proof if you must, but also find mine: take the drug and tell me what you see." His eyes softened. "Believe me, mine will be the hardest part in our trials."

I did not want to know what he meant by that, but there was a melancholy sadness in his words that made me shiver.

He left the church, and by the time I had followed him out onto the street he had disappeared. I reached into my coat for the laudanum bottle, not caring if anyone could see me. Nor did I look to see how much was left in the bottle since I had refilled it this morning. Would the Dr. Bond of even a year ago recognize himself now, I wondered. Would he be disgusted?

The priest was right: only answers would bring me the peace I craved. I had to see our mad adventure through to the end.

It was nearly six by the time I arrived at the wharves, but they were still busy, with men rushing this way and that, loading or unloading great crates and boxes in and out of the warehouses that lined the river's edge. They started early and worked late here, long hours of heavy labor lugging things on and off boats and into storage or onto vehicles.

Finally I found someone who could point me in the right direction, and I headed toward James Harrington's office. Outside steps led up to the offices. I kept my eyes away from the river—I had never visited the wharves before and I had not realized just how close James worked to the water. The closest I had come before now was Bluegate Fields, the maze of alleyways where the opium dens were hidden, but my focus had always been elsewhere.

Harrington's secretary, a rather nervous man of indeterminate age, was sorting through a large pile of invoices and noting them in a ledger. He eyed me rather suspiciously until I declared myself a friend of the family, and then his smile warmed.

"Mr. Harrington is in his office, sir," he said. "Come with me." He led me up a further flight of narrow wooden stairs overlooking the warehouse below, where various crates were being stacked, no doubt from a just-arrived ship. I had not paid that much attention to Harrington's business affairs, but it looked as if his father had left him with a successful enterprise, just as Juliana had told me. The men at work below looked up, and again I caught a sense of unease in their glances. What were they wary of? Who did they think I was?

James was behind his desk when we came in, and he jumped slightly at our interruption. There were papers everywhere, but he had been staring into space rather than at them. The secretary closed the door behind us, and although I smiled jovially in greeting, Harrington's face was wary.

"If you've come about Juliana, then I had rather you just left," he said bluntly.

"Juliana?" I was thrown slightly. "No, I was simply passing and thought I would come in and take a look at your empire—you know so much about my world, and I . . . What about Juliana?"

"I'm sorry," he said, now feeling awkward in his turn. "I thought she might have come to you," he said. "I know she feels close to you."

"Is everything all right?" I might have come here because of my suspicions of Harrington, but my own feeling for Juliana overrode everything else. My stomach tightened at the thought of her having come to any harm.

"Yes," he said, "she's fine—we had an argument." He frowned, and he moved some papers around on his desk. There appeared to be no order to them, and the cause of the worry on the faces of his secretary and the men who worked for him below started to become clear. "She wanted to help me," he said. "There have been a few . . . problems. Confusion over some bills. Nothing that cannot be sorted out." He sat up straight in his chair and forced a smile. "But I cannot have her here, not now she's carrying our child. What if something happened to her? I would never live with myself. So I told her no, it would be better if she stayed at home. You can understand that, can't you, Dr. Bond? You can see this is no place for a woman."

"Of course," I said, although I could see no reason why Juliana should not be safe enough up here, away from the docks and boats, and the loads of herbs and spices that came in and out. But I wished to placate him.

"Women get so emotional," James muttered. "I just do not want her to come here—not here. This is where I work."

"I suppose," I said, keeping my tone light, "that she recalls you once told her she could help you in the office. I imagine she misses you. You work such long hours."

"Did I say that?" He looked genuinely confused. Was it the proximity to the river that affected him? Did it make the *Upir* stronger, quashing his naturally gentle personality? Even if there was no *Upir*, he was still a troubled man, and I truly believed he had some involvement with the death of Elizabeth Jackson. I felt it in every nerve that jangled in my tired body.

There was a monster of some kind inside James Harrington, I was sure of it—and whether it was just part of his tortured mind or a real beast from the bottom of a Polish river, it was connected to the water. That was where most of the girls' bodies had been pulled from.

"Yes, you did."

"I do not recall. I forget a lot these days. My illness, I think—that's why I have to work so hard, to stay focused." He looked up at me, and I could see no sign of that happy man I had met in the street only days before; he did not exist in those glassy eyes. Perhaps in the wake of their good news, Harrington had been able to fight his personal demons for a while, but now that he was back in London, whatever plagued him was settling back in.

"That's why I cannot be distracted by Juliana," Harrington continued. "You know how it is: we men must concentrate on our work. Our work is *important*."

"It certainly is."

"I do not remember saying that at all. How strange." Harrington was staring into space, the frown still etched on his forehead, and then suddenly his eyes snapped back to me. He smiled again. "But speaking of work . . ." He gestured at the mass of untidiness that covered his desk. "I really must get on, or I shan't be home before midnight. If I had known you were coming, I would have put some time aside to give you a tour, but . . ."

"Of course," I said, "I understand perfectly. I am sorry to have disturbed you." I glanced again at the disorganized papers on his desk. For someone who apparently worked such long hours, he did not seem to be on top of his affairs at all. "And I am quite sure Juliana will be fine when you get home."

He did not get up to see me out. As I opened the door, his secretary almost tumbled in. He muttered his apologies for his clumsiness and started, "We need somewhere to store the tea that's just come in. I was thinking warehouse three. That's nearest the—"

"No. That's being used."

"Is it? I was sure that—"

I closed the door behind me and left them to figure out which was the cause of the confusion. I imagined it was Harrington. This was not the self-deprecating young businessman I had met last year.

I had no desire to go home and sit alone with my thoughts, so I decided to call on Juliana and the Hebberts instead. I was now almost part of the family; they would not object to my arriving unannounced. My concern was obviously for Juliana; the way Harrington had immediately jumped to the conclusion that I had come about her implied that he had done more than just politely ask her to leave. She must have been in quite a state for him to think I had come to berate him, when I had never spoken an ill word to him in all our acquaintance. I could not imagine any circumstance wherein anyone could be angry with Juliana, and the thought of it upset me. My feelings for her were stronger than they should be, that I knew, but they did not lie about her nature: she was sweet and intelligent and warm—and she was also pregnant.

Summer having full reign, it was still light when I arrived, but as I stepped into Charles's house, the temperature dropped, and any brightness was shut outside with the closing of the door. The lamps were already lit, but their light was dull, and shadows clung to every surface. I joined Charles in his study, where I found him in a not-dissimilar position to Harrington: at his desk and surrounded by reports and folders.

"I'm trying to put together a paper on the Jackson girl," he said, "but I just cannot concentrate. I think we need a thunderstorm, don't you? Something to clear this air, anyway."

Although the day was warm, I had not found it muggy, but inside the house, the air felt oppressive, and the book-lined walls started to close in on me, almost as if threatening to tumble and crush both me and my superstitions under the weight of science. My heart began the strange beat I dreaded, and my face tingled. What was it about being in this house that made my anxiety surge? I surely had enough laudanum in my body that it should not even have been possible. I took slow deep breaths, pretending to study the spines of the dusty volumes, until some semblance of calm had returned.

"I have decided to take a holiday myself," Charles announced abruptly. "I am taking Mary away, the day after tomorrow—somewhere by the sea. I think I shall sleep better by the sea." He was smiling, but his eyes were tired. "I think I shall sleep better out of London for a while."

"You have been working very hard," I said.

"You should consider a holiday too, Thomas. If you do not mind me saying, you are a shadow of your former self—do not think I have not noticed. I am a doctor, after all." He smiled, and it was almost the cheery expression I always associated with him . . . but not quite. We had both become ghosts of ourselves, I feared, and the smile sat like it was drawn on tracing paper stretched over his face.

"Did you know that Elizabeth Jackson used to work in a house on the street where James lives?" I asked.

"Really?" Charles dropped his face to his papers. "No, I didn't. Still, people have to live somewhere. Juliana is resting, by the way. I think she's suffering slightly with this pregnancy. She won't rest enough, that's her problem. She was always so active, even as a child." He tossed his pen down and pushed away from the desk. "I think we should have a drink."

His words came out in a cheerful rush, almost as if to drown my words in their surge. He was not going to comment further? Surely there should be some discussion, even if only to decide it was simply a strange coincidence. I stared at my friend's back. Or had he already known? It was hardly confidential information; if I knew, then there was no reason that Charles would not. But why had not he mentioned it? Simply because he thought there was no reason to, or because he too was caught up in a whirl of suspicion? And if he did already know, then why not say so when I brought it up?

He turned and handed me a brandy glass.

"This house is so *full*," he said. "It will be good to be alone with Mary. I asked Juliana if she would like to come, but she would rather stay here with James. That's natural, I suppose."

It had been only a few days since the young couple had moved in, and the last time I had been here they had all been full of mirth at the thought of a new arrival. How much had changed in so short a time: this house was not small—there was plenty of room for them all, and several more besides, before it would feel crowded. However, I would have to agree that there was definitely something oppressive in the place. I noticed that my breaths were shorter, as if the air itself were heavy and resisting inhalation, wanting to suffocate, rather than provide life. It was dark too, despite the curtains being open and the early evening sun still shining outside. I sipped my brandy.

"I imagine she would not want to be far from her own house," I suggested. "If James is always working, then she will have to oversee the labor there."

"True," Charles said, "but I am sorry she won't come with us. The seaside would do her good."

"She's just been to Bath. That will have refreshed her."

Charles looked distinctly unhappy at the thought of leaving Juliana behind, and I wondered if he realized how much he sounded like he was running from something rather than simply taking a well-deserved break. The one person he was leaving behind was Harrington—was he running from his son-in-law? Was he even aware of it? The priest said the *Upir* brought mayhem with it; if it really was attached to Harrington, then perhaps it was no wonder that Charles felt so despondent while he was in the house. Maybe that was why he was suddenly plagued by nightmares, when he had always been the most optimistic of men.

What had Kosminski said? That the *Upir* was stronger than the man now? Could Charles somehow feel the wickedness in his house? If I had been so plagued by thoughts of darkness in the streets of London that they had driven sleep further than ever from me and led me to the opium dens, was it so irrational to think Charles might be similarly affected too?

"I can keep an eye on Juliana if you like," I said. "She and I are friends now, and I think she would not find my presence an imposition."

"Would you, Thomas?" He looked at me with a strange mixture of relief and desperation. "I hate leaving her behind, but I have to . . . I have to get away, if I am to be of any use to my profession." He smiled again, that strange expression that did not quite fit, like a reflection of sunshine on the filthy river.

He was terrified, I realized—terrified enough to leave his daughter behind in the city. "And I must finish this paper." He gestured at the pages behind him.

"It would be my pleasure," I said. It would also give me a chance to study Harrington more closely, if I had been charged to watch over them both by Charles. The young man would not be so rude as to tell me to leave under such circumstances. Charles had returned to his desk and was shuffling his notes around.

"Why the Jackson case?" I said. "Why present a paper on her?"

"Why not?" Charles said. "We found all but her head, and she has a name. We know who she was." He drained his brandy.

"A name to haunt us," I said softly.

"This year has been filled with names to haunt us, Thomas," Charles said. "I see those women in my dreams. I see their blood. I could live without another summer like the last one quite happily."

I nodded in agreement and swallowed the last of my own drink. It might be the Ripper victims he saw in his dreams, but he was fixating on the dead girl who'd known his son-in-law. Somewhere in his subconscious, Charles was wrestling with knowledge he did not want. I was not sure if I envied him or not. Was it better to be in my position or his? At least he could leave London with no sense of abandoned responsibility. I was trapped in a world of madness and superstition, steeped in murders that I had a terrible feeling might lead to one more—one in which I would play a part, even if it was not my hand that committed the deed.

Suddenly I wanted out of this house, even if it meant a return to pacing my own and staring out at the night. At least the air was *clean* there; it lacked the stagnant tang that filled my nostrils suddenly.

"I shall leave you to your preparations," I said, "and hope the sea air does you good."

We shook hands, and both our palms were clammy with cool sweat that held more honesty than any of the words we had spoken to each other.

I did not go home until much later. For the first time in a long time I took a hansom to Bluegate Fields. My nerves were surprisingly calm but I sought oblivion—some peace, if not rest. I knew, whether I wished to admit it or not, that this would be my last opportunity until this miserable business was done, one way or another.

The priest was right of course: the *Upir*—or the monster within the man, both demons regardless of which was driving the actions—would kill again, and I needed to reach my conclusions before then. I hoped beyond all things that we were wrong, that I had found Harrington a suspect simply to satisfy the mad desires of we fellow hunters. The next time I saw him, I would take the drug the priest had given me; I would fulfill that obligation—but I would not trust my eyes. After all, the sea creatures I had seen around the heads of the sailors in the dens had been so realistic, but my rational mind had known that they did not truly exist, so it would surely be the same with anything I saw around Harrington. Despite Charles's strange behavior and the undeniable atmosphere in that house, I had to prove Harrington guilty or innocent on *physical* evidence.

My decision to start the following day left me with a feeling of vague, doomed calm; what would be, would be. If I had attained any kind of tranquility, it was that of the condemned man.

I let the sweet smoke caress me, and this time no monsters came to plague my visions as I lay back on the filthy cot. I had missed the simplicity of this place, back when I was plagued only by insomnia and unease, when the priest was simply a curious stranger in a long black coat. Tension eased from my limbs as I saw the ocean and swam in its depths, drifting in and out of oblivion, calling for the Chinaman to refill the pipe every time my conscious mind came too close to the surface. I do not remember leaving the den, but I must have, for I wandered through the streets to Whitechapel, where I weaved my way between the drunks and other unfortunates who tumbled loud and toothless from the public houses and brothels that filled those streets.

Strange street theaters acted out gruesome scenes, my drugged mind seeing only tortured people behind the actors' made-up faces. Everywhere around me I saw life and death battling for control of each filthy, hacking body. Women walked past me, leering and laughing, their faces so close to mine, for they were only several feet away, and I could smell their rancid breath. Through my revulsion I wanted to kiss them: this was humanity in all its brutal beauty, with mankind's matchless ability to laugh, even while trapped in such a pitiless existence. I had seen men and women like these at Westminster Hospital, their miserable lives plotted out for them by the accident of their birth, their lives doomed to failure and sickness even as they clawed their way through each day. These lives might have been better off snuffed out at birth, and yet they were all so determined to cling on, to hope for some happiness, however elusive or improbable that might be.

I wanted to suck in their warmth; I wanted to take their raw grit away and arm myself with it. Was this how Jack felt when he walked these streets? Was that why he butchered these women? Did he want to rip this hungry energy from them for himself?

I walked until I was exhausted, and slowly the world slipped back into some kind of normalcy. My eyes stung as dawn creaked into life, the early birdsong soon drowned out by the throb of the city. It was past eight in the morning by the time I returned to my house. I scribbled a note for my housekeeper, claiming to be unwell and asking her not to disturb me, and then I crawled into my bed, where I slept like the dead.

When I awoke it was past four, and the day was lost. I was still tired, and although I had slept for eight hours—something of a miracle for me—I felt disoriented and bleary.

"You're up then, sir," Mrs. Parks said, appearing silently in the doorway in that way that only a housekeeper could manage. "I shall get you some coffee if you're feeling better. I shall take the tray to your study."

"Thank you."

"Miss Hebbert called earlier to see if you'd care to join them for dinner tonight. I told her you were unwell but that if I saw you, I would certainly tell you. She said there would be a place for you if wanted it." She raised an eyebrow. "I presume you will not be requiring me to prepare you any supper?"

"No, no, thank you, Mrs. Parks. I do feel much better now. Perhaps some company will do me good."

Mrs. Parks stared at me for a moment longer, her expression unreadable. "Very well, sir," she said eventually, and she disappeared back toward her own domain.

Tonight. If I had to take the drug and study Harrington, then I would do it tonight. I had prevaricated for longer than Hamlet, and my own inability to act or to know what to believe was driving me just as mad as the Danish prince. I would appease the priest by taking the drug, and I would appease my own curiosity by questioning Harrington about Elizabeth Jackson.

I waited until Mrs. Parks had left and then bathed and dressed before taking the narrow box containing the opium equipment from the back of the drawer in my locked study desk and tucking it into a pocket cunningly set into the lining of my waistcoat. I resisted the urge to take some laudanum, but I did pour myself a brandy. I stood by the window and looked out at the heavy summer sky before pulling the curtains closed to shut the view out.

I sometimes wish I had allowed myself to gaze on more of that dying day . . .

Charles was dining with colleagues from the hospital at his club, it transpired, to discuss covering his duties during his absence. Like me, Charles rarely took time away from work, and the staff would probably feel his absence far more than they realized. As would I, should there be—though I prayed there would not be—any more grisly discoveries dredged from the Thames.

Juliana and Mary kept the conversation going, talking about the preparations for Whitby, and how early Mary and Charles would have to be up in order to catch the right train. Harrington and I commented occasionally as we ate our soup, politely interjecting as and when required, and I noticed that he appeared much calmer and more relaxed than when I had seen him at the wharves. Every now and then, when someone else was speaking, Juliana's eyes would dart nervously from James to me and then back again, making me wonder what had been said about our meeting the previous day. I imagined she would have been embarrassed to hear that her husband had told me of their argument—maybe James had not believed me, and he had confronted Juliana when he had gone home. He had certainly been in a strange enough mood. I realized that this dinner invitation was perhaps a conciliatory attempt to smooth out any awkwardness there might be, and I wondered how much I might soon be adding to it.

Between the first and second courses, I made my excuses and locked myself in the bathroom. I worked fast, and within moments I was sucking the strange-tasting smoke deep into my lungs. My skin tingled, and the last remnants of my exhaustion disappeared, and the world sharpened. I opened the small window to dissipate the scent and smoked some more, inhaling fast. When I was done, I put the hot pipe back into its wooden box and slipped the box back into its hiding place before splashing water on my face.

I took a deep breath. I was ready.

The beef was being served as I returned to the table, preventing any discussion of my well-being, and I kept my head down as I took my seat. When I was sure that I could maintain a steady expression, whatever sights might greet me, I looked at James Harrington.

I saw nothing.

There was not even an aura of color around his head. I stared harder, willing my imagination on, but still there was just a young blond man sitting opposite me. My heart thumped hard in my chest. Had the drug failed? Had I become immune to its effects because of my new dependence on its sister drug, the seductive laudanum? I looked over at Juliana, and I had to stop myself from sighing in relief. Around her head yellows and reds shone like sunlight: beautiful summer colors with lines of blue darting here and there. These were the colors I always associated with Emily, the girl lost so many years ago—they were colors I associated with love.

"Aren't you hungry, Thomas?" Juliana asked, breaking my reverie. "Are you still unwell?"

"I am actually much better, thank you," I said, "and this looks delicious." In fact, my appetite had totally deserted me, and my mouth had dried up—the effects of the drug, perhaps, or my own nervousness. I sipped my wine before cutting into the meat, which was very rare. I tried not to look at the blood that seeped out across my plate, or to think about it in my mouth as I chewed a large forkful. All my senses had become heightened, and I could hear my fellow diners' lips smacking noisily as they ate, the wet, slick sound of meat being devoured—a pack of beasts, tearing the victim of the hunt apart.

"This is delicious," I said, and I smiled at Mary, my outward calm quite at odds with my inner revulsion as the virtually raw beef slid down my throat. I thought I could feel it squirm like a live thing, but I knew this was just the drug; everything was normal. The food was perfectly cooked; it was exactly as I would choose to eat it myself. I distracted myself by looking at the scenes that danced around Mary's head. The colors were duller, more world-weary than those around Juliana, but within the folds of the muted pinks and blues were flashes of homely items, like baby clothes. This was Mary: a mother and wife.

I looked once again at Harrington, who had already almost finished and was clearly hungry enough for more.

"Speaking of illness," I said. "I am so glad to see you so fully recovered, James—especially with the wonderful news of the baby."

"Thank you. Let's hope I can keep it at bay for longer this time."

That was a strange turn of phrase to use when talking about illness, I thought. "Perhaps you should let someone else in your offices take on more of the running of your business for a while," I suggested, then sipped more wine, trying to loosen my throat. Somehow the absence of any kind of vision around him was more disturbing than the colors that spun and twisted around the two women. "I was impressed by what a large operation it is—but it must put quite a strain on you."

"Perhaps, but it was my father's business and I want to run it the way he did: from the helm." James picked up his own wine glass and smiled at me. His teeth were white, and his eyes were sharp, like blue crystals. I shivered as we looked at each other. I could still taste the blood from the beef in my mouth, and I imagined it in Harrington's too—and quite suddenly, I felt like prey.

"I think James is not the only one who works too hard, Thomas," Juliana said. "Like all physicians—my father included—you are quite unable to take your own advice. You have not been well yourself, have you? You have certainly lost weight." She looked at my plate. "At least James has not lost his appetite."

"You are right of course," I concurred. "Doctors always make the worst patients. But these are exceptional times."

"I suppose that's one way of putting it," Juliana said. "*Awful* times might be better. I shudder when I think of the sights you and Father have seen—those poor women."

This was it: my chance to probe Harrington, and I had not had to steer the conversation there myself. I could see that Mary was about to reprimand her daughter for bringing up such an unpleasant topic at the dinner table—the colors around her head had darkened and her mouth had started to open—when I seized the moment.

"Poor girls indeed. Your father told you about the last one—Elizabeth Jackson?"

"Told us what?" Juliana frowned, and Harrington's fork froze momentarily between his plate and his mouth. It was the slightest hesitation, but I saw it.

I kept my eyes on him as I continued, "She used to work on the same street where you live—she was a housemaid, and a very good one, by all accounts."

"But that's awful," Juliana said.

"How terrible," Mary added. "And what a strange coincidence. But I thought Charles said she had been living on the streets?"

Harrington put his fork down and looked up at me, and now I was sure I could see the tiniest flicker of a smile twisting one corner of his mouth.

"She had been. She ran away from her job and her home in November of last year."

"But why?" Mary asked. However much she might disapprove of the topic in general, her curiosity was now piqued. "Had she got herself in trouble?"

"The police do think a man was involved." I kept staring at Harrington, who raised another forkful of food and chewed it slowly, his eyes firmly fixed on mine. "Something made her suddenly drop everything and leave it all behind."

"That was when we decided to move back to the house, isn't it, James? It was around then, I'm sure of it." There was no accusation in Juliana's voice, just wonder at the way life weaves people together in the form of coincidences.

"Yes, it was," he said calmly. "How strange."

"She was in service there for several years. I wondered if you might have known her?" I kept my tone light, and I made a pretense of eating by pushing my food around my plate, but tension crackled in the air between us. I wondered if the women were aware of it.

"I barely knew the names of our own maids, let alone those of others," Harrington said. "And I was away from home a lot, first my studies, then my travels."

A simple "no" would have sufficed, but he had felt the need to elaborate on his reasons. I certainly did not know the names of the servants who worked in the houses around my own, and I doubted Mary or Charles did either—why had he needed to give more than that?

Blood heated in my veins and my face burned as my mind raced. There was a secret here—drug or no drug, I knew that. He *had* known Elizabeth Jackson; *he* was the reason she ran.

"Why would you think James knew her?" Juliana laughed, and I could hear a slight nervousness in her voice. Was my directness forcing her to peel back layers she had built up to protect her own suspicions? I did not think for a moment that she would ever consider James a murderer, but given his strange behavior recently, she might wonder if he had a sordid secret in his past—a servant girl in trouble would certainly fit that bill. It had crossed my mind that Elizabeth Jackson might have been the root cause of Harrington's travels into Europe. Juliana was a clever woman, and I imagined that thought might also be occurring to her.

"Because his mother did." It was an aggressive approach, but I wanted to get a reaction from Harrington. "She called on Elizabeth Jackson—just a day or so before she and your father died."

"But that would have been some time before this servant ran away from her house," Harrington said. His eyes were still fixed on mine, but I could make out nothing from his expression. "And I must say, it seems highly unlikely that my mother would ever call on a serving girl."

"That's what I was told," I said. "Of course, it's always possible that the person who told me was mistaken—people do get details muddled over time."

"Well, that must be the case. My mother might have called on a neighbor, but certainly not a maid."

When he had finished speaking, I saw his lips pinch together slightly, a downward frown of displeasure and irritation, and I had to stop myself from smiling in triumph. He knew I was questioning him, and I knew that he was hiding something. I would win this, I thought, for Elizabeth Jackson's sake if nothing else.

Suddenly I felt a chill in the pit of my stomach. Harrington flinched, and his eyes drifted, looking confused for a moment. Then his spine stiffened as *something* shifted behind him—and then he refocused.

He frowned, picking up his knife and fork and cut angrily into the remains of his beef before thrusting a large chunk into his mouth. A greasy trickle of pink liquid ran down to his chin as he chewed hungrily, but he ignored it. As his lips smacked together, it clung to the contours of his skin and slid down to his neck.

My eyes followed it, my attention focused on the blood so that I did not have to look at the darkness that was creeping up over Harrington's shoulder. My heart raced and I swallowed hard as a black tongue smelling of something rotten darted around Harrington's neck and squeezed like a garrote for a moment before pulling back, licking up the blood as it did so.

I was assaulted by the thick, sickly stench of stagnant water, which coated the back of my nose and throat, making me want to gag. My collar felt tight, and I could not catch my breath. What was that *thing*, that awful dark shape that was too dense behind him? The bulbous growth was just out of sight, but my eyes hurt just *trying* to look at it, the sharp pains stabbing behind my eyeballs forcing me to blink rapidly.

Harrington continued to eat, refilling his plate from the bowl of buttered potatoes in front of him and cramming them into his mouth two and three at a time. I had seen him eat like this before, and I had thought there was something unnatural about it then. Now I knew why.

My ears buzzed with the noise of Juliana and Mary's chatter, but I could not make out their words. I felt distant from them, a world apart, as if I were lost under the Thames and they were still on the surface.

The *Upir* was showing itself. It clung to Harrington's shoulder, dark talons gripping him as it peered around the back of his neck, an awful parody of a baby carried in a sling behind its mother, that style so often seen amongst the Orientals.

It did not emerge fully, and only one side of its face was visible. That eye came to rest on me and I could feel my heart pounding rapidly. I tried to stay focused on Harrington; unlike the red orb that glared angrily at me from the apex of his neck and shoulder, the man's eyes were blue, and wholly human. I concentrated on them, rather than the awful wickedness in the corner of my vision, for I could not bear to look directly—even if I had had that desire, I *could not*, for it was death; it was madness; it was everything that was wrong with the world, all wrapped up into a dense black shape. The whole world's shadow had been sucked into this awful clinging gargoyle. The head bobbed up slightly, and the black tongue flicked out again, catching an invisible fly in the air, and then it hissed, and I felt a fine spray of poisonous spittle land on my skin. As the rotten stench of corruption assaulted me, bile rose up my throat and I fought not to be violently ill.

"Of course," I said, forcing the words out, "I thought it must be a mistake too. Servants can have such vivid imaginations at times like this—they get carried away with the excitement of it all."

I suddenly hated having to open my mouth to speak. The thought that any of that awful spray might get inside me was too much to bear, and I suddenly gagged slightly.

"I'm so sorry," I muttered, reaching for my wine glass. My hand trembled, and I quickly put it back down again. For a brief moment my eyes landed on the *Upir* and I wanted to sob at the sight, for it was staring right at me.

But my words must have appeased it slightly, for after a long moment, it crept back down in a series of jerky movements until it had disappeared behind Harrington. The terrible stench abated, but I still found it hard to breathe. My whole body was cold and my face felt clammy. Black spots darted in the corner of my vision, and for an awful moment I thought I might pass out.

"Are you all right, Doctor?" Mary asked.

"Yes," I breathed as I dabbed at my face with my napkin that came away damp with sweat, "I am so sorry—I think I might have a slight fever after all."

"You certainly look pale."

"Have some water." Juliana touched James's arm. "Pour him some water, darling."

"Of course."

Harrington got to his feet and brought the water jug round to where I sat. As he leaned over my shoulder to pour it, I could not stop a slight shudder at his proximity.

"Thank you," I muttered, and he turned away and walked back to his side of the table. I could not help but stare at his back as my heart beat fast in my chest, but there was nothing there; no dark, misshapen creature clung to his spine. I picked up my glass and drank, but though the water was clear and clean, I hated having it in my mouth—not after seeing that *thing* that had lived for so long at the bottom of some river somewhere. Had Harrington stopped for a drink somewhere? Or maybe it been a hot day, and he had bathed in a private stretch somewhere on his travels? I pitied him and feared him in equal measure.

For the remainder of the meal, I steeled myself to ignore my terror and instead steered the conversation back to the subject of Mary's holiday. I no longer wanted Harrington to know I suspected him; I wanted to run as far away from him as I could. Was this what had happened to poor Elizabeth Jackson? Did she see something crawl over her beau's shoulder—and did she realize that it would come for her?

The colors and shapes still danced around mother and daughter's heads, but I knew they were as much a part of me as anything to do with them. What I had seen with James was different: it might have vanished now, but this time it was a *reality* that I no longer trusted, for I had seen the *Upir*. I had *felt* its existence in my poor soul, and I did not believe that it was just a figment of my drug-addled brain, a vision thrown up by auto-suggestion. I knew my own mind was too rational to have created something like that. I did not have that level of monstrosity lurking at my core. This had been real and old and full of menace. My throat tightened once more.

It was just before midnight when I finally said my good-byes, politely refusing the offer of a bed for the night if I was still feeling out of sorts. The fresh air would do me good, I declared; I would walk a while before finding a hansom cab. My smile had felt like a rictus grin. Nothing on this good earth could have persuaded me to spend the night there, not then—not so soon after seeing what shared the house with them.

I walked until I was out of sight from the windows, and then, shuddering uncontrollably, I leaned against a wall. My teeth chattered in my head and my eyes watered. I had felt fear before in my life—on the Prussian battlefields mortal fear was a daily occurrence—but this was something different: this was base and primal. This was like standing at the doorway to hell and gazing inside at all the conceivable horrors as they shifted in the endless dark and knowing you were to become one of them. This terror was rooted in the death of my own humanity.

"You saw it."

I almost shrieked as the words cut through the night, and then my shoulders slumped with relief at the sight of the priest. He had followed me—of course he had. All my animosity toward him had vanished with the first glimpse of that rotten tongue licking the blood from Harrington's neck, and now I almost sobbed with relief. The priest was strong—he knew what to do. He would destroy it, for that was his calling.

"Yes," I said, "and it was truly awful."

With his good hand, he pulled a box from somewhere within his heavy coat and then lit a cigarette and handed it to me. I breathed the smoke in, eager to wipe all trace of that awful stench from my mouth and nose. We smoked in silence for a few moments, both staring back down the street at the Hebberts' house, until I had regained my composure. When my cigarette was finished, he handed me a small bottle of liquid and I drank from it, dulling the effects of the opium that was still in my veins. I felt almost like normal: the terror had not left me, but it had settled into a quieter place inside for now, and I could breathe properly once again.

"We shall have to watch him," I said. "The three of us must know where he is at all times. We will have to be ready for when he next tries to take a woman—"

"Or we could take him now." The priest's voice was cold.

"You may have destroyed your soul, Father," I said quietly, for the first time acknowledging his status in the Church, "but I still have mine. I must see Harrington and the *Upir* at work together—I must see that he is in some way complicit."

"Very well." I had expected an argument, but the priest knew me well enough now to understand my need for the rational in all of this. Even now—*especially* now—it was vitally important. If I believed Harrington to be innocent of the *Upir*'s guilt, then I could not be part of taking his life without damning my own soul. We stood there a while longer, both lost in our thoughts, before a second shudder ran through me.

"Do you think it saw me?" I asked. "The *Upir*?"

"Perhaps—probably." The priest shrugged. "But that should not be your concern. It is not whether it saw you that matters; let us just hope that it does not realize *you* saw *it*."

I did not sleep that night.

39

The Times of London
July 17, 1889

MURDER IN THE EAST-END

Shortly before 1 o'clock this morning a constable on his beat, while passing through Castle-alley, in Whitechapel, noticed the form of a woman lying in the shadow of a doorway. He at first thought it was one of the wanderers so numerous in the neighbourhood, especially at this season, and was about to rouse the woman, when he was horrified to discover that she was dead, blood flowing from a wound in the throat. The body was in a pool of blood, which flowed from a gash in the stomach, evidently inflicted with a sharp knife or razor. The officer at once gave the alarm and within a few minutes several other constables were on the spot.

The New York Times
London, July 18

THE WHITECHAPEL VICTIM

London, July 18—At the inquest held on the body of the woman found murdered in the Whitechapel district yesterday morning, the fact was developed that in addition to two large gashes there were fourteen other wounds on the body. The greater number of the wounds, however, were only skin deep.

Marion Daily Star—Ohio, USA
July 17, 1889

ANOTHER MURDER ADDED TO THE LONG LIST IN WHITECHAPEL

One more murder has been added to the long list credited to Jack the Ripper in Whitechapel. The body of a woman, evidently one of the disreputable frequenters of the district, was found in Castle-alley last night, only a short distance from where the other murders were committed. The body was horribly mutilated and bears undoubted evidence of the mark of the fiend, whose atrocities in Whitechapel have terrorized the whole district repeatedly.

40

London, July 18, 1889
Dr. Bond

The rain of the previous days had done nothing to abate the muggy atmosphere and as I closed up my bag, I was glad to be getting out of the sweaty wooden shed that was being used as a mortuary. Despite Bagster Philips's best efforts, the mutilated corpse of Alice McKenzie laid out on the table had begun to decompose, and the air was filled with a sickly sweet tang. She had not been a pretty woman, and death was never kind to a face, but I took one long last look at her. I had begun to lose my professional distance with the dead before all this madness started, but now each dead woman added to the burden of my exhaustion, keeping me awake. At least I could be certain that this murder had not been committed by Harrington: it had been midnight before I had left the family, and then the priest and I had stood in the street for the best part of half an hour afterward. It was during this time that this woman was losing her life in a different part of London. Harrington and the creature attached to him were an abomination, but they were not Jack the Ripper.

The door opened as I headed toward it and Moore stepped inside. He cast a look toward the corpse, his nose crinkling slightly with revulsion, and left the door ajar.

"Where's Philips?" he asked abruptly.

"Stepped outside. We have had something of a professional disagreement."

"To do with her?" Moore looked surprised, and I did not blame him. It was hard to argue with Bagster—he was jovial and well respected, and in the main I trusted his judgment—but not this time, however.

"He thinks her killer was left-handed."

I let that sink in. Jack, we had all agreed, was right-handed, and that meant Bagster was eliminating her as a Ripper victim. "He thinks the bruises on her chest and the left side of her abdomen, above the mutilations, were from where he held her down while he attacked her." I stepped back alongside the corpse and demonstrated. "Like this." He watched me. "However," I continued, "I am not convinced. The bruises could be the result of the way she fell, or any number of other things. Also, we must take into account the sudden frenzied nature of the attack, the area where she died, and of course the nature of these injuries. This is Jack again. I can guarantee you that."

"I thought as much," Moore snorted. "Commissioner Monro thinks so too. You'll be putting that in your report?"

I nodded.

"Philips says that the killer is an anatomical expert—his words. Some kind of doctor, maybe?"

"You know my views on that," I said. "I doubt it. These kind of injuries could be caused by anyone with a half-decent idea of the human innards." I thought of Harrington: his business was import and export; he had no experience with knives or saws as far as I could tell, and yet he had become more than capable at dismembering bodies. I wondered if the *Upir* guided him in that too? How many other victims had there been that we had not found? Or maybe he had just availed himself of some of Charles's anatomy books, stealing them out of the house under his coat and studying them under the blanket of night as his young wife slept, oblivious to the creature at his back. I shivered again, despite the heat. Suddenly I was finding comfort in this poor dead woman's demise: at least hers was a simple murder. She died at the hand of a madman, perhaps, but a human one; there was no unnatural monster involved here.

"If you say so." Moore sniffed again, a thick snort, like a summer cold. We agreed on most things, but on this issue of medical training, I would say he took Bagster's side, and of course he was entitled to his opinion, as was my colleague, even if I was sure they were both wrong.

"I presume you will be at the next inquest?" he said. "Not that we have anything to add to it yet—we have an extra forty or so constables drafted onto Whitechapel's streets, but we still can't catch the bastard. I was hoping he had died." He almost smiled. "Him and the other one. What makes killers so hardy, Doctor? Are they born with a stronger constitution than the rest of us?"

"You do not seem to be doing too badly, Inspector." I may have faded over the past year, but Inspector Moore remained a solid man. He might get overworked and tired occasionally, but he retained his earthy sensibilities.

"Well, I certainly do not have the energy for that kind of activity after work." He glanced once again at the dead woman. She did not look back—she would never look at anyone again, but I still felt her disapproval as we talked about her so casually. She had had a rotten life and a rotten death, and now she was simply rotten; there was much of this she probably did not deserve.

"I cannot muster that kind of rage these days," Moore added. His face had grown serious. "Not even for whoever did this. Mainly I am just weary."

"That I can understand."

He looked at me, suddenly distracted by a thought. "Andrews said you missed a dinner with him last night?"

"Oh good God," I said, "I did—how utterly rude of me. I have been rather unwell of late, and it completely slipped my mind. I shall apologize straight away."

"I'll pass that on when I get back to the station. As long as you're all right. I think he enjoys your dinners. You have similar minds, I think, and an eye for detail."

"Yes, perhaps." Of course I had forgotten: yesterday had passed in a blur of exhausted fear. After returning from dinner I had spent the night sitting in my study armchair and staring out of the window, sure I would see Harrington and the *Upir* coming for me at any minute. But they did not, and as dawn rolled round and I was once again brave enough to step outside, I had gone to meet the priest and Kosminski to discuss how we could watch Harrington. News of the new Ripper death was all over Whitechapel, the gossip flowing like blood in the gutters, running from street to street, and as well as injecting more fear into my troubled soul—the Ripper was another reminder of the mayhem the *Upir* brought with him—I knew that my days would once again become filled with postmortem examinations and inquests and writing reports. Much would fall on little Kosminski, who would no doubt be called back in for more questioning now that there was a fresh victim for the hunt. Kosminski was still plagued horribly by visions; he had been as eager as the priest for us to take action now, but I would not allow it. We had to *catch* him. We had to act like policemen, not vigilantes; that was the only chance we had of retaining our sanity.

By the time I had got home, all thoughts of dinner with Andrews had been forgotten. Those plans existed in a different life, one before I had *seen* the truth.

"I shall have to find some time to rearrange it," I said, adding, "but I imagine that you are all very busy after this new development."

Development. Death was what I meant: this woman had died in terror while fighting for her very existence. That was not a *development*. I wondered if perhaps I had lost my humanity already. Were any of us capable of feeling anything much at all anymore? I thought of the *Upir*. I might no longer be shocked by murder in its various forms, and my senses might often be dulled by laudanum, but I had plenty of fear left. Every time I closed my eyes, I saw that *thing* attached to Juliana's husband, and when I did snatch moments of sleep, my dreams were terrible. The *Upir* might have cursed Harrington, but it was also haunting me now.

The open door was doing nothing to ease the smell. I closed my bag and picked it up. I was tired, and I wanted to be alone with my thoughts, even though I knew that when I got the solitude I craved, I would immediately wish for company to ease my anxiety. Perhaps I had been foolish not to let the priest and Kosminski have their way; this *waiting* for Harrington to strike was leading us all into despair.

"I should go and prepare my report. I believe I am expected tomorrow morning." I walked toward the door, and Moore stepped aside to let me pass. "I also want to write to the Commissioner. It would be a terrible error to dismiss this woman as an isolated killing. I am sure Bagster will be back shortly—he is not a man to harbor ill feeling for long. Rather like Charles Hebbert in that regard." I smiled. "They are good men, both."

"You do not want to stay and clear the air yourself?" Moore asked. His nose wrinkled again. "Although I think more than fair words might be required to make this place smell sweet."

I should have stayed, of course, but the room was feeling claustrophobic, and there was something about Inspector Moore's earthy gravitas that made me feel uncomfortable—as if he could see some invisible guilt clinging to me. Not that I had done anything to feel guilty about—not yet, at least—but I had not shared my suspicions with him. I wondered how he might react if I did. I imagined he would question Harrington about his relationship with Elizabeth Jackson, and then let him go. I could hardly tell him the legend of the *Upir*, or that Harrington was possessed by it. But still, when Moore looked directly at me, I felt as if my soul was exposed. That skill had served him well as a policeman, but I could do without his glances plucking at my frayed nerves.

"I have spent enough time in here, Inspector—and despite what people might think, no one ever gets used to the smell."

"Are you sure you're all right, Dr. Bond?"

"Of course," I said. "I am just getting long in the tooth, as you yourself have said. I may get tired, and occasionally under the weather, but I have seen worse than this, I am sorry to say."

Moore nodded and his thoughts drifted, perhaps scrolling through the catalog of his memory to all the awful cases of his past. London was not short of grim sights, after all. I doubted anyone who had been inside Mary Jane Kelly's room would forget what they had seen any time soon—at least the inspector had been spared that.

"True," Moore said, "but I think the secret of survival is knowing when you have had enough—your soul's survival, I mean. All of this—I have seen it destroy good men in the past."

"It won't destroy you, I'm sure of that." I edged to the rough wooden steps, wanting to get away.

"No, I doubt it will. But it is good for a man to know that it can." He stared at me for a long moment as I searched for a glib remark with which to finish our conversation, but I found none. Instead, I smiled lamely and bade him farewell.

I was quite sure he was still watching me as I strode away, panting, as if I had been running.

The next two days passed in a flurry of work, liaising with the police and standing my ground with Philips on the nature of Alice McKenzie's death. I found the days easier—there were whole hours when I was lost in the mêlée of people and life around me and forgot what I had seen across the dinner table less than a week before. This new murder, so soon after the Jackson case, had lit a new fire under the tired officers who had spent so much of the year before unsuccessfully hunting the killer. Old evidence was reexamined and lists of suspects were once again trawled through. I heard Kosminski's name voiced here and there, and once again I gave my two-penn'orth on his personality versus my own analysis of Jack. I did not convince everyone I spoke to, but I was always pleased when I came out of a conversation without any eye of mistrust falling on me. I was sure someone would start to wonder why I was defending the dirty Polish hairdresser, or why my hands sometimes trembled when I mentioned his name, but it looked like my reputation had remained intact.

The nights were different: there was no respite from my fear then. The warm, damp air sat like treacle in my lungs, and my skin itched as if tiny bugs crawled over it. I refused to accept that my increasing dependence on drugs might have any part in that sensation. I stayed at home, in case there was any call for me in the night, in case any more poor women were attacked, and I tried to find comfort in the knowledge that the priest and Kosminksi were watching Harrington.

My heart rattled in my chest, and as the hours slowly passed I focused on the tick of the clock. My breath was too loud, and I could not concentrate on any of the books that lined my shelves, pulling them down one after the other and flicking aimlessly through the pages before tossing each to one side.

Mrs. Parks's dinners went mainly uneaten, save for the bread and potatoes. Kosminski had found water revolting after his dreams of the *Upir*; for my own part it was meat: the texture of it, the grease— the *blood*. I could no longer put meat in my mouth. Even the very thought made me feel like the *Upir* itself, devouring the organs of all those dead women, feeding its endless hunger. Anything I tried to swallow would lodge itself in my throat and threaten to choke me until I hawked it back up and spat it out onto the plate.

I checked the locks on the doors and windows and drew all the curtains. The gas lamps flared all night until dawn, when the rising sun rescued me from my fear, allowing me to sleep for two or three hours in relative peace. Daylight might not offer much protection against the *Upir*, but I was sure that, like all things of wickedness, man or beast, it preferred to hunt in the dark, when the world handed itself over to superstitions and the hustle and bustle of the days vanished like fading dreams, leaving men with only their own thoughts to occupy them.

Several nights had passed since the dinner at the Hebberts', and I was just starting to relax slightly and believe that the creature had not seen me when Mrs. Parks came to my study to announce a visitor. I had been so close to sleep that I had not heard the door, and I looked up, expecting Juliana.

It was Harrington. My blood froze in my veins.

"I'm sorry, Thomas, is this a bad time?" He looked young and awkward, and he clutched his hat between his hands, picking at its edges.

I got to my feet, trying to ignore the trembling that settled in my legs.

"Not at all—I was just . . . I was working." I forced a smile to stretch across my face, but it felt more like a deathly grimace. What was he doing here—why would he come? "Is everything all right?"

"Yes—well, no." He started to pace up and down a little, and each time he turned his back to me I shivered, even though I could see nothing but the fabric of his coat. There was no monster clinging to him—yet I could sense it; I could almost *smell* it.

"I wanted to ask a favor of you."

"Of course—what can I do for you?"

He looked almost as tired as I felt. Was he sickening again? So soon? Was the *Upir* starting to devour him?

"We have been having problems at the docks," he started. "The workers are restless, making demands—it's part of why I was rather rude to you when you visited the other day. I have been under a lot of stress." His eyes dropped, and he flushed with embarrassment. "But it means I am having to spend more time at work, having meetings with the other companies, trying to sort it all out."

"I understand—but it is important that you do not make yourself ill again, James." I was glad I sounded so normal; inside, every nerve was tingling as if preparing for sudden flight. My pupils had no doubt dilated with fear, and the air was watery between us. I was talking to an illusion; everything that was important—everything that threatened me—was invisible.

"It is not my own sickness that concerns me. Juliana has been rather unwell since her parents left, and even though some days she can barely get out of bed, she won't let me call them back."

"Would you like me to call on her? If so, that really is no inconvenience. I shall fetch my medical bag and come immediately. Pregnancy can have—"

He shook his head, raising his hands to stop me. "I was hoping for rather more than that." His blue eyes, so earnest and honest, met my own. "I was wondering if you could possibly move in with us—just until her mother returns. I hate leaving her alone for such long hours with just the housekeeper, and Charles and Mary are away for another two weeks."

"*Move in?*" I repeated the words in an attempt to buy myself some time to settle down, for my head had gone into a whirl, and fear sat like a melting block of ice in the pit of my stomach, sending cold rivers of terror tumbling through my guts. The idea of being in the same house as that *thing* was too much to bear. The priest would be delighted—I could watch Harrington from within while they watched from without—but to spend my sleepless nights there? My hand twitched for the laudanum bottle, my automatic response now to any moment of stress.

"I understand if it's too much of an imposition—I know how busy you are with your work at the hospital and for the police. It's just, I have no one else to ask. Not someone that Juliana would tolerate." He smiled, and all the love in the world was there. Were there days when he was simply an ordinary young man? Did his mind block out the awfulness of his deeds? Did the thing on his back sleep, was that it?

"You know what she's like," Harrington continued, unaware of my internal dialogue. "She can be quite—well, *opinionated*, really—even when she's ill."

It was the thought of Juliana that finally persuaded me: she was alone in the house with him, and unwell. I had to make sure it was simply her pregnancy taking its toll rather than anything Harrington might have done. Charles had run out on her and left her behind; I could not abandon her too.

"Of course I can," I said warmly. "I shall come this very afternoon."

He smiled, as if hugely relieved, and shook my hand vigorously before bidding me farewell.

When he had gone, I sat down heavily in my chair. I was about to go into the belly of the beast.

41

LONDON, AUGUST 1889
AARON KOSMINSKI

It was harder to watch James Harrington now that the unrest at the docks was spreading and more and more workers were joining the strike. Before that, Harrington had spent most of his time in his offices by the wharves, where he was easy to keep track of—like most men, he was essentially a creature of habit, using the same way in and out each day. Now his days were far less regimented; he was often at meetings with other importers, and they scurried around in groups, moving from pub to club to offices, no doubt discussing the best ways to get the growing group of dissatisfied dockworkers back to work without giving in to their demands. There were times Aaron simply could not keep up.

There were practical problems too. Dr. Bond had given him some money, but his unkempt appearance made it hard for him to get a hansom cab. It looked like he had stolen the money and was looking for a quick getaway. He knew he stank—most of London did in this heat, but his was a stench that had grown in layers, old sweat and new mingling to create a noisome odor that surrounded him. Matilda was at the end of her tether about it—perhaps that was why she no longer chastised him for spending long days outside. He had told her that he was looking for work, and she had chosen to accept the lie. It got him out from under her feet, and that was enough. He would wash, he had promised her, and himself, but he knew he could not do it until this was over.

At least while Harrington was on the move, it meant that Aaron did not have to spend so much time too close to the river, which made him want to sob. The blood of all those women had fed it, making it a home for the *Upir*, and it terrified him almost as much as looking directly at Harrington did. His fear made him a good spy though; he would never get too close, nor would he risk being seen. He wished the priest would give him more of the calming drug, not just when the visions or his panic overwhelmed him, but perhaps it was for the best: when he was terrified, at least he knew he was alert.

Using the strike as excuse, the dockworkers had been spending a lot of their time and money in the public houses of East London. Now he pressed himself against the wall of the pub beside the window, his small frame hidden by the burly, raucous men around him. He peered through the glass and checked that Harrington was still there. The five men he had arrived with had obviously concluded their important business, because they had beckoned over two women, who were laughing gaily—or more likely drunkenly—at whatever the besuited men were saying. Their dresses were cut low, and they leaned forward to display their assets, but Aaron ignored them. Fear and desire were not good bedfellows, and it had been a very long time since he had last entertained any thought of encounters with the opposite sex. Anyway, how could he look elsewhere when Harrington was there, along with the *Upir*, which had haunted his visions for so long? He had felt it coming across Europe—and now it took all his strength not to turn and run.

The other two did not understand; perhaps they were too absorbed in their own roles. The priest had withdrawn into himself even more as he continued with his preparations, whatever they were—although he would not share what he was preparing for. Aaron presumed he was readying himself to kill Harrington. He himself had never taken the priest for a moral man, for all he was a man of the cloth.

Aaron himself wished Harrington dead: he wished it every morning he awoke, sweating and screaming in fear, with the stink of the river filling him. He was just too scared to do anything about it himself.

Dr. Bond had changed too. They met every few days near Dr. Hebbert's house. Once Harrington had arrived home, the doctor would go out to take the evening air, strolling to the corner where he and the priest would be waiting in the shadows. The changes were obvious; even at his most fevered Aaron could see it. Did Bond realize he had developed a nervous tic in his left eyelid? There was often a familiar sweet scent on him too, and not from laudanum. The dark circles around Bond's eyes were now hollow caverns. If he was sleeping, it was not often.

Inside the pub, a thick-waisted man with a huge silver mustache was ordering more drinks, and the women were laughing more loudly. Harrington was joining in, but his back was stiff, and he was clearly uncomfortable. Aaron had never really considered the man before he had started this almost constant watching. Until then, plagued by his own visions, he had seen only the *Upir*, not the host. Now he knew James Harrington to be a measured man, serious, slightly reserved. Even so, it was hard to separate the man from the monster, and knowing the parasite attached to Harrington made Aaron weep—especially if his dreams had been particularly bad. He could not start thinking of Harrington as a victim, not if they were to succeed in their hunt.

He was thirsty, and the heat was making his head spin a little, so he rested it against the cool bricks. He needed to drink more, but he could not bear the touch of water. He would deal with it after this was all over—*is that what Dr. Bond thought about the laudanum too*, he wondered, *that he would stop when this was all over?* In the middle of the night, Aaron could not help wondering who was really the hunted who was the hunter. Were they three all part of the *Upir*'s game, or was everything exactly as it should be? His grandmother used to talk of destinies. Perhaps she had been speaking directly to him.

He glanced back in the window—and his idle thoughts vanished. Harrington and another man were getting up to leave, and one of the women was standing between them. Aaron noticed how pale Harrington's skin was—and that two small purple patches were starting to bloom on his neck.

Aaron turned to race round to the front entrance on the main road and instead collided with a woman standing behind him, sending her tumbling backward to the filthy ground.

"Oi!" she called out, "watch yerself!"

Aaron muttered an apology and started to push through the gaggle of drinkers, but a burly arm pulled him back. "You stinking bastard," the man growled. The hand was a dockworker's hand, thick and muscular, and Aaron's arm felt as brittle as a stick in the man's strong grip. Aaron's face twitched nervously, and he spat a little as he spoke, spluttering out more apologies in a string of words, some English and some Polish, needing desperately to get away, to see where Harrington was. He turned his head helplessly, trying to see behind him.

"Oh, let 'im go. He's clearly touched." The woman had picked herself up and now she stood over Aaron. "Blimey, does 'e stink— you can wash your 'and before you touch me after touching 'im." She laughed, and suddenly Aaron was free. He did not wait to hear what else the dockworker might say to him. He darted to the front— just in time to see a flash of a red dress climbing inside before the hansom cab took off, following another a few feet ahead.

He stared after the carriages, his chest pounding. Which man had the woman left with? Harrington, or his companion?

His thin shoulders slumped. He would have to tell the priest. He stared for a moment longer, and then realized, with no small amount of relief, that there was nothing more for him to do than go home.

42

LONDON, AUGUST 1889
DR. BOND

"When do you think he will be home?"

I took the dinner tray from Juliana's lap and placed it on the table by the window. It was dark outside, and the street was empty. I glanced to the corner where the priest and Kosminski and I would meet, but the shadows held no waiting figures.

"I imagine he is very busy." I closed the curtains and turned back to her, forcing a smile as I turned up the gas lamp on the wall. Juliana did not object, even though she was settling down to sleep for the night.

"I thought perhaps he would be home more often now that this stupid strike is on. There can hardly be any work for him to do if no ships are being unloaded."

I sat on the side of the bed and checked her pulse, which was strong and even. She looked better than she had in a few days, and she had clearly eaten a little more too.

"But no," she continued, "he is never here." She sighed and leaned back against her pillows, closing her eyes. I thought she looked quite beautiful. "Sometimes I wonder what happened to the man I married, Thomas. I really do. He is like a stranger."

I clenched my fist to stop my hand trembling, digging the nails into my pain.

"Sometimes," she said sadly, "I am quite glad we are sleeping in separate rooms."

"It will be better when you feel better," I said. "And of course when the baby comes. You are both just very tired."

My words seemed to soothe her, and I waited until she had drifted off to sleep before turning the light down and closing the door. It took all my strength to remain composed around her when I loathed every moment I spent in this awful house. Despair seeped from the walls, and I had no choice but to breathe it in. Even the brightly colored wallpapers had dulled, as if the wickedness of what lived here had spread its darkness.

In the study I sought out the small box I had hidden amongst the books. I still had the priest's pipe, and I had taken the precaution of going to my favored den and purchasing a supply of the poppy. As usual, Chi-Chi had remained silent as he sold me what I required. The laudanum might be enough to calm me during the day, but at night, in this awful house, knowing that Harrington and that *thing* were so close to me, I needed something more. I could not increase my dosage— I was beginning to have problems with my bladder, and the trembling was on the verge of turning into convulsion—but I truly needed the oblivion I had in the past sought on Chi-Chi's cot. I needed something to dispel the awful dread that pervaded the Hebberts' house.

I prepared the opium and then sat in Charles's favorite wingback chair and lit the pipe. I breathed deeply of the sweet smoke, and then, with the last of my energy, put the equipment back in the box and closed the lid before relaxing. Tension eased out of the muscles of my neck and shoulders, and my jaw hung slack, a blessed relief from the ache that had settled in from gritting my teeth so tightly all day.

Upstairs, Juliana would be sleeping as the child who was so determined to make her ill grew in her belly. I found the pregnancy disturbing: what was she carrying? Her husband's child? Or was there some part of the parasite that had transferred into her womb too? Was that why she suffered so much with sickness, because she was bearing a monster's child? The lamp was on low, and even as I drifted in the opium haze there were too many shadows for my comfort. I tried not to think about the baby; there was nothing I could do about that. James Harrington was the quarry, and all I could do was watch and wait.

I must have fallen into some sort of unconscious sleep because I awoke with a start, feeling cold and achy, as if I had been in the same position for too long. I was at first completely lost to my surroundings, expecting to be in my bed at home, and instead finding myself dressed and upright. The shapes in the room were all wrong . . .

It was dark.

The fog in my brain began to clear, and I slowly remembered my whereabouts. Had I turned the light down? I did not think so. Pale light trickled in from the night sky outside, but barely crept as far as my feet. I sniffed and coughed, my throat dry from breathing through my open mouth, and I looked around me. My opium box was still there—surely if I had gone to the trouble of turning out the lights, I would have put it back in its hiding place? Admittedly, what I did under the influence of the drug was not always clear but I had to presume I would act as I did normally. My back ached as I leaned forward, and I started to shiver away the drop in my body's temperature. I needed to turn the light on. The house was oppressive enough in daylight; at night I found the tension unbearable.

I went to stand and then froze as my eyes, now growing accustomed to the gloom, locked on something at the other side of the room: a dark outline, a figure, just behind the open door, not quite in and not quite out of the room, bisected down the middle by the dark wood. He remained perfectly still.

With my heart in my mouth, I got carefully to my feet and turned up the lamp. The clock showed it was nearly one o'clock.

Harrington stayed where he was, standing silently just behind the door, his hands hanging by his sides. He continued to stare at me, and I tried not to look at the space around his shoulder. I could not see the *Upir*, but that did not mean it was not watching me.

"James?" I asked, my voice cracking slightly, "are you all right?" His pale skin was coated in a sheen of sweat that looked like grease, and a patch of purple on his right cheekbone was loud against his pallor. His blond hair was untidy: it was obvious the sickness was coming for him again.

He frowned at me.

"I must have dozed off while reading," I said, despite any lack of evidence in the form of a book. How long had he been watching me? Ten minutes? An hour? I shivered. "I should go to bed." I kept my tone light. "So should you. It's very late, and you look rather unwell."

"I had a letter from Charles and Mary. I saw you were sleeping, but I thought you would like to know: they are coming back. In a week."

He turned and walked away without waiting for any response. I heard him make his way steadily up the stairs. Charles was coming back. I could go home. I picked up the box and turned the light down, despite loathing the darkness. I tried not to imagine that the *Upir* had somehow separated itself from the host and was waiting for me in the hallway.

I still had the dregs of the opium floating in my system, but my fear had overwhelmed it. I climbed the stairs with haste, and by the time I reached my bedroom, the furthest along the corridor, I was virtually running.

I slammed the door shut and leaned against it, breathless and twitching, until my momentary flood of relief was swallowed up by the sudden conviction that Harrington was somewhere in the room, staring at me in the dark, just as he had been when I had awakened downstairs. I lunged for the wall light, my trembling hands making it almost impossible to strike a flint to light the gas. I was flinching against an immediate attack: the *Upir* was coming for me, I was sure of it.

I finally managed to light the gas, and I stayed huddled into the wall for several moments before slowly opening my eyes. My bedroom was empty. I looked into each corner and the wardrobe, and then I dropped to my knees to search under the bed, but there was nothing. I was safe. Harrington was not here.

I sat on the bed, sweating and exhausted, and let my shoulders slump. I looked up at the door.

After a moment, I picked up the occasional chair by the washstand and wedged it under the handle. I would leave the light on.

43

LONDON, SEPTEMBER 1889
AARON KOSMINSKI

Sometimes in his dreams he could not breathe. His face was pressed into the floor, and splinters cut into his cheeks. It was dark. He was terrified. He knew this could not end well.

The visions came too fast to keep under control: sometimes he was at the bottom of the lake, his nostrils clogged with mud, anger and hunger itching at every pore as if something wanted to explode free from his skin. Other times, he was walking the streets of London at night, tired, a weight on his back. He wanted to claw the skin from his face, to tear it free and scream his madness from the rooftops. He wanted to be *free*. He wanted to cry. He wanted to *hunt*.

Here and there, in the suffocating dark, he would see flashes of red: crimson red, with lace trim, gone in a second, swallowed up by the yawning, endless eternity of wickedness that wanted to claim him—or washed away in the river . . .

The river. The red. The wickedness.

The visions were trying to tell him something—but when he woke, screaming and sweating and tangled in his sheets, he could only remember the fear.

44

LONDON, SEPTEMBER 1889
DR. BOND

Fate lives in the shadow of coincidence.

We collided, both in full flight, in the middle of Westminster. At first I did not recognize him, but as I crouched to help gather his papers, the familiarity of his face struck my memory. Where had I seen him before?

"I do apologize," I said, handing the ruined documents to him. It had rained heavily in the night and the streets were muddy, and as I picked up a ledger I pulled a handkerchief from my pocket to wipe it down as best I could. The collision was my fault, I was sure of it—as was ever the case these days, my mind was not where I was. I had moved back into my own house a week or so before, but the relief I had hoped to find had not come. I still had the awful feeling that the *Upir* was coming for me, and I had not kept the promises I had made to myself, that I would stop taking the opium and cut back on the laudanum as soon as I had left the Hebberts' house.

That morning I had been at the inquest of a cobbler murdered by his wife after fifteen years of marriage. She had stabbed him as he lay sleeping; then she had dressed, eaten breakfast and walked to the police station. She had told the police inspector that she could not abide the thought of his company anymore. They had wondered if she was insane; for my part, I thought not. She was resigned to her fate, the officers who had dealt with her told me. She regretted her actions, but she did not regret that he was dead. She was not entirely sure why she had done it, but she knew she had.

There was no insanity in those thoughts, but as I headed home at just after eleven o'clock that morning, I wondered whether she would have done it had the *Upir* not been in London. Was her fate just one more ripple in London's water caused by his being in our midst? I certainly had not been looking where I was going.

"I'm so sorry," I repeated. "It is entirely my fault. If there is anything . . ." I paused and frowned. There was something familiar about him: the neatness of his dress, the slight roll of neck pressed over his collar. "I say, have we met before? You look familiar?"

The man, perhaps ten years younger than I, had thinning brown hair and a narrow mustache, and his skin still retained the youthful softness of someone much younger, though that was perhaps due to his slightly portly physique.

"I do not think so. I—" He stopped as recognition dawned in his eyes. "Oh, you came to the wharves—to see Mr. Harrington. I thought you might be from the bank, or one of our creditors."

"Harrington's secretary!" I said in triumph.

"Yes," he said, and wrestled one hand free from his bundle of papers and held it out to shake my hand. "James Barker. Although I am no longer in Mr. Harrington's employment, I am afraid to say."

"I am sorry to hear that—is this a result of this awful strike?" Nearly all the dockworkers in East London were striking; they had been out for more than two weeks, and it was causing merry havoc for businesses who relied on supplies coming in and out. The business owners had hoped to starve the men back to work, but the newspapers were reporting large sums of money coming in to support the dockworkers from places as far-flung as Australia to lend support. I had paid it little attention beyond the effect it might have on Juliana and her husband.

"That was the reason given, yes." Barker's mouth pursed slightly. "But the business was not doing well before that—there was only so much I could manage on my own, and old Mr. Harrington, God rest his soul, he was a stickler for detail. His son . . . well, let me just say he is not a natural businessman."

My exhaustion faded slightly. "But he is always at work—he must be trying."

"Perhaps." The secretary looked as if I had said something mildly amusing. He was clearly bitter about the loss of his position because of Harrington's incompetence. "But he spent very little time in his actual office. You saw the state of it yourself: hardly the desk of a man on top of his affairs."

"So what does he do, then?" The question was light, but inside my every nerve tingled.

"I should not speak out of turn—my work so often relies on discretion, and I would hate to get a reputation for idle gossip."

"I understand that completely." I smiled to reassure him. "I work closely with the police, and I, more than most, understand the need to keep information private. But between you and me, his family are worried about him."

"You will probably think it silly," he started after a moment. "There may well be a perfectly reasonable explanation for why he spends so much time there . . ."

"Where?" I wanted to grab him and shake the details free.

"In one of the warehouses—the smallest one, actually, nearest the river. There is no list of anything going in or out of it, but he refused to let me allocate shipments to it. I do not know what he keeps in there—perhaps he just sits inside and drinks. I've heard of stranger things." His mouth curved again into a tight, unpleasant smile. Barker clearly had no love for Harrington.

"And he spends most of his days there?"

"Not always—but there are periods of time when he does—those are the times he has the least interest in his crumbling business. And the evenings, of course—I know, because I was so often working late. I had wondered if perhaps he was unhappy at home, but I hear there is a child on the way."

A warehouse: *of course*. All thoughts of going home and trying to sleep vanished and as soon as I had said my farewells, I hailed a hansom cab and headed east.

The priest's room was shabbier in daylight, and I thought I could see small dark splashes on the floorboards where he had bled while whipping himself. He moved carefully too, no doubt the cuts across his back causing him much pain beneath his rough clothes. I did not ask the purpose of his birching; there were many things about the priest I did not understand, and I guessed many were things I did not *want* to understand. If this was part of the preparation he had to make to face the *Upir* then I would not challenge it; I had to presume he cared as much for his own welfare as I did for mine. He might not show his fear as Kosminski and I did, but he would be as monstrous as the creature he had followed across Europe if he had none.

"A warehouse?"

"Yes." I was pacing up and down the small space, and between my agitation and the stifling heat, my collar was sticky with sweat. I had already abandoned my coat and waistcoat, tossed carelessly over the rickety chair. "We should have realized—the wharves are close to the river, and it is his place of business, so it would not take very much to lure a woman back there. It must be where Harrington kills and dismembers them. It *must* be."

"And from there the *Upir* can feed both himself and the river." The priest was nodding. "We must get inside."

"The strike may make that easier. There will be fewer people around to question what we're doing."

A sudden, furious banging interrupted us, and from outside came a flurry of foreign words. I pulled the door open, and Kosminski rushed in. He threw himself onto the bed and rocked backward and forward, tugging at his hair and muttering under his panting breath. The priest spoke to him in his native language, barking words at him, rather than soothing him as I would have, but his sharp tone had an effect, and after a few minutes Kosminski was breathing normally.

"A woman," he said. He looked up at me, his eyes full of dread. "He has a woman—I *saw* her."

"In a vision?" I asked.

"Yes—*no*, I saw her first with Harrington—but I didn't realize he had her still. Not until these visions."

"When?" I crouched beside him, forcing myself not to turn my face away in order to avoid the tangy stench that rolled from him, as thick as winter smog.

"I cannot . . . I cannot remember." He trembled and twitched and tugged at his upper lip with dirty fingernails.

"Think," I commanded, employing the priest's aggressive tone. "Think, man."

"Two weeks ago, perhaps? He was drinking. You were still in the house."

Two weeks—could she still be alive? Nothing had been pulled from the river, and no body parts had been discovered in public places. I tried to focus on Harrington as the quarry in our hunt rather than what he carried on his back—I told myself I must think of Harrington as a murderer, not as anything unnatural, or my limited courage would fail me.

"He must be keeping her at the warehouse," I said. "She may still be alive."

"Warehouse?" Kosminski said, and I wondered again at Fate: two pieces of the puzzle, coming together on the same day—perhaps we were men of destiny, after all.

The priest prepared a pipe of the strange opium for Kosminski, and I sipped at my laudanum.

And then, God help us, as the afternoon slowly drew round toward evening, we planned our attack on the beast.

"I need to meditate," the priest grunted eventually. "I must be mentally strong, ready for tonight."

"But we should go now," I said, getting to my feet. "There is a woman who might still be alive. If Harrington has her in that warehouse, then—"

"The woman is not important." He leaned forward and pulled out a box from under the bed. "The *Upir* is important."

"But if we can save her—?"

"Do not think in terms of *saving*. Think in terms of *destroying*. We are not here for the woman. We are here for *him*. If we save her, then we shall thank the Lord, but we must focus on the creature. It is not yet dark, and if we go now, we may free her, but Harrington will run, our hunt will be taken over by your police, and they will not understand their killer in the way we do."

His dark eyes bore into mine. "Trust me, Dr. Bond. I have seen all this many times before." He opened the box. "Take this." He handed me one of two small bottles of thick brown liquid. I did not need to ask what it was. "You still have the pipe?"

I nodded.

"Good. You must both smoke some. We must all be able to see it if we are to fight it. We will also need his"—he gestured at Kosminksi—"special ability to lead us to Harrington."

"As he led me to you?" I asked.

"But he will need a belonging of the man's, I think, to be able to follow. You will have to find something for him to use." He got to his feet. "I will meet you both at nine, outside Harrington's offices. Until then you must stay together."

"Stay together?" I was appalled at that thought, and I could not keep it out of my voice. "But I cannot take him to my house. He is a police suspect, for one thing, and then there is—" How could I politely comment on Kosminski's physical presence? I compromised by saying, "Well, people will think it strange that he is in my company."

"You must stay together," the priest repeated. He pulled off his outer robes and then his rough shirt and fell to his knees in front of the fire. He reached for the birch by the fireplace and my arguments faded as I stared at the mess that was his back. It was so lacerated with cuts there was barely an inch of undamaged skin. Welts rose high, still bleeding, and several were infected. How many hours a day had he spent doing this—and why? Because we might have to kill Harrington? Because the woman might die? If so, surely we should all three be on our knees and whipping ourselves, for we were in this awful pact together.

I could not stay and watch. As the priest raised the wood up over his shoulder, I grabbed my coat and jacket, then took hold of Kosminski's arm and pulled him out of the room.

The evening air was thick and hot, but I insisted Kosminski wear my coat, in an effort to give him some semblance of normality, though I knew that it meant I could never wear it again myself. As it was, it hung too heavy on his thin frame, making him look like a child wearing his father's clothes and thus likely to draw more attention to us rather than less. I bundled him into a hansom as quickly as I could.

Once home, I opened the front door cautiously. Seeing the hallway empty, I pushed Kosminski toward the stairs, shooing him to make him hurry.

"I thought I had better wait and make sure that you were feeling better." Mrs. Parks appeared from the sitting room just as Kosminski made it to the landing. "I've left some supper out for you—cold pork, some potatoes."

"That is most kind of you—I am afraid today has been rather busy." Disapproval—and a slight hint of mistrust—had lately become Mrs. Parks's normal expression on seeing me, and I was also looking forward to getting back into a normal routine with her. I found myself looking forward to regaining all kinds of normalcy, especially no more laudanum, no more opium—and proper sleep. Perhaps by the next day all these things would be mine once more.

I could have wept at the very thought—but tonight, I had other cares.

"Thank you," I repeated, and then I added, "but please, get home to your family now."

"Well, good night, then, Doctor Bond," she said curtly. "I shall see you tomorrow."

I waited until she had disappeared back into the bowels of the house—she invariably left by the kitchen door—and then I ran up the stairs. Kosminski was standing in the middle of the study. He had taken my coat off and had laid it carefully over the back of a chair. He looked decidedly uncomfortable—my house was not grand, but I had seen the rooms Kosminski and his family shared, and it was a world away from Westminster.

"Please, sit down," I said.

He glanced around, but he stayed standing. I looked at the clock. It was nearly seven. There was no more time for politeness. I ordered him to sit down, and I prepared the pipe.

Within fifteen minutes we had both smoked heavily, and my mind was singing and sharp. I examined the vivid contrasting colors around Kosminski's head that spoke so loudly of a troubled soul, and as I stared at him, I concentrated until the colors faded: I clearly did not deem them real in the way that the sight of the *Upir* had been. My brain was creating them—and then dismissing them. I was glad. That would make the next step of our plan easier.

"You will have to stay here," I said. "I think that is the best option. I will be as quick as I can."

Kosminski, calmer under the influence of the drug, nodded, and he dropped to the floor where he sat cross-legged. He did not speak further, and so I left him there. I locked the study door behind me and pocketed the key. Kosminski was a good man, I was sure of it, but he was not predictable.

"Thomas! What a lovely surprise." Mary was in the drawing room. "Isn't this weather just stifling? I can barely breathe. It kept me awake all night. Charles is not back from the hospital yet, and Juliana is sleeping, I think. The poor thing is having a terrible time carrying this child. And of course James is always out, trying to find some resolution to the awful strike . . ."

"It's not a social call, I'm afraid." I tried not to sound snappy, but I had neither the time nor the inclination for polite chatter. My heart was racing, my tongue tasted of metal and the world had flattened slightly with the drug, though each shape was sharp-edged and vivid. There was *too much* clarity and truth in everything. I was completely outside of Mary Hebbert and her polite company, and suddenly I wanted to get back to Kosminski and the priest—the only people, at least until all this was over, who understood me.

I pulled myself together and said politely, "I think I might have left a pocket watch here when I was staying. Could I go and look?"

"Of course, of course—would you like me to—?"

"No, no," I said with a smile, "this heat demands no movement unless absolutely necessary."

"True—I wish we were still at Whitby. The sea air is so refreshing there. You should try it, Thomas. It will do you the world of good."

I smiled in response, but had already turned away. Upstairs the house was gloomy. I hurried along the corridor, glad Juliana was sleeping, for I could not bring myself to speak to her, not knowing what lay ahead. I would feel like a serpent in her midst, even though the true serpent was the man she had married. At least tonight we would have proof, one way or another, for I would not act without evidence. If young James Harrington truly was the killer, there would be evidence in the warehouse.

I crept into Harrington's room just as the first roll of thunder shook the sky outside: the weather was about to break. With my heart in my mouth I moved toward the dresser, sure that every footfall was betraying me. What should I take? The clothes in the wardrobe were all clean and pressed—would that work? I looked at the bed and was about to search for nightclothes when I spotted a crumpled handkerchief on the table by the bed. I held it against my nose for a second—it was rank with stale sweat and illness. Were those smells really there, or was that just the opium at work? Either way, this would surely do.

Mary was waiting for me at the bottom of the stairs, and for a moment I was sure she could see right into my soul. I almost expected her to hold her hand out for the item I had stuffed into my pocket.

"Did you find it?" she asked instead.

"Sadly no—it must be at the hospital. Or perhaps I lost it at the inquest today."

"Why don't you stay for dinner? Charles will be home shortly, I'm sure, though poor James won't be—he is getting ill again, have you noticed? I do so worry that he will work himself into an early grave."

I shivered slightly at her last words and tightened my grip on the banister. "I am sure he will be fine," I said soothingly. "He is young, after all." The words tasted like gritty mud in my mouth. Outside, lightning flashed, sending shards of white light splintering across the hall tiles as it landed.

"Unfortunately, I already have plans." I looked toward the door. "My hansom is waiting," I said, hoping I sounded regretful enough. "I really should go."

We said our farewells and as I hurried out, large drops of rain splattered around me, the first spits from the mouth of the coming storm. My skin tingled. All the pieces were coming together. One way or the other, it would all end tonight.

45

London, September 7, 1889

Emily had lost all sense of time. How many days had she been here—a week? More? It had to be more. At first, once her terror had settled into something manageable and she had realized he was not going to kill her just yet, she had tried to measure the passing of time by his visits and the sounds outside, but it was always so quiet, with not even the sounds of men working to give her any indication of the hour, and he had painted the windows black so no daylight crept in. There was only the sound of the river for company and after a while, she had lost track.

She was tied to a pipe running against the wall, and she ached, not only from the lack of movement, but also from the slight fever she was running. The damp that came through the bricks had permeated her shivering bones, and there were moments when her panic rose, not from the thought of his return, but from the thought that if her cold got worse she would no longer be able to breathe through her nose, and then she would suffocate behind the stinking gag. Often she cried. Sometimes she just stared into the darkness and wondered if she might already be dead. Then a rat would scurry by, or her bladder would cramp, and she would know that her ordeal was very far from over.

Why had she got into the carriage with him? She had been impressed by his offer to show her around his business, and—she must be honest with herself, that was all she had left—she had hoped for a new dress, a little excitement, a gentleman to look after her for a week or so, just until his interest waned. Times had been so hard, and she was *tired* of hard. Warm liquid leaked out between her legs—her bleeding had started earlier. Her face burned with shame—she was surprised she had any shame left; the bucket in the corner had put paid to most of that.

She cried a little again, mourning herself before she was even dead. Even when her fevered mind came up with reasons for her capture that did not culminate in her demise—perhaps he was going to sell her into slavery abroad, perhaps he would just keep her here forever, like a pet—she did not truly believe them. He was mad. He would kill her. Those were the hard facts. But they still felt like fiction in her head. Someone would look for her, surely?

She cried again after that, for she knew no one was looking for her. She had moved around too much and had no real friends, none that were not transitory themselves. Her family were in York, and she had not seen them in a long while.

This was the truth: she was going to die, and no one would even notice.

He talked to her sometimes. He would turn the lamp on and look at her, his face unhappy. He would pace up and down and cry, tell her he did not know what to do with her. He had not meant to take her—*it* had forced him. At first he had fallen down beside her and pleaded with her, that if he let her go, she would not tell anyone, and she remembered the explosion of relief in her heart, the frantic nodding, the tears. In that moment, she had wanted to hug him, to kiss him, even—

—but he did not let her go, of course, because he knew that whatever she promised, in the end, of course she would tell. That was when she knew she was never getting out of here. Sometimes, when he brought her food and let her use the bucket, he would twist suddenly, as if catching sight of something out of the corner of his eye. He would look frantic then and swipe at his own back, as if to shake something off. Once he cried, and she had tried to run for the door, but he had hissed and grabbed her and she had seen the evil behind those blue eyes, the cold anger.

She was never getting out.

The past few times he had come, he had looked sick in the lamplight, pale and sweating, with great blotches on his face, and this had filled her with a new kind of fear. What if he were taken ill and confined to bed? Who would bring her food and water—would she die of thirst, here in the dark?

A key slid into the lock and her whole body tensed. Her sobs died in her throat. He had been once today already— why was he back now? Her ears throbbed and her face burned with terror.

The door creaked as it opened, and she caught a glimpse of the night outside before he closed and locked it behind him, tucking the key back into his pocket. She could hear him shuffling over to the table where the lamp was, and she squeezed her eyes shut at the sound of the match striking. The yellow glow of the lamp seeped behind her lids and she opened them slowly, unaccustomed to even this small amount of brightness.

"Blood," he muttered, and turned to face her. "It can smell your blood. It must have your blood."

His face was calm and his body still. There was none of the usual anxiety in his manner, just a quiet resolution. Even from a few feet away she could see his eyes were tinged with pink and the blotches on his face now looked like day-old bruises, angry and purple.

"You understand that, do you not?" His expression was dead. "It has to *feed*."

He crouched and opened the trunk, and although she struggled against her bonds, he did not glance her way as he picked out his tools and placed them on the table. A saw. A knife. A hammer. They glinted in the meager light and she thought she could see dried blood on the handles. Her vision smeared with fresh tears, blurring him, and she no longer cared about her unseemly bleeding that smeared her legs and stained her dress.

He turned and smiled at her. "I won't be long," he said, kindly. "I just need to prepare."

She sobbed again—and then she froze, for there was something—

There was something peering up from his back, and it was dark and awful and evil.

And to think she had been afraid of Jack the Ripper.

46

LONDON, SEPTEMBER 7, 1889
DR. BOND

We were all three of us soaked to the skin, but I felt alive and alert. On my return, I had found Kosminski sitting exactly where I had left him, and we smoked more of the drug and drank a glass of brandy each before heading out to whatever the night held for us.

And here we all were, outside the small single-story warehouse, the metal walkways looking down on us from above, and the cobbles beneath our feet slippery from the rain. The storm had persuaded the last of the dockworkers picketing the wharf to give up for the night, and as they trickled away home, I followed Kosminksi and the priest through the darkness. We were alone, the only sounds the heavy patter of rain, the occasional growl of thunder, and the sound of our own breathing. The rest of the world existed on a different plane. For all my belief in the rational, here I was, ready to fight a demon. Perhaps only then would I be able to resume my place in society, as I so badly craved.

Through the gaps by the hinges I could see a pale yellow light: Harrington must be inside. The solid wooden door was no doubt locked, but that was not how we intended to enter. The priest had already moved to stand in front of one of the blacked-out windows, and now he pulled off his coat and shirt, leaving himself naked from the waist up. He abandoned the shirt to the floor but wrapped the waxed coat around his arm. Even here, where sight was reduced to shapes in shades of gray and black, I could see the awful injuries on his back. The rain pounding on his back must have been agony where it hit his lacerated skin.

As we huddled together, my mouth dried. I trembled as we raised the bricks we carried. This was it; there was no time for hesitation. The priest gestured grimly, and with all my might and a silent prayer to a God who would no doubt abandon me for my actions this night, I threw the brick.

The peace of the night shattered with the glass. I flinched away, covering my face, but the priest had moved immediately, using his coat-wrapped arm to knock out the remaining shards, before throwing himself into the room with no concern for what might be on the other side.

I took a deep breath, held one arm over my face, and followed him, hitting the floor hard, my breath punching out of me. A mixture of adrenaline and the drug had me on my feet in seconds, a large shard of broken glass in my gloved hand. I moved out of the way to make space for Kosminski, who followed hot on my heels.

For a moment we stood there frozen, staring at the sight that greeted us.

Before I had leapt, I had, just for a moment, worried that perhaps all this was truly madness, that I would smash my way into Harrington's warehouse only to find him unpacking tea or engaged in some other perfectly normal activity, leaving me horribly embarrassed and having to find some way to explain myself to the innocent husband of my dear friend. That worry evaporated instantly as my eyes met his.

He stood a few feet away, between an open trunk and a table covered with bloodstained instruments, his hands wrapped round a woman's throat. Her eyes were wide and desperate and terrified, and I knew why.

The *Upir* was stretched over Harrington's shoulder, and its tongue, like Harrington's hands, was wrapped tightly around her neck. Between them they were squeezing the life from her. The head turned, red eyes blazing, and it stretched its tongue further and hissed angrily, displaying long, sharp teeth.

The priest pulled a silver knife from the waistband of his trousers and held it high as he chanted an incantation in what sounded like Latin. When the blade flashed in the light, I could see gold crosses inlaid into the blade. The *Upir* squealed at the sight of it, and Harrington turned, throwing the woman to one side. As she dropped heavily to the floor, forgotten, the priest was on him.

I could not stop myself from crying out—I thought he was simply going for Harrington—but instead, he attacked the furious, shrieking creature, and I could see he was using the knife to try to cut the beast free of the man. Kosminski dived past me and ran to the far end of the warehouse, then began yanking at the bolts fastening the door that led out to the river.

I followed my own instincts and ran to the woman lying next to the trunk. As I crouched beside her, I could see her neck was black and blue, and her tongue and eyes were both swollen and protruding, but she was fighting for breath. Her eyes met mine.

"It's all right," I said, although it most certainly was *not* all right; it would never be all right. "I am here—I am a doctor." I squeezed her hand, and she gripped mine back, for just the briefest of moments—and then she was gone. I felt the shift in her weight; all I held now was limp flesh. Her face was frozen in a mask of terror, and as I leaned over her and pressed my mouth against hers, trying to breathe life back into her, I was sure I could see the reflection of the *Upir* in her eyes.

My efforts were in vain, for the life was already gone from her. I turned away, not wanting to look at her, but I did not wish to witness the struggle between the priest and his devil raging behind me. Instead, I found myself looking into the trunk. For a long moment I frowned, unable to comprehend what I was seeing: a collection of objects, leathery-looking, round—with some wispy stuff clinging to them—

—*the heads.*

Inspector Moore had wondered what he did with the heads, and now I knew: he kept them, of course—his trophies, something to gloat over. There were too many here, though—fifteen, perhaps—so how many more poor women had we never discovered? Where were their remains?

In one corner of the trunk was something else, a different shape, set aside from the rest of the gory clutter. The head had been severed from the body and the stomach sliced open, but it was no doubt Elizabeth Jackson's baby, cut from her womb after her death.

I thought of Harrington, and that poor girl, once so in love with him. I thought of Charles and Juliana, and I found I no longer cared about the *Upir*; he was the priest's demon. James Harrington was mine. All of these people had died at his hand—he had killed the mother of his own child, and then mutilated the corpse. He could have stopped himself—he could have gone to the police—but he did not. Man and monster had truly combined, and there could be no redemption for either.

For the first time in more than a year, my mind felt clear. I knew exactly what I had to do.

I got to my feet and turned to the fight behind me. The struggle between the priest and the *Upir* meant Harrington's body was being tossed around like a puppet. I lunged forward and grabbed the young man, pulling his chest into mine and holding him tightly, and the priest swept his knife down, finally severing the man from the beast. Harrington shrieked loudly and slumped onto me as the priest dragged the writhing creature to the rear door.

"Thank you," Harrington gasped, and as I watched, the purple spots faded from his skin. "Thank you."

I looked him in the eye for a long moment, and I saw relief, yes, but no regret. How much would the *Upir* have left its mark on him, I wondered. How could he be trusted not to commit such awful acts again? And could I put Juliana through the terrible trauma of a trial? My mind burned, and I knew I would never be able to free myself of the image of the baby's mutilated corpse—Harrington's own child. Almost automatically, I brought up the shard of glass and thrust it deep into his throat, and he staggered back, blood pumping from the torn artery and splattering over me, feeling warm against my face. His hands waved vaguely in front of his neck, as if trying to indicate where he hurt, as if he could somehow save himself.

He could not. I had known where I was aiming, and my hand had been true.

Harrington stumbled backward, his legs as unsteady as if death were gripping him by the ankles, and liquid gurgled in his throat. He crumpled, and as the light faded from his eyes I tried to feel remorse. I could feel only relief.

I turned away from the dead man in time to see the priest by the far door of the warehouse. He still held the *Upir* tightly, and suddenly I could see the point of the lacerations on his back. Every time the demon reached over to try to get a firmer grip on him, the pain made the priest flinch and turn away. He would hold the beast even tighter with his good hand while beating at it with his bad one, and locked in this strange dance, the two of them slipped across the slick stones of the quay. Each time the *Upir* reached over the priest's shoulder, it melted into invisibility, and each time the priest yanked it back, it re-formed, black and hideous.

I stood, panting, in the doorway and looked out, Kosminski standing next to me. His whole body trembled, and when he gripped my arm, I did not shake him away. He had dreamed of the *Upir* for so long; I was amazed he could stand now that he was so close to it. He was fragile, the little hairdresser, but brave.

Suddenly I felt overwhelmed by our own humanity, and everything that we had been through to reach this point. It was Fate, I was sure of it; what else could have drawn us all together in this madness?

The river was dappled in the moonlight, and though the rain had eased off a little, it still pattered gently against the ground, making it hard to see the struggling figures. The priest dropped to his knees, and though I squinted, I could no longer see the *Upir*—it was too black against the dark of the night—but suddenly the air was cut with the sound of a hissing shriek, followed by a great splash. After a moment, the priest got to his feet and tilted his head back into the rain.

We stood in the glow of the one small lamp surrounded by death. For a long time we said nothing. The river sang to us from outside, and I thought about the creature sinking to its depths. I found I was no longer so afraid. It might not be dead, but it was gone, for a while, at least. I ached with tiredness.

"Why did it vanish like that?" Kosminski's voice was small. He sniffed and then wiped his nose with his sleeve like a child. "When it tried to get onto your back?"

"It was trying to change hosts—perhaps the drug shows it on only one host." The priest was leaning against the table. Scratches covered his chest, and he was wet with sweat and rain. "I do not profess to have all the answers."

"So it could be attached to you?"

I stared at Kosminski and then at the priest. Surely he was not suggesting—?

"I heard the splash," I said after a moment. "I heard the creature scream."

The priest held his silver blade out to Kosminski. "Kill me if you wish to. Believe me, it would be a relief."

Kosminski glanced from the man to the knife, and then he shook his head.

"There has been enough blood shed today," I said. I glanced toward the horrors of the trunk. "And for too many other days."

"What do we do with all this?" Kosminski asked, gesturing at our surroundings.

"Clean up," the priest said. "Harrington can go in the river—it will look like he was attacked here by the dockworkers, perhaps: they broke in through the window, demanded money. That is how the police will see it, at any rate. We will clean this place up. Dr. Bond, if you could take the trunk and burn its contents?"

"With pleasure," I said. Perhaps that way I could eradicate the memory of it from my mind. "But what about her?" I looked down at the dead woman we had not managed to save.

There was a long pause. I looked up at the priest. "What about this poor woman?" I repeated.

"I will dispose of her," he said, "the same way Harrington disposed of the others."

"Surely not," I gasped. "That is monstrous—!"

"It will stop the police looking for other motives for her murder. We cannot take the risk that anything could connect her to us—to *you*, even to Harrington, whom, I should point out, you killed. She must be disguised as a victim." He looked down at her body. "I will do it. She will forgive us."

"And you will clean up here?" I said.

The priest nodded.

I closed the lid on the trunk and picked it up. It was surprisingly light for the weight of human unhappiness it held.

"And after this," I said softly, "I never want to see either of you again. Is that clear?"

I did not look back as I left them.

The fire blazed with the sort of heat I would expect from hell itself, and yet I found the sight of the flames comforting. They mesmerized me even as they destroyed the last of the *Upir*'s depraved work, and as they burned, I began to feel cleaner. In a few days, they would bring Harrington's body out of the river, and Juliana would cry, but she was young. She would recover. We would all recover, even me.

I smiled slightly and then yawned. Perhaps I might even sleep tonight. It was over. It was truly over.

EPILOGUE

The Times of London
September 20, 1889

Nothing has occurred to throw any light upon the circumstances attending the finding of the trunk of a woman under the railway arches in Pinchin Street, Whitechapel. Without the head, all hopes of the body being identified will have to be abandoned, as on the body there are no birthmarks of any kind.

ACKNOWLEDGMENTS

I could never have written this book without the hard work done by so many others. My go-to book was *The Thames Torso Murders of Victorian London*, by R. Michael Gordon (McFarlane, 2002), and, should I ever meet him, I owe him much wine. There was also *The Thames Torso Murders*, by M. J. Trow (Wharncliffe Books, 2011).

The most valuable Internet resource for anyone writing in this period has to be the "Casebook: Jack the Ripper" website where there is a wealth of information and discussion. There is also an astounding body of work to be found on the "Dictionary of Victorian England" website. Beyond these there were many other websites and books dipped in and out of, and I thank all of their authors.

A big thanks to my editor, Jo Fletcher, and to all at Jo Fletcher Books and the extended Quercus team for being so enthusiastic about this book. Jo, thanks for all the hard work and also the friendship. You truly do own a part of my soul now.

And, of course, to my lovely agent, Veronique Baxter, at David Higham. Thanks always.

Central London

Locations of the Torso Killer's Victims 1886–1889

May 1887

September 1889

South Lambeth